DENISE VEGA

ROCK ON

A STORY OF GUITARS, GIGS, GIRLS, AND A BROTHER
(NOT NECESSARILY IN THAT ORDER)

LITTLE, BROWN AND COMPANY
NEW YORK BOSTON

Copyright © 2012 by Denise Vega
"Waiting for You" lyrics copyright © 2012 by Denise Vega

Little, Brown and Company

Hachette Book Group
237 Park Avenue, New York, NY 10017
Visit our website at www.lb-teens.com

Little, Brown and Company is a division of Hachette Book Group, Inc.
The Little, Brown name and logo are trademarks of Hachette Book Group, Inc.

The publisher is not responsible for websites (or their content) that are not owned by the publisher.

First Paperback Edition: January 2013
First published in hardcover in March 2012 by Little, Brown and Company

Library of Congress Cataloging-in-Publication Data

Vega, Denise.
    Rock on : a story of guitars, gigs, girls, and a brother (not necessarily in that order) / by Denise Vega.—1st ed.
        p. cm.
    Summary: High school sophomore Ori Taylor, lead singer, guitarist, and songwriter in a nameless rock band, has always been known as the easily overlooked younger brother of Del, a high school sports star, but when Del suddenly returns home from college just as Ori is starting to gain some confidence in himself, Del expects everything to return to the way it used to be.
    ISBN 978-0-316-13310-4 (hc) / ISBN 978-0-316-13309-8 (pb)
    [1. Sibling rivalry—Fiction. 2. Brothers—Fiction. 3. Rock groups—Fiction.
4. Self-confidence—Fiction. 5. High schools—Fiction. 6. Schools—Fiction.] I. Title.
    PZ7.V4865Ro 2012
    [Fic]—dc23

                                                                                    2011019475

10 9 8 7 6 5 4 3 2 1

RRD-C

Printed in the United States of America

To the guys who influenced my taste in music and/or brought music into my life: my husband, Matt Perkins; my dad, John Vega; my brother, John Vega Jr.; my brother-in-law Wayne Applehans; my brother-in-law Josh Massaro; and my friends Jerry Dunlop, Andy Fordyce, and Jimmy Ray Rich; and to all the musicians out there who play for keeps. Rock on.

Ain't
~~There's~~ nothin' better

Than a sweet guitar

And the music

rolls through

That ~~comes out of~~ it

And the place that it takes me

Far away, but still like coming home

Sometimes I don't want to come back

[chorus]

COLORADO ROCKS

We are an up-and-coming band, name-less but open to suggestions. Feel free to post your band name ideas on our blog. (We don't want to use one of those band name generators — we want it to come from you or us.)

WANTED
Bass guitar player. If you're interested, <u>contact</u> us about audition times.

Countdown to
BATTLE OF THE BANDS:
152
days

BAND NAME: to be named later

| PROFILE | MUSIC | PIX & VIDS | ABOUT/FAQ | CONTACT | BLOG |

BAND MEMBERS

 Orion Taylor, lead guitar, lead vocals

 Troy Baines, second guitar, backup vocals

 Nick Brewster, drums and percussion

UPCOMING GIGS

1/11 – 6 PM Mic Night Monday at the FX Lounge, LoDo

4/10 – 3 PM Matt's Sports, Centennial

6/5 – Battle of the High School Bands, Nicholson Sports Complex, Denver

COLORADO ROCKS

We are an up-and-coming band, nameless but open to suggestions. Feel free to post your band name ideas on our blog. (We don't want to use one of those band name generators — we want it to come from you or us.)

WANTED
Bass guitar player. If you're interested, contact us about audition times.

Countdown to
BATTLE OF
THE BANDS:
152
days

BAND NAME: to be named later

PROFILE   MUSIC   PIX & VIDS   ABOUT/FAQ   CONTACT   **BLOG**

Monday, January 4

So in this blog, you'll hear from me (Nick), Orion, Troy, or Alli (aka A. Wilcox, our webqueen, as she calls herself), or maybe all of us. We'll try to keep you up to date on the latest and greatest.

ORION: I'm not sure who we're talking to, since we've had this profile up for over a month and hardly anyone has found it. But to the two people who might read this, you should know that we are gearing up for the Battle of the High School Bands. We couldn't do it last year, because we didn't have our band together enough, but this year we're ready. Or we will be. The Battle is BIG. It's HUGE. A good showing at the Battle could mean we move out of my garage (aka OT Studios) and into some serious venues.

NICK: That's right. The countdown to the Battle begins NOW. Some past Battle winners have gone on to record and tour, and that could be us. We want it to be us. It SHOULD be us!

TROY: Indeed it will be us. But first we are going to rock FX Lounge next Monday, so everyone should come check us out. And I predict that soon there will be tons of people commenting on this blog.

ALLI: And they totally need a band name because they can't go into Battle without one. Well, they can but they don't want to, so help them out here.

Gold's Guitars supports this band. • 303-555-GOLD.
This site updated and maintained by A. Wilcox.

COLORADO ROCKS

We are an up-and-coming band, name-less but open to suggestions. Feel free to post your band name ideas on our blog. (We don't want to use one of those band name generators — we want it to come from you or us.)

WANTED
Bass guitar player. If you're interested, contact us about audition times.

Countdown to
BATTLE OF
THE BANDS:

152

days

BAND NAME: to be named later

| PROFILE | MUSIC | PIX & VIDS | ABOUT/FAQ | CONTACT | **BLOG** |

ORION: And we need a bass player to go into Battle. Pronto.

DominantSpecies
I have no idea who you guys are, but you sound like losers. Hey, how's that for a band name?

PurpleGrrl
One of my Facebook friends told me about you guys. I listened to the download you have, and it's really good. When will you put up the whole song?
Band name suggestions: Arrowhead, Clocked Up, Buffalo Ridge, Mangled Sweater
YOU sound like a loser, DominantSpecies. Go away.

DragonBreath
Hey, Troy, my man! Cool profile, dude. I'll be there next week. Names: Mordor, Natural Enemy, DunderHeads

Halyn
Hey. This site came up in a search on poetry, but I might stick around cuz I like music and it's cool that you are doing this Battle thing.
I agree with PurpleGrrl. I hope DominantSpecies stays away.

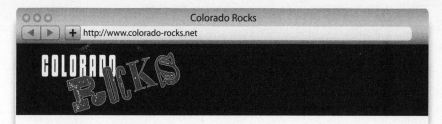

COLORADO RICKS

We are an up-and-coming band, name-less but open to suggestions. Feel free to post your band name ideas on our blog. (We don't want to use one of those band name generators — we want it to come from you or us.)

WANTED
Bass guitar player. If you're interested, contact us about audition times.

Countdown to
BATTLE OF
THE BANDS:
152
days

BAND NAME: to be named later

PROFILE | MUSIC | PIX & VIDS | ABOUT/FAQ | CONTACT | BLOG

BoyMagnet

I was doing a report on the constellations and this site came up. But I love music and Orion is cute on the Pix & Vids page. I'm in Denver so I'm hoping I can come to FX.
Names: Magnetize, Magnetic Connection, Magnetism

ONE

My dad likes to joke that the first word I ever spoke was *guitar*, but apparently it was *Del*.

Not *Mama* or *Dada*, like most kids, but the name of my older brother.

I used to think that was cool. Because Del was cool. Sure, we had the usual brother stuff with shoving, hitting, and his yelling at me to stop following him and his friends to the tree fort, but it was Del who rescued me from Curtis Langford when he shoved my head into a bucket of muddy water and held it there when I was six, Del who told everyone at our elementary school I was going to grow up to be a rock star, Del who took me out to Chipotle the day he got his license before he went to show off to his friends.

The same Del who, just yesterday, told me he probably wouldn't be at my first official gig, even though he'd known about it for weeks and had been really pumped about it.

"I put the word out," he'd said back when I first told him about it. "Lots of people should be there. And we'll have a big party after, even if it *is* a school night." I'd thought that was so great because I knew he could charm my parents into agreeing.

But now he wasn't even interested in coming to listen to us, let alone arrange some stupid party. It was like everything before he quit college never existed—the times we hung out together or when I went to his games or he bragged about my playing. That brother was gone, and in his place was a guy who looked at me like I was an idiot for even playing the guitar and made fun of me for trying to make it as a musician.

I shook my head hard, trying to get rid of thoughts of Del so I could focus, get myself to another place, the place I would need to be if I wanted to pull off this gig. I closed my eyes and concentrated.

It took just a few seconds before I could almost hear the shouts and whistles, the applause, practically smell the fake smoke rising on the stage at Red Rocks Amphitheatre as…

I look out over the crowd, framed by massive walls of red rock jutting into the night sky.

I stroke my sleek black Les Paul, then slam into a killer riff that sends every girl in the front row screaming for a piece of me. The sound reverberates off the rocks that surround the seats, natural acoustics for our music. The music is pure and perfect; record execs will be knocking over one another after the show to sign us.

I look out on the crowd, my voice hitting all the notes. I—

"Ori?"

—look back at my best friend and drummer, Nick "Call Me the Brew Man" Brewster, and—

8

"Ori. Dude. You've got to come out now. We're going on soon."

I blinked once. Twice.

The Red Rocks stage dissolved. I wasn't a rock star. I was a sixteen-year-old dork in a dingy bathroom stall, staring at the F-word scratched into the door in all its glorious forms. It took me a second to remember that we were at the FX Lounge on Mic Night Monday for our first official public appearance.

And I was hiding in the bathroom.

"Give me a minute."

"We've already given you ten," Nick said. "Come on."

I hesitated.

"Don't make me crawl under this door, dude. The floor is disgusting."

"But we don't even have a name," I said. "Or a bass player."

"We'll get those things." Nick thumped the metal door. "Dude, how are you going to play at the Battle with hundreds of people watching if you can't even get out there in front of a few dozen who are mostly friends and family?"

The Battle. Our ticket to getting noticed, to building our career as a band.

But it was safe in here.

The Battle. Our shot at doing what we loved, at making and playing music that other people would listen to.

Okay, so it smelled a little. But it was quiet.

The Battle. Something we couldn't go into cold, never having played anywhere but in the garage or at my sister's birthday party.

Dang.

The Battle. The only thing that would get me out of this stall.

And Nick, of course, knew that.

I unlatched the lock and opened the door.

Nick grabbed my arm, shaking his head as he led me out of the bathroom. "All you need to do is get your hands on your guitar and you'll be fine."

"It's not mine," I said. Which was true. I'd borrowed the electric guitar that sat out there waiting for me. It wasn't the Les Paul, the only guitar I'd ever pictured myself playing at the Battle of the Bands.

"Taylor, dude, you're killing me. Get your butt out there, pick up that guitar, and do your thing." He gave me a shove.

"Thank God," Troy said as I stepped out onto the stage, which wasn't really a stage at all, just a cleared-out area in one corner of the bar. "I was afraid we'd lost you, man." He smacked me on the arm, genuinely relieved and happy to see me, not annoyed at all. But that was Troy.

Next to him was Alli, who was not only his girlfriend but also our band chronicler via video and Internet, my next-door neighbor, and one of my best friends since our moms shoved us together for a bunch of playgroups and such. Back in seventh grade we tried to kiss, totally messed it up with braces snagging and overall weirdness, and agreed we did *not* belong together—except as friends.

"All you need to do is pick up that guitar," she said, pointing to it.

"Why does everyone keep saying that?" I swallowed and

stepped closer to the loaner, a decent Fender Stratocaster that belonged to one of my guitar mentors. I had several who Ed Gold had turned me on to, guys who taught me jazz, classical, rock, blues, and more.

Sucking in a breath, I tried to calm myself as I looked around, the smell of beer mixed with greasy fries wafting toward me.

No girls in the front row ready to scream for a piece of me — luckily, because even though one of my best friends was a girl and I had a sister, girls scared the heck out of me as a general rule. So it was probably a good thing that there weren't any nearby.

And no record execs, just a clump of adults — our parents — sitting at a table, completely ignoring us as they talked and sipped their drinks. To their right was a table full of eighth-grade girls trying to look mature and cool, headed by my sister, Vela.

"Here comes our biggest fan base, thanks to Troy." Alli put her arm through his as we all looked toward the door. It was Troy's crew spilling in, spreading out over the front tables, leaning up against the walls, talking, texting, occasionally glancing our way. They would be half the audience, which was great because we needed as many friendly faces as we could get. Especially since all the people Del would have brought weren't here because Del wasn't here.

"I'm going to hand out our website cards before we start," Nick said. Then he looked at Troy. "Make sure he doesn't go anywhere."

I rolled my eyes, trying to ignore the sudden urge to flee again. These people were looking for some real music and were about to get *us*. True, most of them were our family and friends, but there were a few unknowns and they didn't seem like they had stumbled in here accidentally.

Holy crap.

We weren't rehearsing in my garage, or playing for Vela's thirteenth-birthday party. This wasn't a crowd I could imagine, one that did exactly what I wanted it to do at any given moment.

These were real, live, unpredictable people.

Unpredictable.

Like Del. I glanced around the room, my gaze stopping near the door, then back at the far corner. For a moment I thought I saw him, and my heart sped up.

"He's not here," Alli said quietly before pulling her video camera out of her bag. "I checked. I'm sorry."

"Whatever," I said, turning abruptly back to the "stage." I felt disappointed and relieved at the same time. Mostly relieved, because I never knew these days whether Del would be Dr. Jekyll or Mr. Hyde, and I didn't need that stress at our first official gig.

Alli smiled sympathetically. Part of me wished she didn't know so much about me, but most of me was glad she got it. Got me. Like she always had.

"You're going to rock the house." She squeezed my arm and smiled as Nick strode up, all grins.

"I gave away all the cards," he said. "I think we'll have more people visiting our site, not just a few who found it by accident."

"If we play, they will come," said Troy, ever the optimist.

I hoped he was right. It would help to have some real fans who could spread the word about us and our music. And it would be great to have that support at the Battle.

"Okay, boys." Charlie, the FX manager, walked over to us. "You've got thirty minutes to play, then there's a break and you clear out so I can bring on the next band. Got it?"

"Yep." Nick's eyes dared me to contradict him.

I frowned, then glanced at the loaner guitar. The strings were taut and finely tuned, just waiting for me to run my fingers up and down the frets.

Waiting.

The moment my hand curled around the neck, calm fell over me. I pulled the strap over my head and adjusted the guitar against my body. The room around me began to disappear, the bar sounds receding into nothing. Sucking in a deep breath, I looked back at Nick and nodded.

He grinned, relieved.

"Hey, everyone," Charlie said to a screech of feedback. "Thanks for coming out for Mic Night Monday at the FX Lounge, where we've also got Two-for-One Tuesdays, Ladies' Night on Wednesdays, and live music every Friday and Saturday night." He rubbed his hands together. "We're excited to showcase some high school bands tonight. Keep eating, keep drinking, and put your hands together for—" He turned to look at me. "What's your name again, son?"

"Orion," I said automatically.

"No!" Nick said, standing up from behind his drums, brandishing one of his sticks. "That's not our *band* name! That's *his* name."

But Charlie was already back at the mic, clapping his hands. "Okay, everyone. Give it up for Orion!"

Nick, still scowling, nodded to the mic in front of me. He had this crazy idea that since I was lead guitar and lead vocalist, I should be the one talking to the audience even though I'm not much of a talker.

But his glare shoved me up to the mic. "Um, I'm Orion Taylor." My voice cracked and several people laughed. Before I could get embarrassed, Alli was giving me a thumbs-up from the side, her video camera rolling, so I took a breath and continued. "And that's Troy Baines"—an eruption of screams, Troy's crew giving him his due—"on second guitar and backup vocals, and that's Nick Brewster on drums. You should be familiar with this first one, so..."

I knew Boston's "More Than a Feeling" would bring the old people (our parents) and people who'd learned about the oldies on the now-defunct *Guitar Hero* (everyone else) to their feet, and I was right. I'd only played the first few chords when the crowd erupted in screams and shouts. I was glad Charlie had darkened the room so I couldn't see my mom making a complete fool of herself dancing in the back, singing along like she always did when she heard "her" songs.

I stepped up to the mic and sang, Troy and Nick doing their thing....

And then I was gone, catapulting outside of myself, to that place the music took me so hard and fast I couldn't do anything but go along for the ride. I was teetering on the edge, at the top of the roller coaster, hovering for a second before crashing down, feeling the rush as I flew across the rails.

The last few notes from our guitars reverberated as Nick smashed his way through a made-up drum solo to end the song. Troy and I bobbed our heads up and down in time to the beat, finishing with the necks of our guitars thrust upward.

The screaming, the applause—whoa. I came back to Earth to see girls clapping and cheering for us. Not quite wanting a piece of me, but definitely getting into the song.

"Thank you!" I said into the mic. We played our second cover and got the same reaction. I could see Charlie out of the corner of my eye, nodding approval at the crowd. We played one more cover, and then it was time for our first original song—"Knock It Down, Bring It Up"—my feeble attempt at a danceable rock song with lyrics like "Knock it down, bring it up, rock it off the top, and flip it, yeah, baby, flip until you drop." Not exactly award-winning, but it was catchy and my sister's little middle school friends liked it.

"Knock It Down, Bring It Up" kept people on their feet, and they stayed up for our next tune, "Finals Week."

We were on a roll and the crowd was totally with us. We had two more songs—one that was more of a ballad, and then we'd wrap it up with what we hoped would become our signature song, "Suburban Nightmare"—Alli was even creating a cool multimedia presentation to play behind us when we got big.

But first up was the ballad.

"We're going to slow things down a little," I said into the mic, wiping the sweat from my forehead. I could hear the murmurs of people talking, the sound of forks and glasses clinking as I set down the loaner electric and picked up my acoustic. I pulled in the stool we'd had off to the side, plugging the guitar into the amp. Troy and Nick went silent behind me—they didn't play in this one. It was all me.

"This is a song I wrote called 'Waiting for You.'"

One of the great things about being a musician is you can say things through your music that you would never say normally. Somehow, when you're a guy singing about feelings, you're cool. If I were just telling them to someone, he'd call me a wuss or smack me upside the head.

My songs were the only place I could say this kind of stuff, so I did. But this was the first time I was actually going to do it in public, so I was definitely nervous.

The first few chords were sweet and clear, pulling me in. I closed my eyes, letting the music flow through me.

I'm always alone
Even in a crowd
The voices soft
But mostly loud
. . . around me
I always felt
There was someone for me
I was waiting
And so was she
. . . somewhere

A few shouts and whistles rose up from the crowd, but mostly people were quiet, listening. The chords echoed through

my body, and I started the second verse feeling more confident, so I took a chance, looking out into the crowd....

And saw him.

Del was leaning against the bar, his face illuminated by
the neon beer signs, grinning at the bartender, who was smiling and nodding like he and Del were old buddies. Then Del
turned back, smirking at me.

Just a smirk, a small facial expression. That was all.

But that was all it took.

My fingers fumbled over the strings, an off-key note
whining from the guitar, a wounded animal that needed to
be put out of its misery. People cringed.

I opened my mouth, but nothing came out. My mind was
blank. I stared at the floor, as if the words to a song I'd played
a hundred times would suddenly rise up and show themselves.

"'I'd seen someone,'" hissed Troy.

I'd seen someone. I'd seen someone. It sounded familiar. But
what came next?

"I'd seen someone," I whispered into the mic. Another laugh.
Chairs scraping, front-row eyes dropping in embarrassment.

I sat there, frozen, for several more seconds. Then Charlie
was beside me, grabbing the mic and extending it upward.
He covered it with his hand and looked back at me.

"Some nights you got it, some nights you don't," he said.
Then he faced front. "Let's hear it for Orion! The next band
will be up in thirty minutes. Get yourself another drink,
another basket of fries. Stay close and stay tuned." He flicked
off the mic. "You boys have twenty minutes to clear the stage
for the Pissant Pirates."

TWO

I was heading toward the side door with my guitars when I was knocked from behind.

"I am *so* sorry!"

"'S okay," I said, eyes averted. I was in no mood to look at anyone who'd witnessed the Choke, especially a girl. But I could feel her looking at me, eyes locked on my face.

"Oh my God," she murmured before ducking down the hall toward the restrooms.

I got that reaction from a lot of girls. And I hadn't even had time to jump into my usual there's-a-potentially-cute-girl-nearby panic, which transformed me into either a blathering idiot or a frozen mute. This one had lunged away from me upon first sight. It might have been a record. Maybe I should have given her a trophy.

Pushing the door open with my shoulder, I sucked in the

cold January night air, letting it hurt my lungs. It felt good to be outside, leaving the Pissants, my screwup, and the girl I'd repulsed behind the solid metal door.

We all loaded Nick's drum set into the Brewsters' truck. My parents were helping me put my guitars and amp in the trunk of their car when Vela and her friends came around the side of the building.

"You were a rock star, Ori," Vela said, grinning as she gave me a hug. "Except when you messed up."

"Thanks, Vee. Appreciate that."

"I loved that last song you were singing," her friend Jacqueline said. "It was amazing."

"It's true," Alli said as Troy slipped his arm around her shoulders. "If you could have seen their faces..."

Before hung in the air, unspoken. It was quiet—one of those awkward-moment kinds of quiet when everyone's remembering the thing you want everyone to forget.

Then Jacqueline spoke again. "So does she walk in? Later in the song, I mean. Does the girl show up and you get together and everything?"

The other girls nodded, eyes on me. Gotta love eighth-grade groupies.

"Something like that," I said, feeling a little better that they, at least, didn't think I was a total loser. "I'll play it again sometime. All the way through."

"Cool," Jacqueline said.

"You were great." My dad clapped me on the shoulder. "These things happen."

I scowled. "Can we just stop talking about it?"

"Did you see Del?" Vela asked, tugging at my sleeve. "Wasn't it great that he came?"

Yeah, great. Seeing Del was what caused the Choke.

"Must've missed him," I said quickly, then turned to Nick. "Let's get out of here."

"I thought you wanted to listen to our competition," he said. "The Pissant Pirates are in the Battle, too, you know."

I frowned. The last thing I wanted to do was go back in there and stand next to the people who had just witnessed my humiliation.

"I'm done," I said. "You guys go."

They exchanged looks, but I didn't care. I had to get out of there.

"Oh." My mom frowned. "We thought you were coming home later with Troy. We don't have room in our car for you with Vela and all her friends."

And Nick's dad had already taken off with his equipment.

I was even a failure at being a failure, unable to run away with my tail between my legs.

"I'll be down the street at that burger place," I said to Alli. "Text me when you're leaving." Without waiting for anyone to respond, I took off down the sidewalk. A few seconds later, I heard footsteps hurrying behind me, like someone was trying to catch up. I picked up my pace, picturing a heckler, or worse—Del.

"Orion Taylor?" The woman's voice was firm but nice. I stopped and turned around. She strode toward me, sticking her hand out when she got closer.

"Courtney Calavera, online music critic for *DMS—Denver Music Scene.*"

"I know *DMS*," I said, taking her hand.

"And I know you," she said. "Lead guitarist, lead singer, lyricist of a band with no name, and possible music prodigy."

I raised an eyebrow at her.

"I talked to your parents."

"Great." Hopefully my mom hadn't mentioned the time I used Alli's Fisher-Price karaoke player to practice my singing.

"Don't worry," Courtney said. "I won't use the karaoke thing in my piece."

Wonderful.

"I just had a few questions to round things out," she said. "Can we talk?"

"I'd rather not." I yanked open the door to the restaurant and stepped inside, assaulted by the heavy scent of sizzling burgers and french fries. Courtney Calavera followed.

"Look," she said. "Everyone messes up at least once during their career. You're lucky you got it out of the way early, when it doesn't count."

"Is that supposed to make me feel better?" I stepped up to the counter and placed my order, tugging a few wadded bills from my pocket.

"Well, it should. I've seen major acts bite it big-time during a performance. You just keep going."

I didn't say anything. Just paid and waited. When my food came, Courtney was still there.

"You really don't want to talk, do you?"

I shook my head.

"Okay. I'll see if I can catch one of the other band members. In the meantime, here's my card." She held it out to me. "Call if you change your mind. My deadline's tomorrow at five."

I sat down at the table farthest from the windows and ate, even though I wasn't hungry.

Ten minutes later, Alli sent me a text: ✉ **NO COMPETITION. WE'RE LEAVING. MEET US @ THE CAR.**

I stuffed the last of the french fries in my mouth and headed out the door. I was almost to Troy's car when I saw him. Del was at the corner just a few yards away, leaning against the car that was supposed to be mine after he went to college, that I'd gotten to drive for a whopping five weeks after getting my license in November, before he had screwed up, come home, and taken it over because he needed it for work. It really sucked that my parents had agreed to this, basically rewarding him for blowing it while I had to ride my bike or bum rides off my friends.

And what was he doing hanging around? He'd told me he wasn't coming—like he had better things to do than be at his brother's first real gig—and then he was there, smirking, making me choke, staying after to see his handiwork.

My steps slowed. Maybe if I took long enough, he'd go away.

I was getting closer and he wasn't moving. He was looking over his shoulder, waving as a girl came around the corner smiling at him, a girl I recognized, a girl who spun me back to last year, when I was a freshman and she was a sophomore....

Freshman year. Del 17, Ori 14. Ori had taken the long way around to geometry again, hoping to catch sight of Amber Greer. This time he was going to say more than hi to her. He was going to ask her about her new car. He knew she'd turned sixteen and just gotten her license.

As he turned the corner, he saw her with a group of friends near her locker. He took a breath, gathering his courage.

"Hey, Amber."

"Hey." She barely glanced at him.

One of her friends whispered something in her ear, and she turned to look, her face flushed. Ori followed their gazes to his brother.

"Hi, Del," Amber said.

"Hey," Del said, glancing from her to Ori, then back to her. "Did you know Ori's in a band?" He stepped behind Ori and clapped a hand on his shoulder, forcing Amber to look at him. "You should check them out. They are smokin'. They're going to be playing some gigs soon. When's your first one?" He looked at Ori.

So did everyone else.

"Um." There wasn't a gig. There wasn't even a band yet. Ori and his friends had just started talking about it.

"Soon," Del said, smacking his shoulder again. "Ask Ori about it sometime, okay?" He looked right at Amber.

"Sure," Amber said, her eyes on Del.

Del didn't look back at her. "Any of you seen Tara?"

Amber shook her head, clearly disappointed that Del had mentioned his girlfriend.

"I think she's near the gym," Ori said.

"Thanks, buddy." He punched Ori's arm, their eyes locking briefly—Ori's saying "thanks," Del's saying "no sweat, bro."

My feet dragged me closer to Del and the girl he had his arm around—Amber Greer. She was kissing Del's chin, her chest pushing against his bicep. Goody for her. She finally got the Taylor brother she wanted. At least for a little while. Del was pretty fickle with girls these days.

Okay, maybe he'll be in a good mood. Maybe it will be fine.

I took a breath and forced a smile.

"Hey, Del," I said. "Thanks for coming out."

"Wouldn't miss it, little bro," he said. "Nice work." He smiled his lopsided, engaging Del smile, smacking my arm. I let myself relax.

"It was amazing," Amber said, and she looked like she meant it.

"Well, except for . . . you know." Del chuckled.

And just like that it was as if all those looks and comments of the last several weeks were wiped away and the old Del stood in front of me, laughing and joking.

"I know," I said, shaking my head. "I don't know what happened during that song. I've played it a million times." No way was I going to say that seeing him had goofed me up.

"Yeah, I've heard you." He smiled over at Amber. "He

plays constantly." He looked at me. "But you can't be perfect all the time. It's cool."

Del thought it was okay, that I was okay.

"That song," Amber said, stepping a little away from Del. "It was so beautiful. It really got to me." She smiled and our eyes locked. "I'd love to hear the whole thing sometime."

Del reached out and grabbed her arm, forcing her back to him. "Let's go get something to eat," he said to her. "You and me."

"Great!" Her full attention was back on Del.

"Orion?"

I turned to see Courtney Calavera standing beside me.

"Just wanted to remind you about my deadline at five tomorrow. Call, e-mail, text—whatever—if you change your mind and want to talk."

"Who was that?" Del asked after she'd left.

"Just some reporter for an online thing," I said. I was about to ask if he wanted to hang out later, play some video games, when he grinned at Amber.

"Reporters called me all the time," Del told her. "Especially after we won state and I was voted MVP. Phone rang off the *hook*."

"I'm sure," Amber said. "That game was so awesome!"

"You were there?"

She nodded, then looked at me. "You'll play that song for me sometime, won't you, Ori?"

"Sure he will," Nick said, coming to stand beside me. "Hey, Del."

Del didn't answer, didn't seem to notice him. He raised

25

an eyebrow at me, then nudged Amber gently down the sidewalk, away from us.

"Don't sweat it, man," Nick said as we headed to Troy's car. "She'll come around to the real Taylor brother. She's totally into your song."

"Right." I climbed into the backseat, looking straight ahead as we pulled away from the curb. Troy flipped on the radio as Alli started talking to him, her hand resting on his arm.

Nick shook his head. "I have so many memories of the three of us—you, me, Del. *Good* memories. I mean, it wasn't like you guys totally got along or whatever. He pushed you around some and was a jerk sometimes. But he was cool most of the time, you know?" He looked over his shoulder, as if he could see the old Del back there on the sidewalk. "It's like— what happened? Did an alien replace him?"

I snorted. Easier to accept that than the truth.

That ever since he'd screwed up his first semester of college, my brother had started to hate me.

Mic Night Monday at FX: A Mix of Talent and "Don't Quit School"

by Courtney Calavera, *DMS* reporter

Many of us have been big fans of Mic Night Monday at the FX Lounge. A few bands that started out there have gone on to play at larger venues, and it's always fun to see new talent.

Last night was a mix of pretty good, okay, and "don't quit your day job" — or "don't quit school," as was the case here, because FX was showcasing high school talent this month.

The first band was introduced as Orion, but there was a bit of a question as to whether this was their actual band name, since it's also the name of the lead singer and guitarist.

They started out with two decent covers, lead Orion Taylor able to hit all the right notes. Nick Brewster kept up the rhythm on drums, smacking out a solo that the audience really got into. Their first original was a rock-pop tune called "Knock It Down, Bring It Up" — a little too Daughtry for my taste, but the crowd ate it up (though I gathered a good percentage of the crowd were family and friends of this group).

"Finals Week" had a good beat, and Taylor and Troy Baines on second guitar knocked out a killer riff in the middle.

Then they slowed things down with "Waiting for You." Unfortunately, Taylor lost his concentration partway through and couldn't recover. Too bad. It had the makings of a nice ballad, with a classic sound and decent lyrics. The band exited early, leaving most of us wanting more, which is a good thing.

The Pissant Pirates came on next, lead singer Dave Carson screeching out their first cover — "Walk This Way" by Aerosmith — and strutting back and forth in the small space like a Steven Tyler wannabe. Not even close, Carson baby.

click here for full story

COLORADO ROCKS

We are an up-and-coming band, nameless but open to suggestions. Feel free to post your band name ideas on our blog. (We don't want to use one of those band name generators — we want it to come from you or us.)

WANTED
Bass guitar player. If you're interested, <u>contact</u> us about audition times.

Countdown to
BATTLE OF THE BANDS:

144
days

BAND NAME: to be named later

| PROFILE | MUSIC | PIX & VIDS | ABOUT/FAQ | CONTACT | BLOG |

Tuesday, January 12

NICK: Yeah, so we had a little hiccup at FX last night, but so what? It happens to the best of them. BTW, thanks for the band name suggestions. We'll put them in the mix and see if we can ever agree on one. You know I'm picky. (I still can't believe I was outvoted on Nick's Stix and Drummurd — that's *drum* spelled forward and backward. I thought it was cool, but no one else did.)

ORION: That whole choke experience at FX inspired a new song I'm calling "Focus" — art can often come from pain and extreme humiliation, eh? The song's about powering through even when you have stuff pulling you in different directions. You've got to keep your focus, eyes on the prize, that kind of thing. Don't know if it will be ready for Matt's Sports in April, but we'll see.

TROY: We'll be checking out some local bands at the Grog and other places in the next couple of weeks, so maybe we'll see some of you there.

BASS AUDITIONS FEBRUARY 5! Get your name in by January 29 so we have you on the list!

COLORADO ROCKS

We are an up-and-coming band, nameless but open to suggestions. Feel free to post your band name ideas on our blog. (We don't want to use one of those band name generators—we want it to come from you or us.)

WANTED
Bass guitar player. If you're interested, contact us about audition times.

Countdown to
BATTLE OF
THE BANDS:

144
days

BAND NAME: to be named later

| PROFILE | MUSIC | PIX & VIDS | ABOUT/FAQ | CONTACT | BLOG |

♛ DominantSpecies

I repeat: How about calling your band the Losers? I heard you play at the FX, and you suck! Pissant Pirates shoulda got an oncore.

✎ PurpleGrrl

Sorry I missed your big debut. I'm sure you were great! BTW, DominantSpecies, it's *encore* not *oncore*, you idiot. And why are you back?

🔥 DragonBreath

DS needs to take a chill pill. You all ROCK.

❄ Halyn

Obviously, DominantSpecies is either one of the Pissant Pirates or a deluded fan. I was @ FX, and the Pissants SUCKED. That guy can't sing at all.

Cool that you can take something painful and turn it into a song. I do that too in my poetry. It's such a great release, like when something bad happens you can get it down and it's like you've gotten rid of it.

🎸 BoyMagnet

Orion is pretty cute in person! I'm planning to go to their gig at Matt's Sports. Who else is?

✎ PurpleGrrl

Hey, BoyMagnet, aren't you a little full of yourself? And the best you can do is a magnet avatar? Makes me think you really aren't a boy magnet or you'd show some of your stuff.

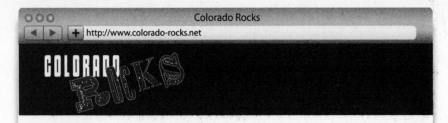

BAND NAME: to be named later

PROFILE	MUSIC	PIX & VIDS	ABOUT/FAQ	CONTACT	**BLOG**

BTW, I'll be at Matt's in April. Look for me. I'll be the one with the purple hair.

BoyMagnet
Purple hair is SO last decade. GMAB.
I'll be the one with the boys ALL OVER HER, including Orion.

Halyn
Take this offline, girls. This is supposed to be about the music.

BoyMagnet
Then why are you talking about your — snore — poetry?

We are an up-and-coming band, name-less but open to suggestions. Feel free to post your band name ideas on our blog. (We don't want to use one of those band name generators — we want it to come from you or us.)

WANTED
Bass guitar player.
If you're interested, <u>contact</u> us about audition times.

Countdown to
BATTLE OF
THE BANDS:
144
days

THREE

Since the FX gig, I'd seen Del only in passing until Wednesday, when Mom brought in a box of stuff she was getting rid of, including an old baseball. I decided to try to be nice.

"Remember when we threw this through the Davises' window?" I asked, pulling the baseball out of the box.

He laughed. "And we both had to work it off cleaning their other windows, and they had, like, a hundred of them that hadn't been cleaned since the turn of the century." He tore open a new bag of potato chips, spilling a few out onto the counter.

"Oh geez, that's right." I smiled and grabbed a few chips. "Remember how pissed Mrs. Davis got when you wrote messages to me in the dirt on the windows? 'Please clean me. I'm disgusting.' 'Help me, I'm melting.'"

"'Young man,'" Del said, doing a perfect imitation of Mrs. Davis, "'you do not make fun of someone you've harmed. I'll speak to your mother about this.'"

My mom chuckled.

"Did she?" I asked her.

"Probably," she said. "I don't remember that specifically. I do remember our discussion about the window cleaning as repayment."

"It took *forever,*" Del said. "I've got to believe we paid for about ten windows, not one."

"It would have been faster if you hadn't used so much soap," I said. "It took twice as long to rinse it off."

He laughed as Vela walked in carrying our mom's laptop.

"Check this out," she said. "Ori's famous!" She turned the screen toward us, displaying the *Denver Music Scene* article.

"How wonderful!" Mom gave me a sideways hug as she read the screen. "She's really got some good things to say about you and the band."

"No one even reads those online reviews," Del said. He hadn't even looked at the computer, the review.

And just like that, the moment was gone. And so were Del and the chips.

"Why'd you have to bring that out here?" I asked Vela.

"Sorry," she said, looking hurt. "I thought you'd be excited."

"I am," I said. "It's just..." I looked back the way Del had gone.

"Oh," Vela said, getting it. "I didn't think about that."

"You shouldn't have to," Mom said. "He's a big boy." She touched my arm. "Celebrate your success. He'll come around."

I grunted. Del was right. No one read those online reviews. There were a zillion sites like those, and who really looked at them? What was so great about it? It wasn't like I'd scored the winning goal in the state lacrosse championship and gotten a partial scholarship to the University of Northern Colorado, like he had.

Still, it would have been nice for him to be happy for me, even if it was just a stupid online review.

I spent the next two days working on "Focus," finally getting enough of it together that it was actually a song. I was trying to get all the way through it one afternoon in the basement, my right hand flying over the strings, my left hand running over the fret like it had a life of its own when—

Snap.

The *thwang* of the off chord made me cringe as a string popped off its peg, flinging itself back toward me like the line on a fishing rod.

I set my guitar down and opened the case, flipping through bags of strings.

Every size but the one I needed.

Groaning, I grabbed my guitar and headed up the stairs, hesitating in front of the kitchen doorway.

"You carry that thing with you everywhere," Del said, motioning to the guitar I gripped in my hand. "Is it, like, your girlfriend?"

I frowned. "I broke a string."

"Why do you have to bring the whole guitar with you?"

I bit my lip, mumbling.

"What?"

"Nothing."

He snorted. "Let me guess. The screwup could never understand the tortured artist."

"You're not a screwup."

"But you're a tortured artist."

"I didn't say that."

"'I didn't say that,'" he mimicked in falsetto. "You're such a girl."

My shoulders tensed. *Let it go.*

He rolled his eyes and walked out, not offering to give me a ride, which was fine by me. Being in an enclosed space for an extended period of time with my brother was the closest thing to hell I could imagine, at least these days. Weird how a few short months could change everything. Before he went to college, he drove me just about everywhere I needed to go and didn't seem to mind. We'd laugh at stupid things and I'd watch him work his magic with girls. The Del Spell, I used to call it in my head, feeling like a little was cast over my average-lookingness when I was with him.

But that was before.

I heard the Honda peel off down the street, leaving me with my only other mode of transportation: my bike.

I headed down the hall to the garage, stopping to stare at the Ultralite Guitar Carrier—Del's name for it—hanging from a hook near the back door. He had retrofitted one of his old rafting life vests about three years ago so I could strap my guitar to my back when I rode my bike. It wasn't one of those bulky orange vests—this was a sleek gray and blue Extrasport Riptide. (*Riptide.* Huh. Possibly good band name.) He'd taken the padding out of the front and added some wide adjustable straps to the back so I could grow into it. I thought it was the coolest thing he'd ever done for me.

I hadn't worn it since he'd been back, but if I wanted to get a new string and finish the song I had no choice. Tugging it off the hook, I strapped my guitar to it, making sure it was secure. Then I slid it on slowly, wondering if it would feel different because *he* was different.

But it felt the same—just a little snugger than the last time I'd had it on—and I couldn't figure out why that bothered me so much.

Gold's Guitars was the closest thing to heaven this side of the Rocky Mountains. It smelled like music—sheets of paper, wood, brass, metal, plastic, and more. The walls were covered with every guitar you could possibly imagine— Fenders and Gibsons, Martins, Rickenbackers, Yamahas, and, of course, Gibson Les Pauls—acoustic, electric, twelve-string, bass. You name it, Ed Gold had it. And if he didn't have it, he could get it for you. Which he was going to do for me when I'd saved enough for *the* Les Paul, one Ed didn't normally carry in his store.

Del had thought it was the baddest guitar ever when I showed it to him online last year.

"You're going to shred on that thing," he'd said.

Now he probably wasn't even thinking about it, couldn't care less whether I shredded or not. And why did I care if he cared?

Argh.

"OT, what's shaking?" Ed came out from behind the

counter, his brown ponytail bouncing against his neck. "You're not on the schedule today." I'd been coming into the store for years and had begged and begged Ed to hire me. He finally had when I turned fifteen, after talking to my parents. Over a year later, I could practically run the place myself, if I wanted to and Ed would let me.

"Hey, Ed." I unsnapped the vest and brought it and my guitar carefully around front. "I need a string. I was right in the middle of a jam session and—"

"Say no more," Ed said, striding over to a carousel where the guitar strings hung. "We'll get you fixed up and playing in no time." He flipped through the bags. "So I heard you started off strong at your gig." He had wanted to come and cheer me on, along with all my guitar mentors, but I had asked them to wait. I knew I'd be way too nervous if they were out in the audience. It had been hard enough with just family and friends.

"Then you also heard I choked in the middle of 'Waiting for You.'"

He shrugged. "When Rod Stewart sang for the first time with the Jeff Beck Group in 1968, he sang the first song while hiding behind some speakers." He clapped me on the shoulder. "You got the first-gig jitters out of the way. It's smooth sailing from now on." He and Courtney Calavera must have been sharing brain waves.

I thought of Del. How I'd wanted him there and hadn't wanted him there. And then he was there and when I'd seen him I'd blown it.

"I hope so."

Ed jabbed the bag of strings toward the Jam Room — a nearly soundproof room he had added last year where people could play as loud as they wanted and not disturb other customers. "Have at it." Of course he would know I had to finish the song I'd been playing when my string broke. And I had to do it on the guitar I'd been playing it on because it was all about the sound I had already created, the sound that still echoed in my mind, waiting to reach its natural end. Ed got this, which was why he hadn't said anything when I walked in with a guitar strapped across my back.

"Thanks, Ed," I said as I took the string from him. When I got inside the Jam Room, I plugged my guitar into one of the amps. It didn't take long to get myself right back where I was, teetering on the edge, ready to fly into oblivion. I backed off a few feet, thrumming my way along, hovering for a second before leaping skyward, feeling the rush as I flew over the clouds, around the sun, and across galaxies.

Step back from me
You can't hold me in your grip
I've set myself free

I strummed harder, strumming thoughts of Del right out of my mind until I reached the end, breathing heavily as I wiped my forehead with my shirt.

I was exhausted but euphoric, grinning from the sheer high of playing. I felt GREAT. Like I could do anything.

"Thanks, Ed!" I shouted as I strode by him, pushing out into the pale January sun as my breath swirled in front of me.

Swinging my leg over the bike seat, I felt ten feet tall. I put on my helmet and slipped on my shades—ever the cool band man. True, we had no name, and we didn't have a bass player, and we didn't know all of our songs yet, and there was a lot of competition for the Battle, but...

We would totally rock.

I felt so amazing as I pushed off down the street that when I saw a white Ford Taurus stopped at a light, with a blond girl wearing sunglasses looking my way, I didn't freak or look away like I usually did.

I looked right at her and kept looking, letting her see my coolness. This was how it would be onstage.

"Ori! Orion Taylor!" The girls scream my name, throwing articles of clothing on the stage. I pick them up and wave them in the air and the screams grow to a deafening shriek.

I am the Guitar Man.

I am the Rock Star.

I am—

Grinning like a maniac because the girl in the Taurus was still looking at me and I was still looking at her.

This rock band dude was definitely cool with the ladies.

This rock band dude just might talk to her if he decides to.

This rock band dude might—

Ride smack into a telephone pole.

FOUR

I caught myself before I hit the ground, a sharp pain shooting up my right arm as I pushed my butt up to keep the arm of my guitar from hitting the sidewalk.

"Oh my God, are you okay?" The voice was female, concerned but not overly so. She was crouching beside me, her hand resting lightly on my shoulder.

Please, God, tell me it isn't Taurus Girl.

Taurus Girl. An okay, but not great, possible band name.

But I couldn't really think about that right now.

I waited for the pain to pass, trying not to wince.

"Fine," I managed to get out between gritted teeth. I glanced at her feet because I was too embarrassed to look at her face. She was wearing flip-flops, even though it was January, and her toenails were painted a bright blue.

Why'd she have to come over here? Wasn't witnessing

my humiliation from afar enough for her? Did she have to see it up close?

"Are you sure? My car's right over there. I can take you to the doctor. Or the hospital."

What happened, young man?

Well, I was checking out a girl across the street and rode right into a telephone pole. Yes, the girl who brought me in, the one laughing hysterically in the corner.

I stood up and turned my back on her, making sure the bike rims hadn't gotten bent. "No, it's cool." My voice cracked slightly, and I cursed it for betraying me. I checked my guitar again before swinging my leg over the seat. "But thanks." I pushed off down the street. If Del had been in this situation, he would have smooth-talked that girl and made her think that crashing into a telephone pole was something every cool person did. She probably would have asked to borrow the bike and helmet and tried it herself.

But it wasn't Del, it was me, so I was riding away as fast as I could.

"Be careful!" Taurus Girl's voice bounced after me, her words causing me to sit up a little straighter. At least she didn't sound like she was laughing.

I raised my hand in acknowledgment before turning at the next corner.

I pulled into our driveway, glad to see it empty, which meant Del was still out. While I was punching in the code for the garage door, Alli walked across the grass.

"Saw you ride off with your guitar," she said. "What happened?"

I told her about the broken string, leaving out the part about riding into a telephone pole.

"Was it one of your new songs?" She hardly noticed the guitar as I pulled the carrier off my back. I'd explained it to her once, about the sound of an unfinished song being in my head, about having to finish it on the exact same instrument if I was interrupted. Like Ed, she got it and didn't think twice about it.

"'Focus.'"

"Cool." She took my bike and wheeled it into the garage while I unhooked my guitar from the Ultralite.

"I bet it will be good," she said. "One of your best." She smiled at me, like she somehow knew I needed a boost after Del being a jerk and that girl seeing me humiliate myself.

I smiled back. She always had been one of my biggest supporters, especially when it came to my music.

Fall. Ori 12. Ori was listening to his iPod in the school parking lot, waiting to get picked up, when he spotted the full-length mirror propped against the Dumpster. He glanced around, saw that he was alone, and walked over to it, raising his hands for an air-guitar session. He sang quietly at first, but soon the song took over and he was belting it out, playing the air as hard as if he were gripping a real guitar in his hands. When the song was over, he let out a whoop, raised his fist in the air—

And heard laughter behind him.

He turned to see a group of guys pointing at him and cracking up.

Alli knocked one of them out of her way as she hurried over to Ori, not even noticing that they were making fun of him. "I didn't know you could sing. Wow."

"I can't," he said. He always sang when he was alone, but he'd never thought of himself as a singer. He played the guitar and if a song had words, it just made sense to sing along with it while he played. That was it.

"Uh, yeah. You can." She shook her head, apparently still amazed. "I mean, when the music teacher forced you to be in that talent show back in—what, third grade or something?—you just played and stared at the floor. You never opened your mouth. But you can sing." She was grinning like crazy. "You should take some lessons. Then you can be lead guitarist and lead singer for your band."

He and Nick didn't have a band—yet—but they'd planned on it. And Alli would be their manager. Glancing over Alli's shoulder, he saw the boys behind her, still mimicking him and pointing. She looked, too.

"Jealous much?" she said to them, then waved dismissively. "You totally have to sing, Ori. Seriously."

"I don't know," he said. But when his mom showed up to take them home, Alli said something to her, and the next thing he knew, he had agreed to see a vocal coach. After that, he was singing and playing and loving the way his voice and the music worked together.

All because of Alli.

"Can't wait to hear it when it's done," Alli said, pushing the door open for me.

"You'll be one of the first." I slipped inside, hanging the Ultralite back on its hook. "Thanks for the help."

"Anytime." She smiled again. "Got to get back and finish that essay. See you later."

"See you." I carried my guitar downstairs to the basement and returned it to its stand, having a brief flash of running into the telephone pole again. I'd been so embarrassed by it that I hadn't looked at Taurus Girl once. I had no idea how tall she was or if her fingernails were blue like her toenails. Del would have known all those things and more.

Del again. I picked up my guitar and played a few more songs, but I couldn't really get into it. I kept imagining what I must have looked like to that girl, checking her out and then riding smack into that pole.

It was humiliating. And even her words — *be careful!* — had taken on a mocking tone in my mind. Maybe she'd been laughing at me after all.

Vela came down a few minutes later. "We have to set the table."

I nodded, putting my guitar back in its case.

"Want to play Family Feud after dinner with me and Del?"

Was she joking?

"No thanks," I said.

She frowned. "You could at least try."

"Every time I do he shuts me down."

"Not every time."

I looked at her. She sighed. "Okay. See you upstairs."

43

Dinner with the new Del could go one of two ways: happy and upbeat Del monopolizing the conversation with stories that made everyone laugh in surprise, or annoyed and sullen Del monopolizing the conversation with his silence and grunts, reducing the talk to "How was your day?" "Fine." "Pass the potatoes."

Tonight it was annoyed and sullen Del, so I ate as fast as I could, doing my share of the dishes before popping my earbuds in, cranking my iPod, and plopping myself in front of the family computer.

From: AlliCat098@gmail.com
To: GuitarFreak@earthlink.net
Subject: FW: Does Orion e-mail people off the web page?

Ori —
I got this through the Colorado Rocks site a few minutes ago. She sounds nice (I'm assuming it's a she) and you've met her, so you should write her back.
L8rs,
Al

- -
A. Wilcox, Webqueen for the Band to Be Named Later (but that's not their name so don't call them that!)

Original Message
From: HalynFlake34@yahoo.com
To: Awilcox@34756.colorado-rocks.net
Subject: Does Orion e-mail people off the web page?

Hi, A. Wilcox,

I'd like to get in touch with Orion if I can. I ran into him today and he had to leave in a hurry, so I didn't really get a chance to talk to him.

You can tell him I'm into writing poetry so maybe we can talk about writing, since I know he writes his own songs.

Anyway, if you could pass this along, I'd appreciate it.

Thanks!

Halyn

P.S. Orion is a cool name. I assume it's after the constellation?

I stared at the screen. Good grief. Taurus Girl—who had just seen me get intimate with a telephone pole—was Halyn from the website.

My first thought: *Why is she writing me?*

My second thought: *How cool is it that she didn't say anything about the telephone pole?*

My third thought: *I'm so humiliated that she saw me ride into a telephone pole.*

My fourth thought: *How cool is it that she writes poetry?*

My fifth thought: *I can never write her back.*

My sixth thought: *She told me to be careful.*

My seventh thought: *What would I say to her?*

My eighth thought:

I closed down my e-mail and headed up to my room.

COLORADO ROCKS

We are an up-and-coming band, nameless but open to suggestions. Feel free to post your band name ideas on our blog. (We don't want to use one of those band name generators — we want it to come from you or us.)

WANTED

Bass guitar player. If you're interested, contact us about audition times.

Countdown to
BATTLE OF
THE BANDS:

139

days

BAND NAME: to be named later

| PROFILE | MUSIC | PIX & VIDS | **ABOUT/FAQ** | CONTACT | BLOG |

Okay, so Alli's been bugging us about getting this page up, so we had to cheat and check out the FAQs of other bands on COLORADO ROCKS to decide what we were going to include here. We're new, so sue us.

How did you get started as a band?

Orion's been playing since he was in the womb. Okay, maybe not that early, but early, dudes, seriously.

Nick and Ori have been friends since forever, and when they were about twelve, Nick got his first drum set. Next thing you know, they were jamming together after school and on weekends. When they got to high school, they saw Troy in the school talent show. He played guitar and did some vocals, and a band without a name — YET — was born.

Nick is the "mastah drummah," as he calls himself. According to his mom, he was banging on pots and pans as a baby. He still takes lessons and plays as much as possible.

Troy got his first guitar when he was ten, after trying out the violin, oboe, and ukulele. He still has his ukulele and pulls it out every so often to drive Nick crazy, who claims it's a sissy instrument.

Do you write all your own material?

Orion writes most of the songs, with help from Nick and Troy. He started writing when he was in eighth grade during a poetry unit in school. Everyone thought poetry was boring, but we (O and N) had this really cool teacher who mixed in song lyrics and said that they were poetry, too. We ended up doing an original song for our final project that eventually became "Suburban Nightmare." Back then it was called "Eat Your Wheaties." We got an A.

Gold's Guitars supports this band. • 303-555-GOLD

This site updated and maintained by A. Wilcox.

COLORADO ROCKS

We are an up-and-coming band, nameless but open to suggestions. Feel free to post your band name ideas on our blog. (We don't want to use one of those band name generators — we want it to come from you or us.)

WANTED
Bass guitar player. If you're interested, contact us about audition times.

Countdown to
BATTLE OF
THE BANDS:
139
days

BAND NAME: to be named later

| PROFILE | MUSIC | PIX & VIDS | ABOUT/FAQ | CONTACT | BLOG |

Which bands influence your sound?

Our music is a weird mix of folk, southern, and hard rock, largely due to parental influence. Orion's and Nick's parents are totally into classic rock and own practically all the songs on every version of *Guitar Hero* either on their original vinyl, CD, digital download, or all three. Yes, *GH Encore: Rocks the 80s* is a parental fave. As Orion says: When you've been lulled to sleep to the sounds of Jeff Beck, the White Stripes, Skynyrd, Zeppelin, Big Head Todd, Incubus, and more, your tastes tend to run the gamut.

Nick likes to drum to a lot of different rock and heavy metal bands.

Troy's into some classic rock, but he also likes some of the new bands and less well-known ones, like Green River Ordinance out of Texas. They opened for the Goo Goo Dolls at Red Rocks, and it was love at first chord.

And we love to support the locals who have made it big or are on their way: the Fray, Big Head Todd and the Monsters, Flobots, 3OH!3, Tickle Me Pink, kosmøs, and more.

If we think of more questions or you have some, we'll add them. Otherwise, this is it.

FIVE

The following Wednesday, I was at my locker between second and third period when Alli came up beside me.

"Did you reply to Halyn's e-mail?" she asked. "When did you two run into each other? What's she like?"

"Slow down, Al," I said. "I haven't had a chance to reply." No way was I going to tell her that Halyn had seen me bite it big with a telephone pole.

"Well, she seemed really nice, so I hope you..."

She stopped talking as we both noticed some commotion at the end of the hall. Stepping out, I craned my neck—

And had to blink once. Twice.

No. Please tell me Del was not standing in the middle of the Falcon High School hallway with a bunch of seniors laughing and talking. The girls were all looking at him with that stupid look girls get when they're around Del or guys like him. The look they never gave me.

"What's Del doing here?" Alli was peering down the hall, too.

"How would I know?"

"Well, he *is* your brother, and you, like, live with him."

I narrowed my eyes. "So?"

"Right," she said, biting her lip. "Sorry. Sometimes I forget you two aren't getting along."

I braced for more comments from Expert Alli. When Del had first started his Dr. Jekyll and Mr. Hyde thing, I'd made the mistake of complaining to Alli about it. She, of course, thought we should talk it out, and I, of course, looked at her like she'd grown another head.

"Okay, fine," she'd said. "I get it. Boys don't have those kinds of conversations. But they should. That's all I'm saying."

Of course, that wasn't all she was saying, because she had plenty of other advice to give me and plenty of examples from girl world about when two people were mad or one was pissed about something and took it out on the other, blah, blah, blah.

So I waited, but she didn't say anything, just kept staring down the hall at Del. "I know it sounds totally corny and stupid, but it's like he's got some spell over them," she said finally. "The girls are drooling and the guys are idolizing."

"You did your share of drooling, if I recall."

Alli rolled her eyes. "I was twelve. What do you expect? I guess we all had to go through our Del-crazy phase." Like it was some kind of inevitable rite of passage. Ages two to three: Lose the diaper. Age six or seven: Lose your front teeth. Age twelve: Lose your sanity over my brother.

I wanted to ask why, but then didn't because I really didn't want to know. I had spent most of my time at Falcon scrambling to get out from under the Del shadow and now here it was again, casting long and wide.

"Remember at the beginning of last year when everyone thought you would be like Del and paid a lot of attention to you?"

Until they got close and saw right away that even if the hair was the same, the eyes, the nose, the mouth, the body—everything else was different. Then I was virtually ignored.

"Gee, I'm so happy you reminded me." I adjusted my books against my hip and turned to head to class.

"Ori!"

He was *not* talking to me. Not in the school that he used to own but that I had partially claimed after he left, a small corner for myself that had nothing to do with him.

"Ori! Bro!"

Two girls were giving me a look like "Are you crazy? Turn around and talk to the god who is your brother."

So I did. Because I'm stupid or I didn't want them to think I was stupid, which was basically the same thing.

"What are you doing here?" I didn't look at him as he fell into step beside me.

"I called Coach to see if he might need some help with lacrosse this spring. He told me to come by."

Did that mean he'd still be here in the spring? What about going back to college? Moving out? Moving on?

"Del Taylor! What's up, dude?" A senior who had been

on the lacrosse team with Del last year clapped him on the back. "I thought you were up at Greeley."

"UNC was holding me back, man," Del said with his easy smile. "Got new plans on the horizon."

"Cool," the guy said, grinning back. They talked a little bit more before the guy had to leave. "See you around."

"Holding you back?" I asked.

"Works for me," Del said, smiling and waving to a group of girls. He looked around, shaking his head. "God, sometimes I really miss high school."

"You're sick," I said.

"You don't know how good you have it," Del said. "This is where it's at. Top of the heap and all that."

"I'm a sophomore," I said. "Not exactly the top of the heap."

"I was at the top when I was a freshman," Del said, saluting another group who recognized him.

He stated it as a fact, as if he'd just said they painted the lockers this year (which they had and which Del, of course, hadn't noticed). Not bragging. A statement of fact, according to everyone who knew him then. A hugely annoying true statement of fact.

"I'm going to be late for class," I said, speeding up to get ahead of him. I didn't look back even though a part of me wanted to, to see if he was still there, if he was watching me or if his attention had already turned to something or someone else.

"Okay, so how weird was it that Del was here?" Alli asked as we all sat down in the cafeteria for lunch a few hours later.

51

"Alumni visit their alma maters all the time, Alli girl," Troy said. "It's cool."

Alli was looking at me, and I knew she was expecting me to say something. But I didn't want to think about my brother.

"New app?" I asked Nick, whose fingers were sliding all over his iPod Touch.

"New version." Nick tilted it toward me. "Check it out."

I shook my head as I watched him play *Fruit Ninja*. "What is it with you and slicing up fruit?"

"It's a skill."

"You do realize you aren't actually wielding a knife."

Nick scowled. "Did you even look at the graphics? They're *amazing*."

I took the banana off my tray and set it in front of him along with a plastic knife.

"Let's see what you've got."

"That knife is not going to cut it." He grinned, suddenly aware of his lame joke.

"It's a banana. It's soft."

"I have to get through the skin." But he picked up the knife and carved the air like it was a miniature sword, lowering it until it touched the banana skin.

I snatched his iPod and began running through his apps. "Do you still have that driving one on here?" I liked vehicle simulations, whether they were cars, planes, or spaceships, though the car ones were my favorites.

"I took it off," he said. "I needed room for other apps." He was hunched over now, still focused on the banana. "I think the only way to do this is by using a sawing motion."

"That defeats the whole exercise," I said, sliding the iPod back to him. "What do you have on yours, Troy?"

"The usual," Troy said. I grabbed it and started to play *Tetris*, the old standby.

"You should really save to get your own," Alli said.

"I don't mind if he borrows mine." Troy took a bite of his sandwich. "But you should think about getting one, Ori. Remember that songwriter app I told you about? Totally up your alley."

"True," I said. "Maybe after I get the Les Paul I can save for one of these."

Alli glanced up. "Do you think Del would stay for lunch?"

"No way," I said, but my head flew up anyway. I hated how my heart beat faster at the mere thought that he might be here. I hated how I panicked, how I might have sunk under the table if he *had* been here. I dropped my eyes back down to the screen.

Alli looked at me, but I didn't return her gaze. "You just need to tell him how you feel, get it out in the open. Then maybe you won't dread having him around."

I groaned. "Give it a rest, Al. Seriously."

"Okay, fine," she said. "But one of you is going to have to do something at some point."

"It should be Del."

She smiled. "But you're the bigger man."

I refused to get caught in her trap. I shifted my gaze to Nick, who was now poking the banana skin with the knife.

"So? What's the verdict on the Great Banana Slice Caper?"

"There's only one way to do it." He held the plastic knife

like a dagger and plunged it into the banana. The skin split, and he pulled it back before slicing the fruit inside into neat discs.

"That was a pretty violent entry," I said.

"It had to be done," he said. "The skin is just too tough. The only way to get to that soft center with one of these is to jab your way through." He slid the knife under a banana circle and held it aloft. "Want a piece?"

I shook my head, glancing over my shoulder in a way I hoped looked casual, like I was just stretching my neck, not double-checking to make absolutely sure Del wasn't in the cafeteria.

He wasn't, and relief flooded through me, which was kind of annoying. I never used to be on edge when Del was around.

Now I felt like that all the time.

That afternoon, Del sauntered into the kitchen behind me, clearly still on a high from his top-of-the-heap experience at school. I relaxed a little.

"Oooh, excellent."

He slid a chip into the cheese and jalapeño pepper mound on the counter and scooped up a big mouthful, chewing loudly. "You make a mean *queso*, Ori." He smacked me on the back before yanking open the refrigerator door. "Remember my great water balloon fight at school last year?" He pulled out a can of Coke, nodding. Being at Falcon today must have dislodged a boatload of memories.

"Yeah," I said, because I did remember. Everyone but the

seniors had been stuck in classes that period, but some of us could see them out on the grass through the classroom windows. "You nailed Chad pretty good a few times."

Del chuckled. "He got me back, though. I was soaked." He took a swig of Coke. "Maybe you'll do something like that, keep up the Taylor tradition of crazy senior pranks. Fun times."

I raised an eyebrow. "Are you kidding? You could get away with stuff like that, Del. If I did it—bam. Immediate suspension."

Del grinned. I could tell he liked that he could get away with things that I couldn't.

"Don't sell yourself short, Ori. I think you could pull a pretty good prank or two, especially with some guidance from a pro." He tipped the can at me in a semisalute before heading up to his room.

A part of me hated how much that meant to me—that grin, that little gesture. I was just like the people at school, wishing a little bit of the Del light would shine down on me.

But another part of me, a bigger part, just let it ride because it felt good.

When the doorbell rang twenty minutes later and I was the only one downstairs, I got to welcome Amber Greer into my house.

"Hi, Ori. Can I use your bathroom?"

I pointed her in the right direction, relishing the fact that I could have this effect on women: See Orion Taylor, must head immediately to the nearest bathroom. At least she'd said hi first.

Del was all grins as he came down the stairs.

"She here?"

I nodded.

"Can you believe she's still into me after all this time?" he said. "She told me when I saw her at your gig, says I didn't even notice her at Falcon." He shook his head. "I don't know what was wrong with me."

I stared at him. He seriously didn't remember that I had liked her and that was why he'd stayed away from her? Well, that and the fact that he was going out with Tara. And he seemed to have forgotten that he'd even tried to steer her in my direction. Because the old Del Taylor had had my back.

The new Del Taylor couldn't give a crap about my back.

When Amber was finished in the bathroom, they made out in front of me in the kitchen.

I lost my appetite for the meanest *queso* ever.

◀ ▶ ➕ http://www.colorado-rocks.net

COLORADO ROCKS

We are an up-and-coming band, nameless but open to suggestions. Feel free to post your band name ideas on our blog. (We don't want to use one of those band name generators — we want it to come from you or us.)

WANTED
Bass guitar player. If you're interested, contact us about audition times.

Countdown to
BATTLE OF
THE BANDS:
132
days

Countdown to
LES PAUL:
92
days

BAND NAME: to be named later

| PROFILE | MUSIC | PIX & VIDS | ABOUT/FAQ | CONTACT | BLOG |

Sunday, January 24

NICK: Remember, bass auditions are coming up on Feb. 5, so if anyone wants to bribe me, feel free. JK

ORION: And keep those band names coming.
By the way, I think everyone should know that I'm saving up for a screaming new Les Paul. Black, beautiful, with a mahogany body, ebony fingerboard. Can't you just feel it? Follow along with us, kids, as we count down to the big day. Yes, my savings account will reach critical mass around April 11, at which time I will pay for it. Then it will be two to three weeks after that. But I'm convinced it will arrive on April 26, so that's what I'm using for the countdown.

ALLI: April 26 was the first time Orion played a real guitar when he was, like, 6 or 7, in case anyone is wondering. Don't ask me why I know — it's embarrassing to have such a useless fact stuck in your brain.

TROY: We'll keep you posted on the new bass player.

We are an up-and-coming band, nameless but open to suggestions. Feel free to post your band name ideas on our blog. (We don't want to use one of those band name generators — we want it to come from you or us.)

WANTED
Bass guitar player. If you're interested, <u>contact</u> us about audition times.

Countdown to
BATTLE OF
THE BANDS:
132
days

Countdown to
LES PAUL:
92
days

BAND NAME: to be named later

PROFILE   MUSIC   PIX & VIDS   ABOUT/FAQ   CONTACT   BLOG

PurpleGrrl
Nick, I think your band names are great. But maybe that's because I love the drums. And your rehearsal video is great, but the videographer needs to span all the band members next time. Too much Troy! (Not that you aren't great, Troy, but I think the others deserve some face time.)

BoyMagnet
PurpleGrrl loves Nick. PurpleGrrl loves Nick.
Orion, do you have a girlfriend?

PurpleGrrl
BoyMagnet, it was a comment about liking drums. End of story.

DominantSpecies
You guys can't be serious about auditions. Who wants to be in a high school band except your lame friends?

GuitarFreak
DominantSpecies: Feel free to show up and see who wants to be in our band.

Halyn
DominantSpecies: What's with you? I'm guessing you tear other people down because you feel like a nobody. Go away.

BoyMagnet
GuitarFreak: Are you Troy or Orion? Either one, answer my question, please (about the girlfriend).

COLORADO ROCKS

We are an up-and-coming band, nameless but open to suggestions. Feel free to post your band name ideas on our blog. (We don't want to use one of those band name generators — we want it to come from you or us.)

WANTED
Bass guitar player.
If you're interested, contact us about audition times.

Countdown to
BATTLE OF
THE BANDS:

132
days

Countdown to
LES PAUL:

92
days

BAND NAME: to be named later

| PROFILE | MUSIC | PIX & VIDS | ABOUT/FAQ | CONTACT | BLOG |

🏆 DominantSpecies
You're all a bunch of girls, including GuitarFreak, no matter which one he is.

🦢 BoyMagnet
You guys should block DominantSpecies. He's a jerk. But I still want to know if you have a girlfriend! And PurpleGrrl wants to know if Nick does!

🏆 DominantSpecies
Go ahead, block me. I'm not coming back anyway.

SIX

Like most people in our suburban development, we had a three-car garage. And like most people, we couldn't fit three cars in it, because one bay was jammed with stuff—in our case it was a hodgepodge of rafting and camping gear, boxes, tools, paint cans, and such. But my rock-maniac parents were more than happy to clear it out to make more room for the auditions. Pulling cars out on one side had been fine for our rehearsals, but we needed more space if we were going to fit the bass players and any friends they brought along. So here we were, the weekend before the auditions, creating audition space.

"This is really exciting," my mom said. "Kenny Wayne Shepherd recorded his first album when he was seventeen."

"I'm not recording an album, Mom." I shook my head even as I smiled. "We're just trying to get a bass player."

"I know, honey." She scooped up a few fishing poles and

tucked them under her arm. "I'm just saying. And he was playing clubs at fifteen or something, I think," she murmured as she walked back into the house. A font of music trivia, my mom.

A few minutes later, Vela and I were carrying some boxes from the garage to the basement when Del came down the stairs. He rubbed the top of Vela's head. "You still want me to take a look at your history report?"

She nodded. "Mrs. Jensen said you were really good at history and that I should ask you."

"I got an A in that class," I said.

Vela shrugged. "She said Del."

Del grinned. "Sorry, bro. The expert has been called." He glanced at the boxes in our arms. "So you're really going through with this audition thing?"

I stiffened, wondering where this was going, especially because I hadn't been too thrilled about the audition idea when Nick first brought it up.

"Why would people audition for a high school rock band?" I'd asked him. "It's not like it's *American Idol* or something. Why don't we just ask someone we already know?"

"What fun is that?" Nick had said. "We've got to create some buzz about our band. Holding auditions makes us look big, legit."

I had had to admit that legit was what I wanted. We all did. We wanted to be taken seriously as a band by the time we got out of high school. Having a good bass player who mixed well with us would really help. And winning the Battle would be a huge step in that direction, with an opportunity to connect with people in the industry, get them to listen to our stuff.

Of course, it would also help to have a band name.

"That just adds to the mystery," Nick had said when I pointed this out.

And that was that. He put the word out on craigslist and Facebook and at music stores, and people started signing up to audition. It was crazy cool.

Del actually seemed to be waiting for an answer. "Nick" was all I said.

He laughed. "Say no more." Which made me laugh, too, because Del knew Nick almost as well as I did. "Gotta love Nick."

"Yeah," I said. "Gotta love him."

"So, how many people? Two or three?"

"Actually, we've got about twelve coming." Plus their friends, because we thought it would be good to see how they played in front of a semiaudience.

"Twelve? Really?" Del shook his head. "Where do these people come from?"

"All over." I kept my voice neutral, waiting for his next move.

"Unbelievable." He shook his head again before pounding up the stairs to his room.

Why did I suddenly feel like this was a stupid idea? *It's not stupid*, I told myself. *People are coming. For* our *band*.

"Will you be nervous if he comes to check it out?" Vela asked as we headed out to the garage for more boxes.

"He won't come." No way would he waste his precious

time watching potential bass players for his brother's band. And I didn't want him there.

"He might. And remember what happened at FX."

"That didn't have anything to do with Del." *How did she know?*

"Oh. Okay. I just thought…well, whatever." She dropped her head to grab another box, her hair hiding her face.

After we were both loaded up, we headed right back to the basement, stacking the boxes next to the others. Vela looked thoughtful, running her fingers over the side of a box. "Remember how he used to say you and Nick could play with boxes and string? That you were so good you didn't need instruments?"

The memory was like a punch in my gut. Del *had* said that. More than once. Boxes and string. Nick on the boxes, me on strings—just like the guitar my mom helped me make out of cardboard years ago. I glanced over at the closet door. Was it still in there?

"You really *could* play with just boxes and string, you know." Vela smiled at me.

"Thanks," I said, smiling back. But I didn't have the same feeling of pride I used to get when Del said it.

She started back up the stairs. "Coming?"

"In a sec," I said. "I want to do a few things down here first."

After she'd gone, I walked over to the closet and opened the door. Bending down, I tugged at the piece of cardboard stuck beneath the bottom shelf and the floor. It crackled as it came loose—my cardboard guitar. It was bent, with two of the strings unwound from the makeshift pegs. Placing my hand on the "fret board," I plucked one of the strings. It didn't make a sound out loud, but I could hear the chord perfectly in my mind, just as I had all those years ago.

Spring. Del 10, Ori 7. Ori sat in the corner of Mr. Keenan's living room while Del had his guitar lesson, "playing" his own guitar. After the first lesson, Ori and his mom had made a cardboard one, so now Ori followed along, placing his fingers on the strings they'd attached. His mom thought it was cute that he wanted to be like his brother. But for once Ori didn't want to be like Del, because Del wasn't any good. And Ori wanted to be good. He wanted to be the best guitar player in the world.

After about six lessons, Del started getting impatient.

"You've really got to set time aside every day for practice," Mr. Keenan said, looking at Mrs. Taylor. "They usually don't do it on their own."

"Ori does." Del looked at Ori. "Let him play."

It was true, the practicing on his own. Ori played his cardboard guitar every day, mimicking the movements he'd seen Mr. Keenan do at the lessons.

"That's just a toy," their mother said.

"Here." Del held out his guitar to Ori. "Try this."

Ori looked at Del, then at his mother, then at Mr. Keenan.

"You've paid for the lesson, and we still have ten minutes left," Mr. Keenan said.

Their mom sighed. "Are you sure this is what you want?" she asked Del.

He nodded.

"Okay," she said. "But I think the guitar's too big for him."

Ori took a deep breath and reached out for the guitar. It was heavier than he'd imagined it would be, and Del had to hold it while he got his bearings.

"Let's try G," Mr. Keenan said, reaching out to place Ori's fingers on the correct strings. But Ori beat him to it, snapping them into place and strumming a near-perfect sound.

Mr. Keenan raised his eyebrows as Ori found all the chords easily, strumming the notes.

"See, Mom?" Del said. "Let Ori play guitar. I want to play lacrosse."

I stood up, holding the cardboard guitar in my hands as I took a few steps toward the large trash can in the corner of the basement. I stopped in front of it, looking at the first guitar I'd ever had, at the ridiculous white strings where my fingers had practiced my first chords. Turning to the closet, I tucked the guitar back where I'd found it.

SEVEN

The days flew by, and when the afternoon of Friday, February 5, rolled around, Alli and I grabbed our bikes from the school rack, racing to get home and get ready for the auditions. It was cold with some snow on the ground, but the roads were clear, so we were expecting a good crowd.

"I'll be over after I dump my stuff!" Alli shouted as she rode up her driveway and I rode up mine, swerving to avoid the Honda that meant Del was home. But the Brewsters' truck was there, too, which meant Nick had arrived. That made me feel better.

"This is amazing," Nick said, standing in the middle of OT Studios, taking it all in.

"I know." I was really happy with what we'd done. It still looked like a garage, but it was bigger with all the junk put away, and we had set up some chairs, brought in a few space heaters, and put down a padded tarp where the auditions would take place. We'd also set up our equipment because we planned to play one of our originals at the beginning to give everyone a taste of our sound.

Alli and Troy arrived and started setting up lights in front of the tarp stage. Then Alli set up her "instant office"— a TV tray and a laptop—in her usual corner before taking her camera out of its bag and setting it on a tripod.

Two hours later, OT Studios was packed with people— the bass players had definitely brought their friends and fan clubs.

Alli tugged my arm.

"Can you believe what the band atmosphere will do to people?"

"What do you mean?"

"Look at her," Alli said, pointing to the girl attached to Nick. "First of all, she would probably never wear that Metallic Barbie outfit in public, and second of all, she's all over *Nick*. Hello?"

"Some girls actually find the Brew Man attractive," I said as the girl stroked his arm. I could tell he was close to hyper-ventilating. He put a hand on the wall to steady himself.

"She just wants you to pick her boyfriend as your bass player," Alli said, pointing to a guy standing a few feet from Metallic Barbie. "Kind of like sleeping with the director, only she's just flirting with one of the judges."

"Huh," I said.

"But they aren't all like that," Alli said. "Maybe we can find someone who's more *your* speed."

I knew she didn't mean anything by that, but it still stung.

"Like *her*. I bet *she's* nice." She nodded to a girl with stringy brown hair. "Quietly understated."

I shrugged. Why was she trying to find me someone anyway? I was perfectly happy being incognito, admiring girls from afar without having to engage in any actual conversations that might show my geek side.

Shifting my gaze to the Goth girl next to Stringy Hair, I noted her ripped T-shirt, long gloves cut off at the fingers, tight jeans, heavy boots. Her hair was so black it was almost purple, and—wait a minute—she held a *serious* bass guitar in her hands. Whoa. You didn't see too many girl bass players. From this distance, I couldn't tell the brand of her guitar, but I had a feeling it could scream. It would be interesting to see if Goth Girl could make it scream.

"Man, that's awesome."

"I knew you had the ability to look beneath the surface," Alli said.

I looked at her, furrowing my brow. "What are you talking about?"

"What are *you* talking about?"

"The bass guitar that girl has," I said. "What did you think I was talking about?"

"Figures you'd be talking about a guitar," Alli said, laughing.

"Even you have to admit it's sweet."

Alli looked back at it. "Yeah, it is. I'll give you that. But back to my original topic. I just don't get why you are such a dork around girls. Sure, you're not Del-hot, but it's not like you're, you know, gross or anything."

"Why am I friends with you again?"

Alli grinned. "Because of my brutal honesty."

"Right," I said. "But I'm not a dork around girls."

"Trust me," Alli said. "You are."

I just sighed. It was hard to argue with Alli when she was right.

"He's not a dork around girls," Nick said as he passed me to check his drums.

"That's the tragedy of dorkdom," Alli said. "Residents don't recognize each other."

Nick raised an eyebrow.

"I think she just called you a dork," I said.

He smacked her on the arm.

"Go back to your laptop and write something good about us on the blog," I said.

"I always do." She smiled, then glanced toward the front of the garage. "Boobs," she muttered as she headed toward her makeshift desk. "They're everywhere."

I looked over my shoulder at a brunette poured into a black minidress with thigh-high boots to match. If her V-neck plunged any lower, we would have been able to toss raisins at her belly button.

"Isn't this fantastic?" Nick spread his arms wide to encompass the entire garage. "Girls everywhere, all wanting to get close to me. I'm a genius." I didn't remind him that once I was on board with the whole audition thing, *I* was the one who had pushed for open auditions—he'd wanted them closed to bass players only because he thought that seemed more "professional." But I'd convinced him with the audience aspect.

He picked up a stack of papers from the workbench. "These are the score sheets," he said, handing them to Troy and me. "They're already labeled with each person's name."

I nodded, glancing down at them as Nick strode to the mic and announced over the sound system that we'd be starting in five minutes. Then he moved through the chairs to sit next to a girl who'd been signaling him.

I was about to go check my guitar when some action near the garage entrance caught my eye. A blond girl tripped over something I couldn't see, grabbed a guy with a bass guitar who shrugged her off with a scowl, then spun away, shouting "Sorry! I'm so sorry!" before landing in Nick's lap.

Nick grabbed her, startled. She tried to push off him but lost her balance again, apologizing a mile a minute. Nick was laughing and shaking his head. Even from here I could tell she was cute. If I knew I wouldn't turn into a dork, as Alli had so generously pointed out, I might actually have gone up and talked to her. But the dork possibility loomed large, so I didn't. Instead, I turned back to the equipment and fiddled with my amp. About a minute later, Alli was whispering in my ear.

"Someone has a question for you."

It was the girl who'd fallen into Nick's lap. And she *was* cute—hopefully not cute enough to get her on Del's radar—with big brown eyes and long eyelashes without a lot of makeup.

Cute girl in proximity = loss of brain function.

Alli, wearing her don't-go-to-Dorkville look, got in my line of sight and smacked my arm before walking past me.

"You wanted to ask me something?" If only I were playing my guitar. I always felt more confident when I was playing. But I guess I couldn't go around playing my guitar all the time while I was trying to talk to cute girls. That would be pretty stupid.

"I'm Jane Garfield," she said. "My friend over there, Gwyn, with the killer bass guitar? She'd like to go earlier rather than later if that's okay. She's got a family thing to get to."

I paused for a moment because her voice sounded vaguely familiar. But then I was drawn to her eyes, wondering if she had any idea how amazing they were. I mean, they were *really* brown with yellow flecks in them, and I could tell it wasn't from contacts or anything. And her eyelashes, long and thick, surrounding those eyes—did I say they were incredible?

"Orion?" She waved a hand in front of my face.

"Sorry," I said. "I was, uh, just trying to think if that would work, and I think it will. Tell her sure. No problem."

"Really?" Relief spread across her face. "That's great."

She was gone before I could say anything else, not that I had planned to, but still.

"Did she want my number?" Nick came up beside me.

"No," I said. "She—"

"She was on my lap," he said. "Her butt was touching my legs."

I sighed.

"It *was*," Nick insisted.

"I know," I said, suddenly annoyed. "But she didn't want your number, okay?" I explained about Gwyn.

"Fine. Geez." He glanced her way. "Maybe she's just shy because she fell into my lap."

I gritted my teeth.

"Gentlemen, I think we should start." Troy tugged at both our sleeves and we headed to our makeshift stage.

"Absolutely," I said, almost glad to have to go to the mic to speak as our front man, since it meant not having to hear Nick talk about Jane sitting on his lap.

"Um," I said into the mic, "so, if we could have everyone's attention." I cleared my throat. "So I'm Orion Taylor, that's Nick Brewster on drums, and Troy Baines on guitar."

Vela and her crew clapped and cheered. They'd arrived a few minutes ago, cramming in near the back. I smiled at them as a few others joined in, whistling. Picking up the loaner electric, I pulled the strap over my head. Once the guitar was there, secure against my body, I felt better.

"We know that all of you said you've heard some of our stuff on our site, so you have a sense of what you're getting into," I said. "But we thought we'd play one of our songs so you could see how we play together." I strummed once, then smiled. "You know where the door is if you decide to leave."

There was a ripple of laughter. I looked over to see if Jane had noticed. She was smiling, but she was looking down at her phone, not at me, which meant she probably hadn't heard my witty remark. Or maybe she was so amused, she was texting a friend about it this very second.

Right, Ori.

"This one's called 'Stand Up and Be Counted.'" I glanced

back at Nick, since he opened the song with a sweet drum intro — and we were off. We weren't even halfway through the first verse when people were on their feet, clapping and dancing.

The music sucked me in like it always did, and I played and sang like nobody's business. There was something about moving my hand across those strings, producing these sounds, singing words that fit — confidence flowed through me, and I looked directly at several girls as I sang right to them.

We finished with a flourish, guitars jutting skyward before we brought them down for the final chords, Nick thrumming away like a madman behind us.

The room erupted in applause. People were on their feet, and some of the girls surged forward, surrounding us. They were talking quickly — "Oh my God, that was *amazing*" to Nick, who was eating it up — "You're, like, a real rock star" to me, who wasn't sure what to do — "Play another one" to Troy, who was being blockaded by Alli, her touch-him-and-you-die look lasered across her face. Then girls were squeezing my arm, running fingers over my wrist. Belly Button Girl was there in front of me, so close we were sharing the same air as she grabbed my arm and then squeezed my hand. My eyes dropped automatically to her cleavage even as I jumped to the side, falling into another girl, who caught me in her arms, smiling wide.

As I jostled to a standing position and the crowd stepped back a little, I caught Del watching, his eyes darting from the girls to me and I knew he was thinking, *You've got to be kidding.* He turned, saying something to the girl next to him, but I could already feel my confidence ebbing. Before it disappeared completely, I reached for the mic.

"Thanks, everyone," I said. "We appreciate your enthusiasm." I smiled at the girls in the front row, and they smiled back, one cocking her head as she kept her eyes on me. "If everyone could take their seats again," I said, "we can get started." The girls shifted slightly, jostling for seats in front. I ran my fingers through my hair, taking a few deep breaths. I wasn't used to this kind of female attention. But I tried to act cool about it because Del was still watching. We got busy tearing down our equipment so that the bass players would have room to move, and people chattered as they settled back into their seats.

"They were all over us," Nick said. "That was awesome."

"It was weird," I said as I unplugged my guitar from the amp. "What *was* that?"

"I call it Rock Star Blindness," Alli said, holding out my guitar case. "RSB for short."

It figured Alli would have a name for it. Hmm. *RSB.* That might be a good band name. But we'd have to come up with something else for what it stands for...or not. Let people guess.

"Yeah," Alli said. "Most girls go wild for musicians, no matter what they look like or how they act. Something about the music completely blinds them to reality. Historical Exhibit A: Mick Jagger." She nodded. "For most girls, it wears off pretty quickly. When the music is over, they see you're nothing special." She looked at Troy. "Except you, of course. You're special."

"I got your meaning, Alli Cat." He put his arm around her shoulder and squeezed. "Thanks for protecting me back there."

"Well, I don't know what she means," I said, even though I did. I was hoping she was wrong. It felt good to have girls looking at me instead of at Del.

"Oh, I didn't mean you in particular, Ori," she said. "I'm talking about the RSB theory in general."

"Can we save this philosophical discussion for another time, babe?" Troy asked. "We've got a bass player to pick."

While they made what Vela called goo-goo eyes at each other, I turned to Nick. "Del's here."

He looked over his shoulder, frowning. "He'd better not cause any problems."

Like either of us would do anything if he did.

And so, at exactly five minutes after seven on Friday, February 5, auditions for the yet-to-be-named band of Orion Taylor, Nicholas Brewster, and Troy Baines began.

EIGHT

Of the twelve who signed up, nine showed. The first bass player was okay but sweated like crazy and kept wiping his forehead with his sleeve. The second was good but kept muttering "okay" under his breath and taking little half steps forward then back, like he was doing some stop-motion dance. The third one was Metallic Barbie's dude. She gave him a serious tongues-involved kiss before he went up. There was a lot of whistling and shouting at that.

But if it was a good-luck kiss, it didn't work. He messed up and had to start over twice.

I glanced at Troy and Nick; this wasn't looking promising.

"Let's let Gwyn play," I whispered. "She has to leave early, remember?"

Nick nodded as he stood up. "Gwyn Farcosi?"

Gwyn stepped forward, plugged into the amp, tuned a

little, then paused. She glanced at Jane, who gave her a nod. She nodded back, adjusted the volume on the amp, and kicked off her shoes so she was barefoot.

Everything flew right out of my head when Gwyn began to play.

Actually, she didn't play. She *shredded*.

Mutilated.

Killed.

She was *unbelievable*. The room erupted into cheers and clapping. For a *bass player*. It wasn't like she was up there doing some fast and furious riff like Troy or I might do, but the crowd was freaking out about her. When she was finished, she picked up her shoes and went back to her place against the wall, where Jane gave her a hug.

Nick, Troy, and I whipped our heads to look at one another at the same time.

"We have got to have her," I whispered. "No question."

"Absolutely," Troy said. "Whatever it takes."

"I don't know," Nick said. "She's friends with my girl. That might get awkward."

Troy and I both gave Nick a look.

"What?"

Troy patted Nick's leg and smiled his I'll-break-this-to-you-gently smile. "Nick, my friend, she's not your girl."

"She fell into my lap."

"Yes, we have indeed established that fact," Troy said. "But give her a chance to see the coolness that is Nick Brewster and make sure she is worthy of such coolness before you claim her as your girl."

Troy was truly the master. And the crazy thing was, it wasn't an act. He totally believed everything he said.

Nick sat up straighter. "You're totally right, dude. If she can't appreciate the Brew Man cool factor, it's not going to work." He nodded. "But I still think we should listen to the rest of the bass players."

"Absolutely," Troy said.

"And we should probably look at everyone's videos in case we missed something," I said.

"Exactly," Nick said, standing up. "We're going to take a ten-minute break," he announced, "and then we'll listen to the rest." He explained where the bathroom was and pointed out a cooler of bottled water near the back of the garage.

We stood up and stretched just as Jane wound her way through the chairs to where we were sitting. Nick grinned while I tried to avoid looking at her amazing eyes.

"So it's okay if we take off, right?" she asked.

"*You're* leaving, too?" Nick asked, barely able to hide his disappointment.

She nodded, eyes flicking briefly in my direction before returning to Nick's. Or maybe I imagined it. "Is that okay?"

"Of course," Troy said quickly, elbowing Nick.

"Yeah, it's totally fine," I blurted out. Jane smiled at me, and I smiled back. "Tell Gwyn thanks. We'll definitely be in touch."

"I will. Thanks." And she was gone.

"My destiny has left the building," Nick mourned.

"Remember the Brew Man cool factor," Troy said, patting Nick's arm. "She may not be worthy."

"Her butt touched my legs."

"Her butt may not be worthy."

Nick nodded. "Good point."

The next bass player was good, but not as good as Gwyn. Number six was decent, but again, not Gwyn caliber. When number seven stepped up, I saw movement out of the corner of my eye. Del was still watching, his arms crossed over his chest, the girl with the belly button dress making her way toward him along the wall. She leaned in to say something to him, and he turned, his eyes dropping to survey her body. He smiled at her, then said something that made her glance in my direction.

I could hear her inner commentary: *Oh God. I can't believe I grabbed him when I could have been grabbing* you. *You're his brother? Really? You two don't look at all alike.*

"Dude. Ori!" Nick nudged me in the ribs. "Pay attention."

I turned back around, focusing on the music.

After the last bass player had finished, Nick, Troy, and I stepped up to the mic and got everyone's attention. I felt Del's eyes on me and hated that it made me feel off balance.

"Okay," I said, my voice squeaking. People chuckled. *Dang it.* I was sure Del was smirking at me now. "So we want to thank everyone for coming out."

"Yeah," Nick said, leaning toward the mic. "We'll be calling the bass player we think is going to work for us, and we'll also post it on our Colorado Rocks site. That's www.colorado-rocks.net. Since we don't have a band name yet, just search for one of our names."

I hurried to the wall and punched the button to open the garage door. People spilled out, talking and laughing as I watched from my place on the steps in front of the door leading into our house. Del was gone and Belly Button Girl was looking my way, smiling at me. I smiled back but thought it might look more like a grimace because my lips were stuck to my teeth.

Then she walked toward me.

"I'm sorry," she said when she got closer. "You know, for grabbing you earlier. I guess I got a little carried away with the music and stuff."

RSB. Damn that Alli and her made-up acronyms that turned out to be true.

"That's okay." At least she was talking to me. I wanted to say something clever, but before I could even try, a voice greeted her from behind me.

"Hey," Del said. "Glad you could stay."

"Yeah," she said, smiling over my shoulder. "The guys I came with are cool about it."

"I can take you home later," Del said. "You want something? Water? Coke?"

"Beer?" she asked, raising her eyebrows.

Del laughed. "My kind of girl." He looked at me. "Great auditions from what I saw. The band will rock." Dr. Jekyll was back, probably because he had a hot girl interested in him. And not just any hot girl, but the girl who had grabbed me earlier and now didn't seem to know I existed.

Score another one for Del.

I was tempted to ask him about Amber Greer, but I

didn't. This was actually a new thing, all these girls. With all his girl-magnet stuff in high school, he'd been loyal to his girlfriend, Tara—until a few months into college.

"It's like a candy store of women up here, Ori," he'd told me in October. "Everywhere you look, there's one that's hotter than the last."

"What about Tara?" I'd asked. He'd been going out with her for a year, and I liked her. She was one of the few girls he'd dated who actually talked to me and didn't treat me like a little kid.

"We're good," he'd said. "But we're not married. I can still look."

The looking had lasted about a month. The next thing I knew, Tara was texting me to tell me my brother was an ass and she hoped he got an STD.

I told her I was sorry and that it was probably just a phase.

✉ **WELL I'M PHASING HIM OUT OF MY LIFE,** she had texted back.

But I knew she'd kept tabs on him through other friends, at least for a while.

Later that night, I overheard Del telling Belly Button Girl one of his war stories.

BBG (giggling): "The whole team took their clothes off and drove away in their underwear?"
Del: "My idea. You should have seen the look on my mom's face when I walked in wearing just my underwear, carrying that muddy uniform."

Muddy Uniform. Would have been a possible band name if it hadn't come from Del.

BBG: *"Oh my God." (More giggling.)*

It was enough to make you want to upchuck your pizza.

COLORADO ROCKS

BAND NAME: to be named later

| PROFILE | MUSIC | PIX & VIDS | ABOUT/FAQ | CONTACT | BLOG |

Sunday, February 7

ALLI: Auditions were awesome! Thanks to everyone who came out and shared their talents. Next week the band will be contacting the bass player they think will be the best fit, and I'll post his or her name on the blog by next weekend. If we can get permission, we might even put some of the audition footage up on the site.

See you around the band scene.

We are an up-and-coming band, nameless but open to suggestions. Feel free to post your band name ideas on our blog. (We don't want to use one of those band name generators — we want it to come from you or us.)

Countdown to
BATTLE OF
THE BANDS:

118

days

Countdown to
LES PAUL:

78

days

COLORADO ROCKS

We are an up-and-coming band, nameless but open to suggestions. Feel free to post your band name ideas on our blog. (We don't want to use one of those band name generators — we want it to come from you or us.)

BAND NAME: to be named later

| PROFILE | MUSIC | PIX & VIDS | ABOUT/FAQ | CONTACT | **BLOG** |

 ### PurpleGrrl

Her??? So girls auditioned too? Cool. Can't wait to hear who's in!

 ### PeacefulWarrior

I'll check in next week. Video would be great.

 ### BoyMagnet

Alli — can you get Ori to answer my question about having a girlfriend? Or maybe you know since you guys are friends? And what about Nick and Troy? Are they attached? PurpleGrrl wants to know, esp about Nick.

 ### PurpleGrrl

BoyM, can you quit being so nosy about things?

 ### BoyMagnet

You KNOW you want to know.

DominantSpecies

Good God. Can't you girls talk about anything else?

 ### PurpleGrrl

Shut up, DominantSpecies. Why are you here anyway? I thought you were never coming back.

BoyMagnet

Orion? Alli? Nick? Troy? ANYONE! Where are you???

Countdown to
BATTLE OF
THE BANDS:
118
days

Countdown to
LES PAUL:
78
days

NINE

Wednesday night we all headed over to the Grog on a scouting mission. New bands rotated through there all the time, most of them high school or college, and tonight a band called Late Arrival was playing. We knew they would be in the Battle of the High School Bands with us, thanks to the Battle website, where all the competing bands were listed. Ours said "Band to Be Named Later (real name to come)," which was really annoying, but there was nothing we could do about it. At least they had let us register without a real name.

The place was pretty crowded when we got there. Everyone twenty-one or older wore a white wristband so that they could buy alcohol. We stuck with Cokes and a big basket of fries, managing to find a table near the back, where some of Troy's groupies were hanging.

The Grog had a nicer setup than the FX Lounge. There

was actually a raised platform that acted as a stage. It was small, but at least it looked like a place for performers, unlike the corner we had at FX.

"We need to play here," Nick said.

"Totally." I took a swig of Coke, then chomped down on a fistful of fries. "And then we need to play Ryan's." That was what we all called Rockin' Ryan's, this cool restaurant and bar that had a real, permanent stage with a big dance floor in front of it. It really supported the local rock scene and had given exposure to a lot of great bands, but it only booked the best.

"That girl with bright green hair is staring at you," Alli said to Nick. "I think it's PurpleGrrl from the blog."

Of course we all had to look, making the girl turn her head quickly when she saw us.

"BoyMagnet thinks PurpleGrrl has a thing for you," Alli said.

"Really?" Nick asked, still looking at the green-haired girl. "Maybe I need to check out the site more often."

"Why do you think it's PurpleGrrl when she's green, babe?" Troy asked, putting his arm around Alli.

"I think it's a cover," Alli said. "She's cute. Don't you think, Nick?"

Nick didn't answer. He was too busy staring at Green-Haired Girl aka PurpleGrrl.

"He thinks she's cute," Alli said to me.

Why was she telling *me*?

"They're about to start." I nudged Nick.

"Green is my new favorite color," he said as he returned

his gaze to the band. Alli leaned over to me, lowering her voice. "I think you now have a clear path to Jane."

Oh. So *that* was why she was telling me. But how did she know Nick would—or that I—

"I'm a girl," she whispered. "We have radar for this sort of thing."

"Now that's just plain creepy," I said.

"What is?" Nick asked.

"Nothing."

The house lights dimmed and Late Arrival stepped out, jumping right into their version of "You Really Got Me." About a minute into it, Troy, Nick, and I all exchanged looks. They were pretty good. Not great, but definitely decent.

They played one original song that sounded a little rough; the lyrics were pretty lame and the music sounded like things we'd heard before. Then they took a short break.

"Five minutes till they come back on. Anybody want anything?" Troy asked, just as the crowd suddenly erupted.

"Oh my God! Look!" A few more squeals followed, and then a wave of girls turned their backs on the stage and moved en masse toward us.

"What's going on?" I asked.

"They're coming right for us," Nick said. "They must have seen us at FX."

"We sucked," I said.

"*You* sucked," Nick said. "The rest of us dominated. Do you see PurpleGrrl?" He stepped up, ready to greet his public—

But they bowled right past him.

"Roy Stone, Slash and Burn, right?"

We turned to see this Roy Stone they were mobbing. The guy was a few inches taller than me, going for that rugged look with a few days of facial hair growth, mussed hair— you know, the kind that girls lock in on, push you out of the way to get closer to.

The Del kind.

Hated those kind.

"What the…" Nick muttered at the same time I said, "Man."

"You guys are way better than them," Alli said. "Don't worry."

"I've never heard of these guys," Nick said, a little too loudly. "I bet they can't even play."

"You say something?" Roy Stone now stood in front of Nick. The girls huddled around, some glancing furtively at one another, others with fingers flying over their phones, no doubt letting their friends know that the semifamous Roy Stone was about to flatten the nobody-knows-him Nick Brewster.

Roy looked around at us and started chuckling. "Wait a minute. I know you guys. Especially you," he said, jabbing a finger at me. "You totally choked at the FX a couple of weeks ago. Orion or something, right?"

"That's *his* name," Nick said, pointing to me. "Not the band's name." He glared at me like it was my fault we still didn't have a name.

Roy raised an eyebrow. "Are you the Band to Be Named Later for the Battle of the Bands?"

His buddy grinned. "No. I think it was the Band to Be Named Later (real name to come)."

We scowled.

Roy turned to his buddies. "Two bands we can cross off our list."

"You can cross us off if you want, my friend, but we will jump right back on." Troy stepped up next to Nick. Troy wasn't a big guy, but he was solid, was on the wrestling team, and wasn't afraid to stand up to people in his calm, charming way. Unlike me, who had taken a step backward so that I was mostly behind him.

Roy laughed. "We weren't sure we even qualified for the Battle, since we play a lot of paid gigs. We're *professionals.*"

"We're playing Ryan's in a couple of weeks," one of his bandmates chimed in.

"You should come check us out," Roy said. "Maybe you'll learn something." He turned and smacked my arm. "Hey, no hard feelings, O-rion. I'm sure you'll be fine by Battle time." He motioned to his buddies, and they headed toward the door, followed by the girls.

After the show was over, we all walked back to Troy's car.

"Did anyone see PurpleGrrl come out?" Nick asked.

"No," I said, then turned to Troy and Alli. "Can you believe that Stone guy?"

"They're afraid of you," Alli said.

"What?" Nick and I both stared at her.

"How do you figure, Alli girl?" Troy pulled his keys out of his pocket.

"Didn't you feel that mood change when he realized you

guys were the ones at FX?" she asked. "That you were in the Battle of the Bands?"

"Yeah," I said. "He went from obnoxious to laughing his butt off about how I choked."

"He was covering," Alli said. "He's not worried about Late Arrival, but he's worried about you guys."

"Are you crazy?" Nick asked her. "They don't see us as a threat at all."

"That guy remembered your full band name from the list on the Battle website. Every word." Alli smiled. "Just wait. I guarantee they'll show up at your next gig."

"She's got a sixth sense about these things," Troy said as he unlocked the car. "I believe her."

"Does she see dead people?" Nick asked as we climbed into the backseat. "Because she might be seeing us soon. Did you check the biceps on that guy?"

I shook my head. "So if they are really playing at Ryan's in a few weeks, that means they're good. We need to find out how good."

"I agree," Troy said. "Can you work your magic, Al?"

"I'm on it," Alli said, tapping her laptop. "Just get me to a hot spot."

Troy connected his iPod to the adapter, and soon the car was filled with the pulsing beat of music.

"Maybe PurpleGrrl will come to our next gig." Nick settled back in the seat.

"Does this mean Jane has been deemed unworthy of you?" Troy asked over his shoulder.

"Sometimes you have to make your own destiny, dude.

Jane's butt may have touched my lap, but I'm not getting the vibe from her. I need to move on."

Alli gave me her I-told-you-so look. I didn't smile until she couldn't see me, because even though I was glad she was right, I didn't want to give her the satisfaction just yet.

When I got home, I saw a light on in the family room, but I didn't hear anything. I stepped inside and was greeted by a giant image of Del staring out at me from the TV screen, frozen in pause mode. Picking up the remote, I clicked Play so that Del was moving again, running across the field at the end of the championship game after he'd scored the winning goal. His arms and stick were raised skyward and he grinned beneath his helmet. The team smashed into him, lifting him up on their shoulders as he shouted and pumped his arms. They were chanting his name—"Del! Del! Del!"—and he was smacking the tops of helmets as people shouted and cheered.

I stared at his face on the screen—ecstatic, ready to take on the world. So different from—

"What the hell are you doing?"

He stood in the doorway, gripping a Coke.

"I thought you were upstairs," I said. "I was going to turn everything off."

"So why is it on?" He took a step toward me, his eyes boring into mine, before reaching out to the DVD player to turn it off.

"I just wanted to see, uh…" Why couldn't I complete a sentence around him? "It was a great game," I finished lamely.

"Damn straight." He stepped in front of the television, blocking my view. "And before you think I'm just sitting around reliving my glory days, Coach asked me to review my old game tapes."

"I wasn't thinking that." I set the remote on the coffee table.

"I'm getting really sick of everyone thinking I'm not doing anything."

"No one thinks that, Del."

"Yes, they do, but whatever." He dropped heavily onto the couch. "Why don't you go have one of your little rock-and-roll fantasies and leave me alone?"

I opened my mouth to say something and then closed it. No matter what I said, he'd turn it around on me.

"I'm glad you might get to help Coach," I said as I walked out.

We are an up-and-coming band, nameless but open to suggestions. Feel free to post your band name ideas on our blog. (We don't want to use one of those band name generators — we want it to come from you or us.)

BAND NAME: to be named later

| PROFILE | MUSIC | PIX & VIDS | ABOUT/FAQ | CONTACT | BLOG |

Thursday, February 11

TROY: Checking out the competition, and it's not too bad. But we're working hard to kick some Battle butt!

 BoyMagnet

OMG!!! Did anyone go to the Grog and see Slash and Burn? The lead singer, Roy Stone, actually talked to me. The Magnet lives! I think he would have asked for my number but then he was mobbed.

 PurpleGrrl

What about Orion, BoyM? He was there too.
BTW, Late Arrival was not that great. I had expected better.
So all that commotion was for a band called Slash and Burn? Who are they?

DragonBreath

You haven't heard of Slash and Burn? Have you been living on another planet? That band is going to be the next big thing to come out of Colorado. They play everywhere. I think I heard they are about to sign a record deal.

PeacefulWarrior

Do labels even do record deals anymore now that there's digital download? And wouldn't that make them ineligible for the Battle of the Bands?

Countdown to
BATTLE OF
THE BANDS:
114
days

Countdown to
LES PAUL:
74
days

Gold's Guitars supports this band. • 303-555-GOLD
This site updated and maintained by A. Wilcox.

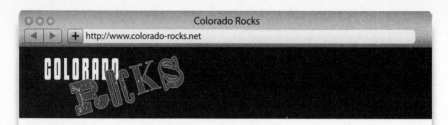

We are an up-and-coming band, name-less but open to suggestions. Feel free to post your band name ideas on our blog. (We don't want to use one of those band name generators — we want it to come from you or us.)

BAND NAME: to be named later

| PROFILE | MUSIC | PIX & VIDS | ABOUT/FAQ | CONTACT | BLOG |

BoyMagnet
Orion is still on my radar but I'm going to see S & B at Rockin' Ryan's. Roy will probably invite me onto the stage.

DominantSpecies
They don't have a deal — yet. So they can still be in the Battle.

Halyn
Hello? Isn't this a blog for the Band to Be Named Later until they get a name? Why don't you all drool over S & B on THEIR site?

BoyMagnet
Speaking of drooling, I saw PurpleGrrl — only she was GREEN — drooling over Nick from a distance because of course she could never get close to him.

PurpleGrrl
I don't know what you're talking about, BoyM. Green is not my color. And I can guarantee that if I wanted to, I could get close to Nick. Who knows? Maybe I already have.

DominantSpecies
What's the big deal talking about S & B here? A little healthy competition is good for this wimpy band.

Countdown to
BATTLE OF
THE BANDS:

114

days

Countdown to
LES PAUL:

74

days

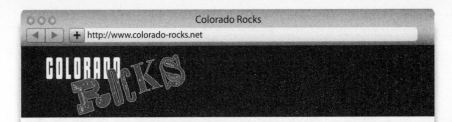

We are an up-and-coming band, name-less but open to suggestions. Feel free to post your band name ideas on our blog. (We don't want to use one of those band name generators — we want it to come from you or us.)

BAND NAME: to be named later

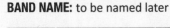

PROFILE | MUSIC | PIX & VIDS | ABOUT/FAQ | CONTACT | BLOG

🎸 BoyMagnet

That's why you've got pics of your green self on your Face-book page. And sure you could (get close to Nick anytime you wanted) NOT. But your comment proves you like him.

✏️ PurpleGrrl

Get off my Facebook page!!! I am NOT friends with you!

Countdown to
BATTLE OF
THE BANDS:

114

days

Countdown to
LES PAUL:

74

days

TEN

On Friday we were in OT Studios, ready to call Gwyn to tell her we wanted her in the band. We had texted the others and gotten a variety of responses:

- ✉ THANKS FOR THE FUN
- ✉ WHO CARES? UR JUST A STUPID HIGH SCHOOL
  BAND
- ✉ NO BIG
- ✉ U SUCK

Troy dialed Gwyn's cell number and put it on speaker.

"You got Gwyn's voice mail. Text her instead."

"She refers to herself in the third person," Troy said, hanging up. "That's pretty interesting."

"She sounded kind of like Jane." Nick scratched his chin, nodding. "That's even more interesting."

"Maybe it's a joke," I said. "Like she's got a secretary or something."

"Could be." Troy tapped on his phone. "But she didn't strike me as the type who would do that."

"Tell her our first rehearsal is next Saturday if that works," Nick said. "And ask her if Jane thinks Ori is a dork."

I glared at him, then at Alli, because how else would he know I might be sort of kind of interested in her?

Alli just smiled.

Troy's phone dinged a text—Gwyn's reply.

✉ EXCELLENT. I'LL BE THERE.

"Okay," Alli said, typing on her laptop. "I'm officially listing Gwyn as your bass player."

We talked for a while about whether we should stick with the same songs for the Battle or have Gwyn weigh in, and then I stood up.

"I need to go to work," I said. "You guys can hang out here if you want."

They gave me a wave, and I wheeled my bike out of the garage.

Like I always did when I got to Gold's, I walked over to the Les Paul in the window. I liked to think of it as the cousin of the one I would own. But when I got to the guitar stand, I found myself staring at a blue Stratocaster instead.

"Ed?"

"OT!" Ed said, walking over to me. "Can you believe it sold yesterday? But don't worry, I've got another Les Paul coming in that you can check out until you get yours."

"Who bought it?" I wondered if they were like me, in a band, trying to make it. Had they admired it for a long time, dreaming of the day they could hold it in their hands for good?

"Some guy got it for his son. Claims the kid is heading for rock-stardom." Ed shook his head. "I'm not convinced the kid ever played an instrument in his life, but there you go."

I frowned.

"I bet they take advantage of my return policy," Ed said. "Guitar like that needs to be in the hands of someone who cares."

I nodded, feeling better. I got to work and was so involved in dreaming about the Les Paul that I didn't notice right away that Ed was talking to someone familiar.

Jane.

My whole body seized up and I did an inventory. Heart rate: slightly elevated. Palms: warm but not damp. Zombification: unknown until I open my mouth.

She walked over. "Hey."

"H-hi." Vocalization lame, but word intelligible. Orion 1, Zombies 0. "Can I help you find something?"

She shook her head. "Actually, I wanted to talk to you."

"How did you know where I was?"

She blushed. "Gwyn had Troy's number from when he called about auditions. He was nice enough to answer my text about where you were."

"Oh." I straightened out some sheet music on the rack, trying to decide if I was supposed to be mad at Troy even though I was happy.

"I would have told you before," Jane said, "but then Gwyn

told me she was going to audition for your band and I didn't want anything to be weird, so I thought I should wait."

"Was I supposed to follow all that?"

She smiled. "Sorry. I get that way when I'm a little flustered. It's just that I have something to tell you and thought I should wait until after auditions."

"Okay…"

"Yeah, so I'm Halyn. You know, on your website."

"You're Halyn." My mind went blank, rewound, then caught up with itself. Jane was Halyn. Halyn was Taurus Girl. Jane had seen me run into a telephone pole.

Wonderful.

"I know. Weird, right? And what's even weirder is that we kind of bumped into each other at the FX Lounge after your set. You probably don't remember, because there were so many people around, but—"

"I remember." The blond near the back door. The one who said "Oh my God" before practically running away from me.

Her face lit up. "You do?"

Wait. Did she actually look *glad* that I remembered?

I nodded.

"I guess I was a little freaked out seeing you up close and personal after talking on the blog," she said. "Kind of like running into a celebrity when you don't expect it."

She was comparing me to a celebrity? She hadn't been repelled?

"The last song you sang was really awesome," she said,

not mentioning that I hadn't finished it. In fact, she acted like she hadn't even noticed I'd choked in the middle. "Did you write it?"

"Yeah."

"I loved it," she said. "I could relate. Having a feeling there's someone out there, waiting for you and you for them." She shrugged. "That sounded really mushy out loud. I promise your song didn't come across that way at all."

"No, it's cool," I said, amazed at how easily she was talking to me when we'd only met briefly at auditions. Amazed at how comfortable I felt with her.

"Sorry to interrupt," Ed said. "But I do need Mr. Taylor to do a little work while he's here." He winked at Jane before pointing to the counter. "Why don't you two get those music books and sheets logged in to inventory and put them on the rack?"

I looked at Jane, who nodded. "Just tell me what to do."

I grabbed the scissors and sliced through the tape on the box. "It's easy. First, read the number on the package, tell me the quantity, and I'll get them into the computer." When we were done with that, I picked up the box and carried it over to the rack.

"So," Jane said, pulling a few books out. "In the interest of full disclosure, I should probably also tell you that I was the one who—"

"Saw me run into a telephone pole? Yeah, I figured that out." It didn't feel nearly as humiliating now. "That's why I never responded to your e-mail. You know, the one you sent through Alli. I was kind of embarrassed."

"That's okay. I probably shouldn't have said that about

running into you. She e-mailed me asking about it, and I said it was outside the guitar store."

"Thanks."

She smiled as we each placed a book on the rack. "I just realized that I might seem like some kind of stalker, running into you all these places. But that last time really was a co-incidence. I was at that sporting goods store across from Gold's. And when I saw you I remember thinking, I think it's illegal to ride your bike on the sidewalk in Denver, and then—wham—you were down."

Did that mean the other times weren't a coincidence?

"Thanks for making sure I was okay."

"That's kind of my thing," she said, almost apologetically. "Helping people. Gwyn says that sometimes I don't know the difference between helping and butting in. I guess I need to work on that."

Jane and I ended up talking for nearly two hours. She followed me around as I worked, and Ed let her, glancing over at us every so often with a little smile on his face that told me he'd have payback the next time we were alone. Whatever it was, it would be worth it because she was really cool.

We talked about stuff I don't even remember, and stuff I did:

HER NAME
Jane: Unlike your creative parents, I was named after my dad's mom's cousin's sister or something like that.
Me: I like your name.

Jane: You don't have to say that. It's, like, an old person's name. Who names someone Jane? It's like naming me Gladys or Martha. I'm changing it the day I turn eighteen.

Me: Jane is not an old person's name.

Jane: (rolls her eyes)

Me: So if you do change it, you'll change it to Halyn, right?

Jane (nodding): I found it on the Internet. It's pretty much the opposite of Jane.

Me: The Opposite of Jane. Sounds like a band name.

HER SCHOOL

Me: Isn't St. Elizabeth's Academy an all-girls school?

Jane: Yeah. It's so great not to have boys around all the time. No offense.

Me: None taken. So you like it?

Jane: Love it. I used to be shy.

Me: You?

Jane: I know. But there's something about really being able to be yourself, and getting involved in all this stuff with other girls who share your vision.... It's pretty cool.

MUSIC

Jane: Who are some of the musicians who inspired you?

Me: Who *wasn't* someone who inspired me? I can't name one without leaving out tons of others. I've listened to and learned from rock guitarists, jazz and blues guitarists, classical guitarists—there are so many amazing people out there.

POETRY

Me: When did you start writing it?

Jane: Fourth or fifth grade. I've won some contests, and only one of those was where the prize is putting your poem along with thousands of others in a book that you have to buy if you want to see it.

AUDITIONS

Jane: Very cool how many people showed up.

Me: Yeah. My brother thought it would be a bust. (Why did I bring up Del?)

Jane: Why? Who doesn't want to be in a band? Well, besides me.

Me: Yeah, it worked out. And Gwyn is amazing.

FAVORITE VIDEO GAME

Jane and me at the same time*: Burnout 3: Takedown.*

Me: Are you kidding? A poet likes to crash cars?

Jane: I'm well-rounded.

We kept talking and working until she finally stopped and looked at me apologetically.

"I really should go," she said. "I told my mom I'd be back in an hour, and she keeps texting me."

"Sorry I kept you so long." I walked her to the door.

"It was fun," she said, leaning against the open door, letting the cold air in.

"So, what do I call you?"

She cocked her head, thinking.

"Jane in person, Halyn online? Does that work for you? Or is it too complicated?"

"I think I can handle that."

"Cool," she said. She pushed through the door, waving once before striding down the sidewalk toward the white Taurus parked about a block away. I liked the way her hips moved, swaying slightly, the way her hair swished from side to side.

"Enjoying the view?" Ed asked behind me.

"Just making sure she got to her car okay."

"Real gentlemanly of you." He squeezed my shoulder before walking over to help a customer.

I got home from work feeling lighter than I had in weeks. I didn't care if Del was home or not, whether he was Dr. Jekyll or Mr. Hyde. I'd just had an awesome time with Jane, and I couldn't wait to talk to her again.

"Your dinner's in the oven," my dad called when I walked in.

"I'll eat in a minute," I said, hustling over to the computer.

From: GuitarFreak@earthlink.net
To: HalynFlake34@yahoo.com
Subject: hey

Thanks for coming by the shop. Way cool that you write poetry. I think it can be a lot like writing songs.
Do your poems rhyme? A lot of songs rhyme, so I feel like mine should, too, even when it doesn't feel right for the song. I think one of the best songwriters ever is Jackson Browne, and he does a lot of

rhyming. And the Indigo Girls have great lyrics, too, especially their old stuff. They're people my parents turned me on to, so they're "classic." Have you heard of them? I study their songs like crazy. How do you write a poem? How do you think of them?
Signed,
Curious (aka Ori)
P.S. Yes, answering the e-mail you sent to Alli: My parents named us all after constellations because my mom's an astronomer. She thinks it's great. We all think it sucks.

From: HalynFlake34@yahoo.com
To: GuitarFreak@earthlink.net
Subject: RE: hey

Dear Curious George,
I do mostly free verse, non-rhyming, but I have problems getting the rhythm — meter, I guess it is — to feel right. I'll say it in my head and it sounds fine, but then I ask my mom to read it out loud and she doesn't hit the beats the same way I heard them, so it's back to the drawing board!
As for how I think of them, most of them are about things I've observed or things I'm feeling. Some of them would probably be considered mushy, but that's okay. I like that I have an outlet for it. And if I do it right with some symbolism and stuff, they sound cool and people really like them.
Signed,
Poetic License
P.S. You said "us" about being named after constellations. Are there other sibs besides your brother?

105

From: GuitarFreak@earthlink.net
To: HalynFlake34@yahoo.com
Subject: RE: hey

Dear Licensed to Write,
So you let your mom read your poems? That's pretty cool. My
parents are really into rock, so we get a lot of support, but I
don't let anyone see my stuff before it's done.
I know what you mean about hearing it differently when it
comes from someone else. Sometimes when I finally start to
play a song and Nick and Troy are trying to figure out their
parts, it just doesn't sound right. So we change it. Back to the
drawing board, as you say.
Signed,
Board (but not bored!)
P.S. My sister's name is Vela and my brother's name is Del —
Delphinius. But don't ever call him that if you meet him or he'll
take your head off.

From: HalynFlake34@yahoo.com
To: GuitarFreak@earthlink.net
Subject: RE: hey

Dear Not Bored (or boring),
It's cool that you have Nick and Troy to work through your songs
with. It must be fun to see how it sounds with all of you
together after only hearing it in your head (or maybe just on
your guitar as you create it?).

My mom used to write a lot when she was in college, so she loves to read my stuff, especially now that she doesn't write her own. She keeps pretty busy with work. My dad died when I was eight — car accident — so it's just me and Mom. My older sister, Beth, is in college.

Halyn

P.S. So, your bro doesn't like his constellation name? I think it's cool. But I'll remember not to ever call him that if I ever meet him.

\--

From: GuitarFreak@earthlink.net
To: HalynFlake34@yahoo.com
Subject: RE: hey

I'm sorry to hear about your dad. That must be hard.

\--

From: HalynFlake34@yahoo.com
To: GuitarFreak@earthlink.net
Subject: RE: hey

Thanks about my dad. It's been eight years, so it's easier to talk about without bursting into tears. It still hurts a lot though. I guess it always will.

Hey, would you be willing to take a look at a poem I'm working on? I would really appreciate your feedback. I know poems and lyrics are a little different, but maybe you can give me some ideas on where to go next.

From: GuitarFreak@earthlink.net
To: HalynFlake34@yahoo.com
Subject: RE: hey

Love to see your poem anytime.

From: HalynFlake34@yahoo.com
To: Awilcox@34756.colorado-rocks.net
Subject: Thanks!

Hi, Alli,
Thanks for sending my message on to Orion. Now that we've
met and talked, we're exchanging e-mails. Are you two good
friends? He seems like a really nice guy.
Anyway, thanks again!
Halyn (aka Jane)

From: Awilcox@34756.colorado-rocks.net
To: HalynFlake34@yahoo.com
Subject: RE: Thanks!

He IS a nice guy, when he's not being a dork. I can say that, since
I've known him forever. I'm glad he's actually communicating
with a "real" girl, since, according to him, I don't fall into that
category, because I'm like a sister to him.
P.S. How did he react to the Jane/Halyn thing?
- -

A. Wilcox, Webqueen for the Band to Be Named Later (but
that's not their name so don't call them that!)

From: HalynFlake34@yahoo.com
To: Awilcox@34756.colorado-rocks.net
Subject: RE: Thanks!

Ha! I know how that is. Anyway, I'm sure I'll see you around.
P.S. Great! We had a good talk.

COLORADO ROCKS

We are an up-and-coming band, nameless but open to suggestions. Feel free to post your band name ideas on our blog. (We don't want to use one of those band name generators — we want it to come from you or us.)

BAND NAME: to be named later

| PROFILE | MUSIC | PIX & VIDS | ABOUT/FAQ | CONTACT | **BLOG** |

Friday, February 12

ALLI: Introducing Gwyn Farcosi, the new bass player! Check out her audition on the Pix & Vids page.
Happy Valentine's Day weekend!

NICK: Alli and Troy are ALL about Valentine's Day, but O and I like to spread the love around, so keep that in mind, ladies.

ORION: I'm not spreading anything, Brewster.

PurpleGrrl

Cool! Will she be ready to play with you at Matt's Sports Bar or are you saving her for the Battle?

DragonBreath

Way cool that you got a girl bass player. Does she rip it up or what?

BoyMagnet

That means Nick and Orion don't have gfs! Did you hear that, PurpleGrrl? They're available!

DominantSpecies

A girl bass player will totally ruin your image. You can't have a chick in the band.
Valentine's Day is for sissies. It sucks.

Countdown to
BATTLE OF
THE BANDS:
113
days

Countdown to
LES PAUL:
73
days

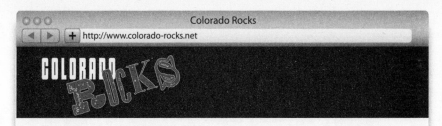

http://www.colorado-rocks.net

BAND NAME: to be named later

| PROFILE | MUSIC | PIX & VIDS | ABOUT/FAQ | CONTACT | BLOG |

We are an up-and-coming band, nameless but open to suggestions. Feel free to post your band name ideas on our blog. (We don't want to use one of those band name generators — we want it to come from you or us.)

PurpleGrrl

DominantSpecies: It makes them enlightened, you sexist pig.
BoyMagnet: What about Roy Stone?

BoyMagnet

I'm like Nick. I believe in spreading my magnetism around.

OzoneLayer

I'm new to this page. I thought it was supposed to be about music. This sounds like girlie crap.

DominantSpecies

It is, man.

Halyn

Hi, OzoneLayer. DominantSpecies likes to come in and criticize everyone and everything.
I like Valentine's candy. Actually, I like any kind of candy.

OzoneLayer

So far it looks like he has a reason to.

Countdown to
BATTLE OF
THE BANDS:

113

days

Countdown to
LES PAUL:

73

days

ELEVEN

When I pulled up in the driveway after work the next day, the house was quiet, except for what sounded like the faint twang of my acoustic guitar. Impossible, though—I was the only one who played. And if someone decided to play, they all knew that if they touched my stuff without asking, they were dead.

I took off my shoes and tiptoed down the front hall and into the kitchen, standing in front of the basement door, where I could clearly hear some poorly executed chords coming from a guitar. *My* guitar.

Avoiding the stairs that creaked, I snuck down, craning my neck around the wall.

Del was sitting on a stool, my acoustic resting on his thigh. I watched his fingers move clumsily over the strings as he tried to remember the chords. His strumming was strong, but the sound was off because he couldn't maintain the pressure on the strings to execute the chord.

"Want some help?"

His shoulders jerked. "Shit, Ori, you scared me."

"Sorry," I said. "I heard you playing when I came in and—"

"I wasn't playing," Del said. "I was just—ah, hell." He stood up. "Don't sneak around like that. You almost gave me a heart attack."

He bent down to put the guitar back in its case.

"Remember when I used to play that cardboard guitar?" I asked, hoping to soften the mood with a memory.

"I remember you taking my guitar," Del said.

"You gave it to me," I said. "You wanted to play lacrosse."

He kept talking as if I hadn't said anything. "You thought you were some musical prodigy or something just because you picked up a few chords and could play them."

I frowned, remembering when we found out I could play by ear. It was shortly after I played Del's guitar for the first time. After that, I stayed in formal lessons with Mr. Keenan—who had introduced me to Ed and the magic that is Gold's Guitars—just long enough to learn all the chords and to read music.

"I was seven," I said, my voice barely above a whisper.

"You still think you're something else," he said, shoving past me up the stairs. I turned to watch him disappear around the door.

That night I sat on my bed, my song notebook in my lap, trying to block out the wall-thumping heavy metal pounding out of Del's room next door. Heavy metal played at those decibel levels meant he was still pissed. I hoped it wasn't still about my catching him trying to play the guitar, but I had a feeling it was. I wished I could tell him it wasn't a big deal, that I was just surprised that he was doing it. I wished I could ask him why now, after all these years? The only interest he'd ever shown since he gave it up to play lacrosse was when *I* was playing. He used to love to hear me play. Bragged about it. Now he thought I sucked and came to hear me only so he could mock me.

Groaning, I leaned back against my pillows and opened my notebook, flipping through until I came to a song—or something—I had started a few weeks ago.

Related Strangers

We used to be friends
We used to be brothers
But that all changed somehow
You don't like what I do
You don't like what I say
The good times we had
Have all gone away
And all that's left
Are two strangers...
Related strangers

"What are you doing?" Vela stood in the doorway.

"Just messing around." I closed the notebook and shoved it under my pillow.

"I got an A on my history report," she said. "The one Del helped me with."

"That's great, Vee." I looked up at her. "Did you tell him?"

"Not yet." She nodded toward the wall that separated Del's room and mine. The music was still pounding out an angry rhythm.

"Right."

She sat down next to me on the bed, pulling her knees up like she was planning to stay awhile. We sat next to each other in silence for a few minutes, listening to Del's music, and then I spoke.

"He was trying to play my guitar when I got home."

Her eyes got big. "Really? That's weird."

I nodded. "And he freaked out when he knew I'd heard him. Got really mad at me."

She sighed. "He just hates everyone."

"Except you." I gave her a little smile.

She smiled back. "What can I say? I'm unhateable." She looked over her shoulder at my pillow, where the corner of my song notebook stuck out. "Can I see it?"

I shook my head. "You know I never share works in progress."

She shrugged before standing up. "It was worth a shot. Will we get to hear it soon?"

We used to be friends.... We used to be brothers.

"Doubtful."

"Why not?"

"I don't think it's a song. Just a bunch of words."

"Do they mean anything?"

I looked toward the wall that separated Del and me.

"Only to me."

From: HalynFlake34@yahoo.com
To: GuitarFreak@earthlink.net
Subject: my poem

So here it is. Well, actually, it's just the beginnings of a poem. Let me know if it flows or if you stumble over parts of it.

> WHO I AM
> If I tell you who I am
> You might not see me anymore
> Could you let go
> Of the person
> You thought I was
> Long enough
> To see the person I really am?

Eek. I'm a little scared. Clicking Send now . . .

From: GuitarFreak@earthlink.net
To: HalynFlake34@yahoo.com
Subject: RE: my poem

Wow. That's about all I can say. Your poem is AMAZING. I thought it flowed well. I actually could almost put it to music. Got a chorus in mind? JK. Sort of.

From: HalynFlake34@yahoo.com
To: GuitarFreak@earthlink.net
Subject: RE: my poem

I'm SO glad you liked it! I was so nervous when I sent it. Though I guess you could just be saying that to be nice. I mean, if you hated it, would you really say so?
Don't answer that. I want to believe you truly liked it, even if it's a fantasy.

From: GuitarFreak@earthlink.net
To: HalynFlake34@yahoo.com
Subject: RE: my poem

Believe it because it's true. You are an amazing writer. I wish I could write lyrics like that. Now I know I won't be sharing any of my stuff with you — ha!

From: HalynFlake34@yahoo.com
To: GuitarFreak@earthlink.net
Subject: RE: my poem

Don't say that! I love the songs I've heard so far. You have a real talent for words, not just music. I'm SERIOUS. I won't push you to send some of your lyrics, but you've got to know they're good.

From: GuitarFreak@earthlink.net
To: HalynFlake34@yahoo.com
Subject: RE: my poem

Thanks for saying that about my lyrics. That means a lot. Let's get back to your poem. Did it come out that great the first time, or did you work on it?

From: HalynFlake34@yahoo.com
To: GuitarFreak@earthlink.net
Subject: RE: my poem

Nothing comes out great for me the first time. I rewrote those lines about a million times, and now I'm not sure where to go next. Does that ever happen to you with your lyrics?

From: GuitarFreak@earthlink.net
To: HalynFlake34@yahoo.com
Subject: RE: my poem

Try all the time! It's like you get this really good idea and jump right in and then it runs out of steam. That kind of happened with "Focus" until I was able to look at it a little differently and make some changes.

From: HalynFlake34@yahoo.com
To: GuitarFreak@earthlink.net
Subject: RE: my poem

I'm so glad I'm not the only one who gets stuck. How did you see "Focus" differently, and what changes did you make? Maybe that will help me with this poem.

From: GuitarFreak@earthlink.net
To: HalynFlake34@yahoo.com
Subject: RE: my poem

I started to write "Focus" because I was really pissed at
someone. But I only got through one verse and got stuck.
Then I started thinking about focusing in general — on what you
want or where you want to go or whatever. Then the whole
song changed and took off. It was really cool.
So if your poem is from something real, maybe you can try to
forget about that and make it bigger.
Listen to me. Like I even know what I'm talking about.

From: HalynFlake34@yahoo.com
To: GuitarFreak@earthlink.net
Subject: RE: my poem

You DO know what you're talking about! I've just gotten a new
idea for the poem thanks to you. I'm off to work on it! I'll check
in with you later.

I smiled and spent the next two hours coming up with a
melody for Halyn's poem, except it was now "Halyn's Song"
and it was coming along nicely, if I did say so myself. I even
came up with a chorus:

Would you want to know the me
The who I really am
The why, the where, the when

119

The person that I am
Would you be there
When the layers
All get peeled away
Would you look at who I really am
Would you look in me, and stay?

Funny how different I felt working on "Halyn's Song" compared with working on that stupid "Related Strangers" thing I was writing in my notebook. Even though the words in her song were pretty heavy, I felt light and happy when I played it, and singing the words was like having her nearby, which felt great.

I went to bed that night feeling good, even though the heavy metal was still banging a beat next door.

The next afternoon, I got a text from Jane. Well, from Halyn—that was the name I used in my phone because it seemed right.

✉ I CHALLENGE YOU TO A RACE – FERRARI F355 DLX AT THE GAME ZONE. *HALYN CELL 4:54 PM*

I wondered if she'd figured out I loved that game because of our shared love of *Burnout*. I rocked at *Ferrari*, high-scored just about every visit. Poor girl didn't stand a chance.

✉ UR ON. WANT TO MAKE IT INTERESTING?

✉ WHAT DID U HAVE IN MIND? *HALYN CELL 4:54 PM*

✉ LOSER BUYS THE WINNER DINNER.

Whoa. That almost sounded like I was asking her out. Had the dork left the building?

When I got to the Game Zone on Wednesday afternoon, Jane was already there, chatting with the guy behind the counter.

"Hey there," she said. "Orion, this is Jake. Jake, Orion."

I looked from Jake to Jane. "You two are friends?"

"I come here a lot." She smiled, looking embarrassed.

"She's a junkie," Jake said. "She practically lives here. If we had something above the Platinum card, she'd have it. Girl earns wicked points, tons of free games."

I shook my head. "I have a feeling I'm in for a serious thrashing."

"Definitely," Jake said. "I won't play against her anymore. Especially any of the driving simulations."

"Great," I said, and then turned to Jane. "You tricked me."

"I did not," she said. "I just challenged you to a game."

"A game you totally dominate."

"Now where's your sense of competition?"

I raised an eyebrow. "We can go to my house and play my old *Guitar Hero* game."

"Next time," she said. "Right now I want to beat you at *Ferrari*."

Which she did. By miles and miles and many crashes. It was embarrassing, but also a total blast because we trash-talked each other and tried to distract each other so that one of us could send the other into a tailspin. Once I found out she had

121

a weakness for french fries, I paid a guy watching us to bring me a plateful. When she smelled them, I could tell I was in the money, the way her eyes kept flitting to them until she couldn't resist and grabbed a handful. That was the one and only time I beat her. After that, she put on what she called her "anti–french fry armor."

"I can resist them if I really focus," she said. "It's all in the mind." She tapped her head.

"You do realize they are only fried potatoes, not drugs or something."

"Maybe to you, but to me they are the food of the gods." She grinned and proceeded to thrash me again.

"I surrender," I said after losing for the fourth straight time. "My ego can't take any more."

"No problem," she said, grabbing her jacket off the back of the seat. "When are you taking me to dinner?"

I groaned. "Geez, can't I wallow a little in self-pity before I have to think about paying up?"

She looked at her watch. "You have exactly two minutes to wallow, and then I want to know."

We decided Sunday would work for both of us.

When we got to her car, she climbed in and gripped the steering wheel. "Okay, so if you keep your hands here and here, then you can turn really fast"—she stopped talking to demonstrate—"and maybe manage to barely clip me before I whip around to demolish you."

"Go ahead, rub it in," I said. "But just wait until we play *Guitar Hero*."

"You know you have a very unfair advantage on that game," she said.

"And you didn't on *Ferrari*?"

She laughed. "See you at rehearsal on Saturday."

"See you." I waved as she drove away, wondering how dorky I looked as I stood there, grinning like a maniac, before heading to my mom's car.

TWELVE

"This is so cool!" Vela squealed, settling into one of the circle chairs she'd carried out from the family room. It was Saturday, and we were getting ready for our first rehearsal with Gwyn. I wasn't sure what I was more excited about, the rehearsal or my "date" with Jane the next evening. I knew it was just payback for our bet, but she definitely seemed glad to be going.

"When is Gwyn getting here?" Vela asked.

"Soon," Nick said, and then turned to Alli. "You were right that BoyMagnet thinks PurpleGrrl is into me. What do *you* think?"

"That you're spending too much time reading the website and not enough time trying to come up with a good band name."

"You're the one who first told me she mentioned me on the website," Nick said. "And I *did* come up with some good names." He scowled at us. "I was just shot down."

"We are hoping for names that apply to *everyone*, not just our esteemed drummer," Troy said.

"Yeah, okay," Nick said. "Is Gwyn bringing her own amp?"

"Yep." Alli fired up her computer, ready to chronicle our first official practice with Gwyn. "Is Jane coming?" She looked pointedly at me.

Alli had seen me come home from the Game Zone and had run out to talk to me. Apparently the giant dork grin was still on my face because she knew right away that something was up.

"That's so great, Ori!" she had said when she pried out of me that we were going to dinner on Sunday.

"She kicked my butt on *Ferrari*."

"Really?" She'd looked surprised. "But you rule that game."

"Not anymore." I had sighed.

She had laughed.

"Yes, she's coming," I said to everyone, and Nick started in with the whistles and whoops. "You'd better not say anything stupid to her." I gave him my best Del glare.

Nick laughed. "That's real scary, Taylor. Intimidating, even. Hey, I think that's what I'm going to start calling you: the Intimidator." He was nodding, proud of himself. "I need a bathroom break," he said. "Don't intimidate anyone while I'm gone."

"Blunt honesty and constant grief. And you're supposed to be my friends." I threw up my hands and finished getting my equipment set up.

Gwyn and Jane showed up just as Nick was getting

settled behind his set. Gwyn was decked out in black jeans and a loose-fitting T-shirt for a band I didn't recognize, a few thick bracelets gripping her wrists. Jane wore regular jeans and a more tight-fitting purple shirt. She looked amazing, and my stomach got a few butterflies.

Yes, you're going to dinner, but remember it's payback. Don't get your hopes up. Friends is good.

Vela jumped up. "I'm Ori's sister, Vela. It's just the coolest thing to have a girl bass player and you're so *good*. I mean, like, beyond awesome!" She smiled. "I watched the video."

Gwyn smiled back.

"She's definitely good," Jane said.

Vela looked at her. "So, are you in the band, too, and I didn't know it?"

"No," Jane said, laughing. "I can't play an instrument or sing at all, which is why your brother is going to kick my butt in *Guitar Hero*."

"That's all hand-eye coordination," Vela said. "No musical ability required. You'll be fine."

"Thanks for that, Vee," I said, but I was smiling. "You ready?" I asked Gwyn. "We can hook up your amp."

"Actually, before you start," Jane said, "Gwyn has something she wants to tell all of you."

I wondered why Jane was doing this sort of introduction thing, why Gwyn wasn't just telling us whatever she had to tell us. I looked at Jane, then Gwyn, who was motioning to Troy to join our little half circle. It occurred to me that we'd never heard Gwyn speak at all, even on her voice mail message, which I was now pretty sure had been Jane.

Gwyn took a deep breath. "I'm deaf," she said. The words were clear, though they had a strange cadence to them.

"Cool!" Nick was grinning like he'd just won the lottery or something. "You're like Evelyn Glennie, except on bass," he said excitedly. "This is so awesome."

Gwyn grinned as Troy and I both asked, "Who's Evelyn Glennie?"

"She's this awesome percussionist from Scotland who's profoundly deaf, which I think means she can't hear much at all," Nick said. "She lost her hearing when she was, like, ten or something, so when she talks you'd never know she's deaf. You should check her out on YouTube."

"She was eleven or twelve when she lost her hearing," Gwyn said, "depending on what article you believe." She made a peace sign and flicked it twice. "I was ten." She made the sign for ten.

"Wow!" Vela said, repeating the sign.

"So how deaf are you?" Nick asked. "You talk really well."

"Nick!" The rest of us glared at him.

Gwyn smiled. "It's okay." She looked at him. "I can't hear much below about eighty decibels," she said, signing as she spoke. "Maybe that's why I like rock. A decent rock concert is about a hundred and fifteen decibels or more, depending on what row you're sitting in and what they're playing." She smiled. "Lawn mower is a hundred and five or so. Normal conversation, about sixty to seventy. But I'm like Dame Evelyn. I don't want to be defined by my deafness."

"This is really cool," Vela said, repeating some of the signs. "You should do a whole song in sign language."

We all laughed.

"What?"

"That would be a pretty quiet song," I said, running my fingers absently over the strings of the loaner.

Vela furrowed her brow, her cheeks turning red.

"It could be an instrumental with actions," Jane said. I thought it was nice that she was rescuing Vela.

Vela smiled at her, then gave me a so-there look.

Hmm. *Sign Language.* Could work as a band name.

"So it won't be a problem? My deafness?" Gwyn asked, signing it as well.

"Why would it be?" I said, enunciating each word. "You shred on the guitar. That's all that matters."

Gwyn smiled. "You don't have to talk that slow. I'm good at lip reading. And sign language. When you all learn."

"People do that all the time at first," Jane said. "Pretty soon you'll talk to her like everyone else."

I nodded, wondering how one brief glance and a few basic words from Jane could make my stomach flip. *Friends. We're just friends—who are going to dinner tomorrow.*

"Right. Sorry."

Jane showed me the sign for "I'm sorry." "I've needed it many times," she said, smiling at Gwyn. I repeated it back.

Gwyn raised her guitar case and amp.

"Let's get me hooked up."

"So I'm just here for moral support, if that's okay," Jane said. "Otherwise, I can run errands and come back."

"You can stay," Nick said. "Right, Ori?"

I ignored his you-know-you-want-her-to tone.

"You should totally stay," Vela said. "I'll go get you a chair." She was off before anyone could say anything.

Jane looked at me. "I don't want to make you uncomfortable."

"You won't," Nick said before I could respond. "Ori's one of the most comfortable guys I know."

I groaned inwardly but acted like I hadn't heard him.

"No, really," Jane said. "It's your first time with Gwyn. I'll come back later. Tell Vela I'm sorry about the chair. If you're still rehearsing when I get back, I'll sit and listen."

Then she was gone.

"What is *wrong* with you?" Nick asked.

"What's wrong with *you*?" I said. "'Ori's one of the most comfortable guys I know'?"

"It was a good line," Nick said defensively. "And *someone's* got to do something or you're going to end up dateless for the rest of your life."

"Not that it's any of your business," I said, "but Jane and I hung out at the Game Zone on Wednesday."

"Hanging out is not a date," he said. "But I'm proud of you for taking the first step."

I didn't tell him *she* was the one who had texted *me* first.

"Gee, thanks, Brewster," I said. "And not that it's any of your business *again*, but we're meeting for dinner tomorrow." Meeting her instead of picking her up kind of sucked. I guess I understood why the law existed, but not being able to be in the same car was so lame. I wouldn't be able to do that until

May, when I'd had my license for six months—unless I cheated, like Del had. But then he got caught and our parents took his license away for a month. No thanks.

"Now that's what I'm talking about," Nick said, grinning. "Pretty soon you'll be able to double-date with me and PurpleGrrl."

"You haven't even talked to her yet."

"But I will, dude. No worries there."

"Well, I've been worried, so thanks for making me feel better," I said. "Now, do you think we could get to work?" I strode over to close the garage door.

We spent the first hour getting Gwyn in sync with us, but that was about all it took. She was a natural. She kicked off her shoes so that she could "hear" the music better through her bare feet. She also watched us really closely. If she hadn't told us, I wouldn't have known she was deaf, which made sense, since we hadn't known at auditions. We played through some basic stuff that everyone knew until we got into a little bit of a rhythm.

Then we took a break, came back, and spent the next hour and a half working through Boston's "More Than a Feeling," which was one of our cover songs for the Battle. Luckily Gwyn knew it already, so we got up to speed pretty quickly.

Just as we were heading into the last bit, the garage door started up. Del pulled into the driveway and stopped.

Why did he have to come through the garage? Why didn't he just park in the driveway and go through the front door like he usually did?

Because he knew we were in here, that's why. Because he wanted to yank my chain.

"Hey," he said as he got out and locked the car. "Is this your little band?"

My jaw clenched at "little."

"This is our *band*," Nick said, a slight edge to his voice.

"Girl bass player," he said, looking at Gwyn. "I remember you. You were good." He gave her the Del skim, eyes dropping quickly, noting the barrier to a breast inventory in the loose-fitting black shirt she wore.

"That was subtle," Gwyn muttered, crossing her arms over her chest. "I'm Gwyn. Who are you?"

Del seemed momentarily put off. Then he smiled. "Del Taylor. Ori's brother." He jerked his thumb in my direction. "You really want to hang out with these clowns?"

"I love the circus," she said, signing it as well.

We all laughed, including Del, who had done a double take when she'd signed.

"I like this girl," he said. "Can you teach me how to say some cusswords in sign language?" He waved his hands around.

"Maybe," she said.

"I'll take that as a yes." He gave her a thumbs-up. "Find me when you guys take a break." He smiled at her before heading toward the door to go into the house.

"You can find me," she called after him.

He laughed and saluted her before disappearing inside.

"Nicely done," Nick said to her. "Most girls just swoon and do his bidding."

"I'm not most girls," Gwyn said, stepping back to her place on the tarp. "How about we finish the song."

"Great idea," I said, pushing the button to lower the garage door, since Del had, of course, left it open.

I set the volume on my amp to Blow Your Stupid Brother Off the Face of the Planet, which made me feel better. When we stopped for a break around five, everyone went inside for Vela's popcorn and Cokes except me.

"I'll be in in a sec," I said, not really wanting to see Del again.

I put the garage door back up because I needed some crisp February air to cool me off, and also because I knew I wouldn't play loud and drive the neighbors crazy. Pulling my acoustic out of its case, I settled on the stool. I found myself playing the opening chords to "Halyn's Song," slowly at first and then up to tempo.

I worked through her verse and then my chorus, then went back to the verse, tweaking a few chords. As I got to the chorus again, I looked up.

Jane was framed in the opening of the garage door, watching me, her mouth wide open.

"Oh my God," she whispered. Her eyes were bright, like she might cry.

I fumbled the music, standing so abruptly that my guitar twanged against my thigh.

"I'm sorry. I know I should have asked first, but I thought I'd just mess around with it a little, see if I could come up with anything before I talked to you. I didn't think you'd—"

"It's amazing." She took a few steps toward me. "Really."

"Oh. Good."

"It's so wild to hear my words, my feelings…in a song. And you wrote a chorus." She sounded almost breathless as she sat down in Vela's chair and moved it closer to me. "Can I hear it again?"

"Like I said, it's pretty rough. And you need to write more of the poem. But…" I sat back down on the stool and began again.

"I *knew* it!" Nick walked toward us, a Coke in each hand. Troy, Gwyn, and Vela followed close behind. Nick looked at Jane. "Ori's idea of taking a break from playing music is to play more music."

She smiled.

"And what was that song, dude? I haven't heard it before."

"It's Jane's. Writing as Halyn."

Jane laughed. "It's a poem I'm working on that I shared with Ori. He's putting it to music." She reached out to touch the guitar. She was only a few inches from me. Her hair smelled like fresh apples, and I couldn't help breathing it in, breathing *her* in. We smiled at each other just as Del came into the garage from the house.

"And the girls keep coming," he said. His eyes flicked to me, then Jane, then back to me, and I could tell something registered. He knew I was into her. But then his eyes were off me and were traveling the length of Jane like he'd done with Gwyn, except Jane's shape was more, well, obvious, and I didn't like the way his eyes stopped where they shouldn't have been stopping. "So, I'm Del, Ori's bro. Need a ride anywhere?" He held up the keys.

"I'm Jane," she said. "And no thanks, I've got a car. But that was nice of you to ask." She was smiling at him. Damn that Del Spell.

"Maybe another time." He brushed his arm against hers as he walked past. Old Del would never have looked her over like that, would never have flirted or brushed against her if he even thought that I might like her. He would have tried to get her to notice me.

March. Del 16, Ori 13. When Ori walked out of school on Thursday afternoon, Del was leaning against their mom's Honda with his arms crossed over his chest.

"No bus today, little brother," he said. "I got my license, and I can drive siblings."

"Cool!" Ori hurried to the car, waving to Nick, who was off to the dentist.

Climbing into the warmth of the front seat, Ori looked out the windshield at a group of girls huddled against the building.

"The one in the red jacket is cute," Del said, inching the car forward.

Ori's heart sped up. The girl in the red jacket was Evie Morris. He'd liked her since the beginning of the year and barely had the guts to say hey to her.

Del stopped in front of the girls, who automatically turned their heads.

"Roll down your window," Del said.

Ori did.

"Hey, ladies," Del called out. They giggled, whispering among themselves before one of the girls pushed Evie, who stepped back, then was pushed again.

"Um, hi," she said. "Are you Ori's brother?"

Del nodded.

"Cool." Evie stared at him the way girls usually did.

"Ori didn't tell me the women at his school were so fine," Del said. "I'm not sure why he went off campus for his girl."

The girls' eyes widened, Evie's most of all.

"You have a girlfriend, Ori?" Her eyes roamed over him, as if she were seeing him for the first time.

"Oh, man. I forgot. You didn't want anyone to know." Del popped himself on the forehead. "Sorry, dude."

"Why not?" Evie asked. "Who is she?"

"She's, well, she's my girlfriend," Ori said, following Del's lead. "And we like to keep it private."

Del chuckled. "He's being modest. This girl is smokin'. And the reason he doesn't tell anyone is obvious. He's a musician. Pretty soon he'll be the front man for his own band, with girls falling all over him. Being single will be better for his image. You know how that is."

Ori had been staring at Del through this whole speech, trying to keep his mouth from dropping. When he felt like his face wouldn't give him away, he turned back to Evie.

"Whatever," he said, shrugging. "We both like it mellow."

Ori's popularity with the girls soared after that day, and he knew he owed it all to Del. He even got to make out with Evie Morris at one of the eighth-grade parties at the end of

the year, when he'd "broken up" with his nonexistent girlfriend and really needed someone.

She tasted like bubble gum.

"Thanks for the lessons," Del said to Gwyn, bringing me
back to the garage. He was giving her some sign. Whatever it
was made her smile and shake her head.

"You're welcome," she said, signing it as well.

"So now he can cuss out everyone with his hands in addition to his mouth?" I asked after Del had driven off.

"Not that most people will know," Nick pointed out.

"Actually," Gwyn said, "when he asked me to teach him 'You
suck,' I showed him the sign for 'Your father is nice-looking.'"

I busted out laughing. "That's brilliant. So the rest of them?"

"All translated into something innocent."

"I knew I liked you, Gwyn Farcosi." I held up my hand
and we high-fived. "But you'll show us the real ones, right?"

"Of course."

"Okay, Intimidator, let's get back to work," Nick said.

Jane raised an eyebrow at me. "Intimidator?"

"That's my new name for him," Nick said. "What do you
think?"

"I, for one, have been petrified of him since day one," Jane
said, looking anything but. "Except when playing *Ferrari*."

I smirked.

"Me too," Gwyn said as she pulled the guitar strap over
her head. "You're a very scary dude."

"You're all being totally unfair," I said. "You haven't seen me in full Intimidator mode."

"You're right," Jane said. "We'll reserve judgment on your intimidationness until we have more information."

"Is that even a word?" I asked.

"It is now," Jane said. She and Gwyn exchanged high fives.

I shook my head but couldn't help smiling. Jane and Gwyn already felt like part of the group. "Fine," I said. "But when you are gathering information, don't trust anything Nick says."

"Hey!" Nick protested, waving a drumstick. "I dubbed him the Intimidator. I'm the main source of info on it."

"Playing music now," I said, cranking the amp and drowning out his voice.

COLORADO ROCKS

BAND NAME: to be named later

| PROFILE | MUSIC | PIX & VIDS | ABOUT/FAQ | CONTACT | **BLOG** |

We are an up-and-coming band, nameless but open to suggestions. Feel free to post your band name ideas on our blog. (We don't want to use one of those band name generators — we want it to come from you or us.)

Saturday, February 20

ALLI: First rehearsal with Gwyn was awesome! She is AMAZING on the bass guitar. It's hard to believe she's deaf. But she "listens" with her bare feet and watches Troy and Ori carefully.

TROY: She knew most of the cover songs, so that helped a lot.

NICK: I'm just worried that Ori might intimidate our audience and they'll miss out on Gwyn playing with us at Matt's Sports in April.

 PurpleGrrl
She's DEAF??? That is AMAZING. I totally want to see her play. Does she have to watch the drummer, too? Or just the guitar players? And why would Orion intimidate anyone? He seems so mellow.

🖐 **PeacefulWarrior**
Any news on the band name? I liked Natural Enemy.

🔥 **DragonBreath**
Hey, that was my name. Thanks, dude!

Countdown to
BATTLE OF
THE BANDS:
105
days

Countdown to
LES PAUL:
65
days

We are an up-and-coming band, name-less but open to suggestions. Feel free to post your band name ideas on our blog. (We don't want to use one of those band name generators — we want it to come from you or us.)

BAND NAME: to be named later

| PROFILE | MUSIC | PIX & VIDS | ABOUT/FAQ | CONTACT | BLOG |

🎸 BoyMagnet
Gee, PG, why do you want to know about the drummer? Not too obvious.

🔊 OzoneLayer
This blog blows.

❄ Halyn
I can't wait to hear the whole band at Matt's Sports. Too bad you don't have a gig before that.

🎸 BoyMagnet
I think Orion needs to let us know if he has his eye on anyone. Should I try, or should I put all my magnetism into Roy Stone?

✌ PeacefulWarrior
And if you plan to post a new song soon or not.

🤘 GuitarFreak
No.

🎸 BoyMagnet
So GuitarFreak is Orion! Hey. Is that "no" that you don't have your eye on anyone or to the new song question? Or that I shouldn't try?

🎸 BoyMagnet
Orion?

Countdown to
BATTLE OF
THE BANDS:
105
days

Countdown to
LES PAUL:
65
days

BAND NAME: to be named later

PROFILE | MUSIC | PIX & VIDS | ABOUT/FAQ | CONTACT | **BLOG**

We are an up-and-coming band, name-less but open to suggestions. Feel free to post your band name ideas on our blog. (We don't want to use one of those band name generators — we want it to come from you or us.)

🖊 PurpleGrrl
Maybe both?

🔥 DragonBreath
I think it was to the second question.

🐾 BoyMagnet
So you're saying he didn't answer MY question? Great.

❄ Halyn
Hello? Can we talk about the music?

Countdown to
BATTLE OF
THE BANDS:

105

days

Countdown to
LES PAUL:

65

days

THIRTEEN

On Sunday Jane and I met at a Chinese restaurant not far from my house.

"I didn't want to have to compete with any french fries," I said.

She laughed. "Now you have to compete with pot stickers."

We ordered them for an appetizer along with our entrees and talked about gaming, snowboarding (another thing we had in common), and poetry and lyrics. Then she asked how Del was.

Just hearing his name made my stomach clench. "I guess he's fine," I said. "Why?"

"I don't know," she said. "I just...sensed something."

"He's Del." I shrugged before attempting to snag another piece of chicken with my chopsticks.

She smiled. "What exactly does that mean?"

The chicken dropped from between the chopsticks just

before I got it to my mouth. Frowning, I went for it again. "He was in college, blew his first semester, and now he's home making my life hell," I said. "That's all you really need to know."

Jane bit her lip, looking down at her plate of fried rice. "I'm sorry."

I didn't know if she was sorry for asking or sorry about the situation, but I didn't want to find out.

"It's fine," I said. "Can you pass the soy sauce, please?"

We managed to shift to other topics, but the conversation felt forced after that, like we were trying to be nice and polite while we inched our way around this giant Del thing that took up the space between us.

I think we were both a little relieved when we said good-bye, heading to our own cars, but I was also feeling angry that Del had once again ruined something that mattered to me without even having to be around.

On Tuesday afternoon I was at Gold's, trying not to think about how the night had ended with Jane, or about how things were with Del, even though it was hard not to think about him because I'd had to ride my bike to work again in the freezing cold, since he'd taken the car. But the band was coming together for the most part, and I'd soon have the best guitar in the world in my hands, so that almost made up for not having the car.

"Can I take five before I start?" I asked Ed when I strode into the store, heading straight for the Les Paul on display.

He had been right about that kid whose dad had bought it. They'd returned the guitar after a week, and it was now back in its spot in the window. I picked it up, feeling the weight of it in my hands.

"Take six," Ed said, grinning as I headed back to the Jam Room.

"Give it up for Orion Taylor and the Whatever-Their-Name-Is band."

Okay. Not the best way to segue into a rock-concert fantasy.

We play for two hours with only a small break. We leave after "Focus," and the stage goes black. We know and the audience knows we'll be back for our encore.

The crowd chants our name, a few of our songs.

We step back onto the stage to a roar. I look to my left, and a hot blond in sunglasses and a ponytail struts toward me, carrying a miniature telephone pole.

Wait. Rewind.

A hot blond with amazing eyes and long lashes (that I manage to be able to see even in the dim stage lights) struts toward me, carrying the Les Paul. The crowd goes nuts. They know what it means when she brings out the Les Paul and hands it to me.

"Welcome!" I shout into the mic, raising the guitar in the air. "Welcome to your 'Suburban Nightmare.'"

The crowd shrieks and claps as the screen behind me grows bright with the image of a typical suburban neighborhood. Yes, this massive multimedia spectacular started as a small light-and-video show Alli put together when we were just a garage band.

Nick starts with his drums, then I plunge in on the Les Paul, the chords screaming through the amp. This guitar is like an extension of me. I barely feel like I'm playing. It's like the guitar takes over, knows what I want to do, and does it before I can even think about it.

"OT?"

We rip the song and the crowd is with us all the way. Then they are chanting my name.

"Orion, Orion, Orion."

"Orion!"

"Huh?"

I blinked, the stage and audience dissolving as the Jam Room came into focus. Ed was standing in front of me, grinning.

"Welcome back to Earth."

My cheeks warmed. "Sorry, Ed. It seems like whenever I get one of these Les Pauls in my hands…"

"I know," Ed said. "It transports you every time." He crossed his arms. "But I do need to get some work out of you. I've got a few customers out there who need some guitar advice."

"I'm on it."

After I'd sold a Yamaha to a happy customer, I went back to the storeroom to unpack inventory. About halfway through, my cell played Jeff Beck—incoming text.

☒ BRO. *DEL CELL 5:20 PM*

Crap. I closed the phone and got back to work.

Jeff Beck announced another text.

☒ NEED 2 TALK WHERE R U? *DEL CELL 5:21 PM*

✉ WORK. CAN'T TALK.

✉ ED'S COOL JUST NEED A SEC. *DEL CELL 5:21 PM*

✉ LATER.

✉ NOW. *DEL CELL 5:21 PM*

Smack. I closed my phone.

Two seconds later it rang, scaring the heck out of me.

"I told you I'm at work," I said.

"I need you to float me a loan."

Just like that. No *"Hi, how are you."* No *"Your band sounded great the other day even though I was scoping out the girls, especially the blond who I have a feeling you might like but so what because I'm the new Del who doesn't care about you anymore."*

Just "I need you to float me a loan."

"I really think you should talk to Mom and Dad."

He sighed impatiently through the phone. "Just for a few weeks. You've got all that guitar money."

I used an X-Acto knife to slice the tape off the box in front of me, wishing I could say what I really wanted, which was *"Exactly. It's guitar money. For my guitar."*

But I didn't want to piss him off, which kind of pissed me off. But there it was.

"You could play music on a box strung with Silly String," Del said. "Come on."

Ah, the nice Dr. Jekyll. But he sounded like he was trying really hard not to turn into Mr. Hyde.

"I could talk to Mom and Dad for you."

He let out an annoyed snort. "I just need a loan. How many times have I helped you?"

"I know." I hated how soft my voice had become. "Really,"

145

I said, trying to be a little louder, more sincere. "Do you want me to talk—"

"Forget it."

Dead air told me he'd hung up.

When I got home, I heard Del and my parents talking in the living room—loudly. Vela was sitting at the kitchen table, shaking her head.

"What gives?" I asked, jerking my head in the direction of the argument.

Vela shrugged. "I'm not sure, but I think Del wants money and Mom and Dad said no."

Huh. Had he actually taken my advice to talk to our parents?

I grabbed a Gatorade out of the fridge and pulled off the top, taking a deep swig as the voices got louder.

"You guys say you want me to get on with my life, but you won't help me." This was the new Del: angrier, moodier, resentful.

"We agreed to let you live at home if you worked and came up with a solid plan," my dad said, "to either go back to college or have some kind of career path you're working toward. If you did that, we wouldn't make you pay back the tuition we lost or pay us rent."

"All I need is a little bit of money and I can move on."

"To where?" my dad asked. "To what? What do you want to do?"

Del groaned. "Why can't you just trust me on this?"

He let the words hang in the air, a challenge.

"It's not that we don't trust you—" my mom began.

"Yes, it is," my dad interrupted. "You lied about your grades and you were skipping classes. You told us you were doing fine right up until we got the letter that you'd been put on academic probation."

"Forget it, then." Footsteps, fast and heavy up the stairs, Mom's "Del!" buried beneath them.

Above us, doors and drawers slammed, and then the footsteps were coming back down. I stepped out of the kitchen in time to see Del yanking open the front door, a duffel bag slung over his shoulder.

"Where do you think you're going?" my dad said, grabbing Del's arm.

Del wrenched free, pushing through the screen door and out onto the porch. "Away from here," he said, striding down the steps.

Vela and I hurried after him, stopping on the front porch. We immediately wrapped our arms around ourselves in the cold of the February night.

"What are you looking at?" he asked me.

"Don't," I said.

"Don't what? Look at you? Yell? Ask for money? Leave? I can do whatever I want, Ori. I *do* things. I don't just sit around fantasizing about being a rock star and hiding out in bathrooms and making a fool of myself. I'm actually doing things." He turned on his heel and strode toward the car. I barely had a chance to register the fact that he knew I'd hidden out in the bathroom at FX when Vela rushed past all of us.

"Del!" Her voice stopped him in his tracks.

He turned and looked at her, his face softening a little, though anger still clung to his jaw.

"Please don't leave," she said softly.

Del sighed, gripping her shoulders. "I'm sorry, Vee. It's not you. I just can't be here right now. I'll call you, though. We'll do stuff."

He smiled and touched her lightly on the cheek before turning toward the driveway.

"You're not going anywhere in that car." Dad strode after him, planting himself in front of the driver's-side door.

Del's face was red, his eyes narrowed.

"Fine," he said. He tossed the car keys over his shoulder, where they landed in the coarse brown grass between our house and Alli's. He hustled inside the garage, wheeling my bike out seconds later. Throwing his leg over the seat, he pushed off, the duffel bag bouncing across his back.

"Hey!" I shouted, jogging across the lawn. "That's my bike!"

But he was already riding furiously down the street.

"He took my bike," I said to no one in particular.

"I'm sorry, Ori." My mom's voice was quiet. When I turned to look at her, I saw Alli step back from her living room window.

Great.

"Goddammit!" My dad smacked his fist into his palm as he stared down the street after Del.

"Steven." My mom walked over to him, placing her hand lightly on his back.

He stepped forward and her hand stayed where it was for

a moment—like his back was still beneath it—before she let it fall to her side. We watched as Dad crossed the grass, plucking the keys from the lawn. I felt movement behind me and turned to see Vela, eyes bright with unshed tears. I made a move to put my arm around her, but she pulled back.

"Why did you have to make him leave?" she said, eyes pinning each of us with her accusation.

"Vela, honey—" My mom started toward her.

"I hate all of you!" She ran back into the house, the screen door slamming behind her.

The three of us stood silently on the lawn, looking everywhere but at one another. Then, one by one we walked slowly back toward the house, no one touching, no one talking.

I trudged up the stairs to my room, pausing outside Vela's door, pressing my ear against it. Nothing. She probably had her nano on, her earbuds in, blocking out the world.

I knocked anyway.

"Go away!"

At least she heard me.

But I'd been her brother long enough to know the difference between "Go away, but come in and talk to me anyway" and "Go away, I mean it." Sighing, I brushed my fingers across her door, averting my eyes as I passed Del's room and went into my own.

Sinking down on my bed, I tried to decide what I wanted to do more: kill him or talk to him. I checked the clock every few minutes, deciding how long I should wait. Finally, after about thirty minutes, I flipped open my phone and typed a text to Del's friend Chad.

✉ DEL AT YOUR PLACE? DON'T TELL HIM IT'S ME

✉ YEAH – VERY PISSED WHAT GIVES? *CHAD CELL 9:45 PM*

✉ LONG STORY – IS HE STAYING?

✉ NO IDEA *CHAD CELL 9:45 PM*

✉ CAN U LET ME KNOW?

There was a light tap on my doorjamb. My mom was standing in the doorway, her shoulders slumped, her face drawn.

"He's at Chad's," she said. "I called over there. Your dad didn't want me to, said to let him be, but I had to know, you know?"

I looked down at my phone.

✉ WILL DO *CHAD CELL 9:46 PM*

"Yeah," I said. "I know."

FOURTEEN

We had rehearsals the next afternoon, but I had a hard time concentrating. Del had come back in the night, snuck into the house, and gotten as much stuff as he could fit in the car, which he then drove off in, using what I could only assume was a spare key he must have had made at some point. Of course, this made the whole tossing-the-keys-into-the-grass thing just for dramatic effect.

At least he'd left my bike leaning against the garage.

But I knew all this before he showed up because I hadn't been able to sleep. I'd been waiting for Chad to let me know what was going on. He'd texted me at 12:21 AM.

✉ HE'S HEADING YOUR WAY TO GET STUFF – STAYING
   HERE 4 A WHILE

When Del got to the house, I'd been too chicken to get up, to help him, to stop him. I pretended to be asleep when he poked his head into my room, whispering my name.

"Figures," he'd muttered. "Sleeping like a baby while I'm…"

I couldn't hear the rest because he'd already turned away, closing my door on his voice. I wondered why he'd peeked in at all, why he'd whispered my name like he wanted to talk to me.

I wondered why I didn't answer.

I had the oddest feeling when I heard the engine start and the car back out of the driveway. I would have thought I'd be glad he was gone, that I wouldn't have to worry about whether he was in a good mood or a bad mood, whether he hated me or wanted something from me so he'd be nice.

I just felt empty.

When my parents woke up and discovered the car missing, they were livid.

"I should call the police and report it stolen," my dad had said. "Maybe a night in jail will wake him up."

"Calm down, Steven," my mom had said. "You know that's not the answer. Filing charges, jail, courts…" Her voice trailed off, the words having the effect she meant them to have.

My dad sighed heavily. "You're right. But it's still tempting. I don't know what to do with him."

"Then let's not do anything, like we agreed last night," my mom said. "At least for now. Let's see what he does on his own."

"But he's sponging off Chad's family. I don't like that."

"I spoke to Michelle." That was Chad's mom. "She apparently told him he gets two weeks as a guest. After that, he needs to start giving them rent and food money."

Dad had nodded. "Good for her. I'm sure we'll see him back here after his two-week freebie is up."

"Maybe." I hadn't been able to tell from Mom's voice whether she was hoping he'd be back or hoping he'd stay away longer.

What a mess.

"Earth to Orion." Nick's voice and his tapping drumstick penetrated my thoughts, bringing me back to OT Studios and our rehearsal. He chuckled. "Get it? Earth to Orion. The constellation."

No one laughed. They were all staring at me.

"Sorry," I muttered. I could feel Alli looking at me, but I refused to look at her. It was bad enough she'd witnessed the scene in the front yard. I didn't want to see the pity in her eyes.

You okay? Gwyn signed to me so no one else could see.

I was surprised I understood.

I nodded slightly and then dropped to a squat to fiddle with the amp cord.

Not surprisingly, the rehearsal didn't go very well. I couldn't seem to get into the music; it wouldn't carry me away like it usually did.

"Any chance we can pick this up tomorrow?" I asked. "I'm a little off today."

After everyone had left, Alli followed me into the house.

"Remember when Del gave you the silent treatment for a week that one summer?" She opened up the refrigerator and pulled out a gallon of milk and some Hershey's chocolate syrup.

"How could I forget?" It was the summer after fifth grade and Del had just gotten out of middle school, already in I'm-in-high-school-I'm-cool mode. He was planning to meet a girl he liked at Cold Stone and wanted to wear his favorite black baseball cap, which he always wore backward. Nick and I had thought it would be funny to hide it, but Del was furious. He acted like I literally didn't exist for a week.

It sucked.

"Yeah, well, this is kind of like that." She had poured the chocolate syrup into a mug of milk and was adding some unsweetened cocoa to the mixture, just the way I liked it. "He just needs time. He'll come back around." She stirred the milk with a spoon and then popped the mug into the microwave.

"Maybe," I said, watching her reach into the cupboard and pull out a bag of marshmallows.

The microwave dinged, and she pulled the steaming mug out, dropping two marshmallows into it.

"Call me if you need anything," she said as she handed the mug to me. "You know where to find me."

I took a sip. It was the perfect blend of not-too-sweet and hot-but-not-scalding.

"Thanks," I said, and I knew she knew it wasn't just for the hot chocolate.

✉ REHEARSAL GOOD? *HALYN CELL 9:48 PM*

✉ SO-SO. HOW'S THE WRITING?

✉ SO-SO. WHEN'S OUR GUITAR HERO CHALLENGE? *HALYN CELL 9:48 PM*

I'd been looking forward to that until she had asked about Del at dinner. And now Del had taken off and things were just weird.

✉ NOT SURE. I'LL LET YOU KNOW.

✉ K *HALYN CELL 9:49 PM*

It was strange how the house felt emptier now than when Del had left for college last August. After his midnight raid, he'd closed the door to his room, and it felt like more than *Keep out*. It felt like *I'm gone and I'm not coming back, but don't even think about going in my room.*

Final.

As I stood in front of the closed door, images stampeded through my mind.

Summer. Del 10, Ori 7. They were playing Horse with the Nerf basketball, the hoop attached to the back of the door.

Del launched the ball and sunk it. That meant Ori had to make the exact same shot from the exact same place. He missed. He got H; Del got to shoot again. It went on like this, with Del missing only one (and Ori suspected he'd done it on purpose, just to give Ori a chance to pick the shot).

"You'll get it next time," Del said, tossing the ball at Ori. "Let's go play video games."

Summer. Del 14, Ori 11. "Some girls will just be after you for your status," Del said. "Those are the ones you want to stay away from. One day they like you, the next they don't and they're on to someone else."

"How can they stop liking you that fast?"

"Who knows?" Del said. "They're girls. They just do stupid stuff."

August. Del 18, Ori 15. "This is so weird." Ori was sitting on Del's bed, watching him put the last of his things in his suitcase for college.

"I'm not that far away," Del said. "You know I'll be down to do my laundry."

"As if you'll be doing it," Ori said. "You'll sweet-talk Mom, like you always do."

Del grinned. "If she wants to do it, who am I to stop her?"

"She always makes me do mine." Ori walked across the room to look at the pictures tacked to the wall above Del's dresser. He'd looked at them a million times—pictures of Del with his friends, with Tara, with their family on the river, skiing, sports photos. Each one told a story.

"Hey, can you take care of this while I'm gone?" Del held out a lacrosse trophy, a smaller replica of the one that now stood front and center in the trophy case at Falcon High.

"You aren't taking it with you?"

He shook his head. "Don't want to seem like I'm bragging or living in the past, you know?"

Ori nodded. "Sure."

I turned away and walked into my room, my eyes immediately falling on the trophy sitting on my dresser. It was the only thing in the whole room that wasn't dusty, because I actually dusted it. I liked the way it shined, the way Del's name stood out from the plate at the bottom. Picking it up, I stuck it into a far corner of my closet shelf, covering it with an old T-shirt.

I wandered around the house, averting my eyes every time I saw something that reminded me of Del—the Goldfish box left on the coffee table in front of the TV, his socks in the hall, his favorite baseball cap decorating the banister knob.

Vela was into day two of the Family Freeze-Out, tucked away in her room, though I knew she'd been out at least once or twice—the Honey Nut Cheerios box had been nearly full yesterday and now it was half empty.

Later that night I knocked on her door. She didn't say "Go away" like she had the night before; in fact, she didn't say anything at all, so I took that as "Come in."

She was lying on her side on her bed, staring at the wall.

"Hey, Vee." I sat at the foot of the bed. "Has he called or texted you?"

She didn't respond, just kept staring.

"Chad's going to keep me updated. I'll keep you posted."

Still nothing. I waited a few seconds, then: "We're having another rehearsal tomorrow if you want to hang out. Bring your friends if you want. We could use an audience." I watched her. "Vela?"

"Maybe."

"Good." I squeezed her arm as I stood up. "Gwyn will be happy to see you."

"Will Jane be there?"

"I'm not sure." We'd had only one other communication since our text exchange about *Guitar Hero*. But even our texts about *Ferrari F355*—✉ NEXT TIME I'LL DRIVE BLIND-FOLDED; NOT ENOUGH OF A HANDICAP—felt forced and phony. Or maybe that was just me, not liking the fact that she had pulled anything out of me about Del at our dinner, that he'd been inserted into our friendship and was now a barrier between us, keeping us at arm's length.

But at least she didn't seem to be one of those girls who made everything about them, who took it personally if you didn't want to talk and thought you were mad at them or didn't like them or whatever. Not that I'd had any experience in that arena. I'd just seen it with Del.

"High-maintenance drama queen," Del had said after a particularly nasty breakup when he was a junior and I was in eighth grade. "I should have known." Then he had smiled ruefully. "Well, I did know, actually. But other things kind of distracted me for a while." We'd both laughed at that.

I remembered being impressed that he cared about personality, about "a good fit" as he called it.

"Not that you are exactly alike or agree on everything," he'd said, "but you kind of know each other, don't let each other get away with crap and stuff." That was about as deep as my brother ever got, but it stuck with me. Tara and Del had "fit." I could see it. She didn't let him get away with anything, and if she started whining, he'd call her on it. But when she was genuinely upset, he was there for her, holding her, listening to her, talking to her. Until last fall, when he'd wanted to be Big Stud on Campus and lost her.

Where had that other Del gone?

And had I lost that chance with Jane before I'd even had it?

"I like Jane," Vela said, bringing me back to her room. She still had her back to me.

I reached out and patted her head like Del sometimes did, noticing the softness of her hair against my palm. I was about to pull away when she reached up and put her hand over mine.

"Will he come back?" she whispered.

"I don't know."

She sighed. "Do you want him to?"

I paused, watching our hands move slightly with every breath she took.

"I don't know that, either."

NickStix88: Should I be worried about our boy?

Allicat21: He'll be fine.

Strummer12: Absolutely, but we need to keep him positive.

NickStix88: Positive. Right. It might help if I had a girlfriend.

Allicat21: Say what?

NickStix88: Al, has PurpleGrrl e-mailed you about me like Halyn did about Ori?

Allicat21: Nick, we're supposed to be talking about Ori. I thought you were worried about him.

NickStix88: I was but you told me he'll be fine, so I'm now focused on the positive that Troy mentioned. If I had some purple goodness coming my way, my happiness would affect Ori in a positive way.

Allicat21: You're hopeless and delusional. Troy, tell him.

Strummer12: Well, you did say Ori would be fine, babe.

Allicat21: But he's not fine NOW.

Strummer12: True. Nick, my friend, let's keep the focus on Ori.

NickStix88: OK. But you'll tell me if she e-mails you, right?

Allicat21: Nick!

NickStix88: OK. OK.

FIFTEEN

The next afternoon, everyone showed up ready to play. My parents had been behind closed doors most of the night, but that morning they both seemed less angry. I guessed letting Del do whatever he was going to do was sitting better with them.

"Let's do this," I said, strumming my guitar. We made it through two of our covers with only a few mistakes, and then Nick said we should try an original.

Before anyone could suggest one, Vela and Jane came into the garage.

"Look who I found out front," Vela said, thumbing at Jane, who waved. She caught my eye briefly, searching my face. I don't know what she saw, but at least she didn't look away. That was nice. I realized I was happy to see her, no matter what she'd asked about Del. I just hoped she wouldn't ask again.

"Is it okay if we're here?"

"Sure," I said. I watched as they settled into folding chairs in the back, whispering and talking like old friends.

"How about 'Focus'?" Nick said, turning to Gwyn. "It's this amazing new song Ori's been working on. I think it's really tight, and we're hoping to play it at Matt's."

"Sounds good to me," Gwyn said. "I'll hang back until I catch on."

"It's still pretty rough." And it was connected to Del, sort of, which made me feel a little weird.

"That's okay," Gwyn said. "Just go for it."

I took a breath and let it out. It was a good song; I should have been able to play it. Just because it started out to be about Del didn't mean it had to be about him anymore, right? Wasn't that what I'd told Halyn in the e-mail? Sometimes you needed to forget about the actual situation so that you could do something different, go in another direction, or just get moving.

"Let's do it."

We had to start over twice because Troy and Nick had played it only a few times, and then we had just been messing around, not really trying to play it. Finally they settled in, and we were able to keep going.

"*I shouldn't let it get to me,*" I sang, "*a face in a crowd, the slightest sound, not even very loud . . . takes away my focus.*" Even as I tried to shove the image of Del from my mind, it came roaring back, stronger than ever. I saw him defying our dad in the front yard, riding away on my bike, and heard his voice, cold and angry on the phone, and the bitter whisper when he'd come back that night, thinking I was asleep.

But I kept singing, letting my emotions bounce between anger and sadness without giving in to them completely. Closing my eyes, I let the song be about whatever I was feeling right then, in that moment.

When we'd played the last chord, there was silence. I opened my eyes to find everyone staring at me. Alli was smiling a sad smile. I knew she wouldn't say anything about Del's meltdown that night, but it still made me feel weird that she knew why the song had come out of me the way it did.

"That was genius, Ori," Troy said, breaking the silence. "You sing all the songs like that, and Slash and Burn won't even show up for the Battle."

"Right on," Nick said as Gwyn nodded.

Jane and Vela started clapping and we all took an exaggerated bow, but I still felt shaky and unbalanced, like I'd just come off a very bumpy boat ride.

"Let's try 'Sweet Child O' Mine,'" I said, wanting the safety of something familiar yet not attached to me personally in any way. "We need to work on the opening."

After we were finished, Jane walked over to where I was covering up the amps.

"That song," she said, grabbing the opposite end of the tarp to help. "Was that the one you were talking about in your e-mail? The one that helped me think of the next verse in my poem?"

"I don't remember." But of course I did.

"It was amazing," she said. "Really amazing."

"Thanks." Soft echoes of what I'd felt when singing it still whispered through my body. Anger, sadness, confusion.

I straightened up. "Speaking of that second verse, I'm ready for it."

She smiled. "I'm working on it. But it's kind of all over the place right now. Just like my feelings."

Was she talking about me? I couldn't tell, and no way was I going to ask.

"You'll get it," I said.

"I hope so. I'd love for you to put more of it to music."

After everyone had left, Vela and I were by ourselves in the kitchen.

"Was that song about Del?" she asked as she pulled a carton of ice cream out of the freezer.

I shrugged.

"Well, whatever," she said, lifting the lid of the carton. "It was really good."

"Thanks."

"Jane's so cool," she said, scooping chocolate ice cream into a bowl. "Are you two going out?"

"We're friends." At least I hoped so. Things seemed to have smoothed themselves out today.

"Good," Vela said. "That means you won't break up and I'll never see her again."

"So this is all about you?" I grabbed a spoon from the drawer.

"Of course." She grinned as she sliced bananas over her ice cream, just the way Del always did. Then he would have poured Hershey's syrup over it—"Because you can never have it too chocolaty," he would say.

"Figures," I said, watching her get the Hershey's out. "And I can't get mad at you..."

"Because I'm unhateable," she finished.

"Exactly." I smiled, but then my smile faded as I looked at that bowl of Del ice cream. It was weird to have it in front of us without him. Vela must have felt it, too, because she looked from the bowl to me, then turned abruptly and opened the fridge.

"Cherries!" she crowed, pulling out a jar of maraschinos. She scooped out several and dotted them over the top of the ice cream, then stirred it all together into one glorious mess.

Del hated maraschino cherries and never mixed his ice cream and chocolate syrup together.

We caught each other's eye, then Vela got two spoons and we dug in.

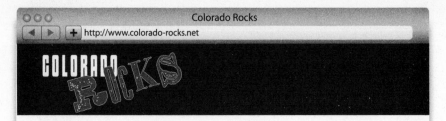

COLORADO ROCKS

We are an up-and-coming band, nameless but open to suggestions. Feel free to post your band name ideas on our blog. (We don't want to use one of those band name generators — we want it to come from you or us.)

BAND NAME: to be named later

| PROFILE | MUSIC | PIX & VIDS | ABOUT/FAQ | CONTACT | BLOG |

Sunday, February 28

ALLI: Thursday the band played "Focus" — remember the song Ori mentioned a while back that he was working on after their debut at FX Lounge? Well they totally kicked that song's butt at rehearsal. And it was like Ori became the song or it was playing him or something. It was AMAZING.

TROY: Keep the good vibes going. This band, though nameless, will be a serious contender at the Battle of the Bands.

NICK: Who else is going to kosmøs on March 5? We'll be there!

 PurpleGrrl

I bet Nick backed up the band on the drums in an excellent way.

 BoyMagnet

You're not even trying to hide your feelings for Nick anymore. I have to give you props for that.

DragonBreath

Can't make kosmøs, but have a blast, dude.

PurpleGrrl

Halyn, are you out there?

Countdown to
BATTLE OF
THE BANDS:

97

days

Countdown to
LES PAUL:

57

days

We are an up-and-coming band, nameless but open to suggestions. Feel free to post your band name ideas on our blog. (We don't want to use one of those band name generators — we want it to come from you or us.)

Countdown to
BATTLE OF
THE BANDS:

97

days

Countdown to
LES PAUL:

57

days

BAND NAME: to be named later

| PROFILE | MUSIC | PIX & VIDS | ABOUT/FAQ | CONTACT | BLOG |

 BoyMagnet

Who cares? She's always trying to get us back to talking about the music instead of the important stuff like IS ORION READY FOR A GIRLFRIEND???

Okay, DominantSpecies, let's hear you say you're outta here or it's all about girlie stuff or whatever.

 BoyMagnet

DominantSpecies?

 PurpleGrrl

You know, I don't think he's been on for a while. Maybe he finally followed through and left for good.

 OzoneLayer

Smart guy.

 BoyMagnet

You think he really quit?

 PurpleGrrl

Looks like it.

 BoyMagnet

That's good. Right?

http://www.colorado-rocks.net

We are an up-and-coming band, nameless but open to suggestions. Feel free to post your band name ideas on our blog. (We don't want to use one of those band name generators — we want it to come from you or us.)

BAND NAME: to be named later

| PROFILE | MUSIC | PIX & VIDS | ABOUT/FAQ | CONTACT | BLOG |

🟣 PurpleGrrl
Sure it is.

⚫ BoyMagnet
Right.

Countdown to
BATTLE OF
THE BANDS:

97

days

Countdown to
LES PAUL:

57

days

HalynFlake34: You there, Alli?

Allicat21: Yep.

HalynFlake34: Just wondering how Ori's doing. He seems a little distracted.

Allicat21: Del moved out, but you didn't hear it from me. Ori will talk when he's ready. P.S. I know this is none of my business, but do you "like" like him?

HalynFlake34: I won't say anything unless he says something first. P.S. Does he "like" like me?

Allicat21: Cool. What did you think of your poem being put to music the other day? P.S. I asked you first.

HalynFlake34: AMAZING. I got all emotional. P.S. No fair.

Allicat21: Are you going to answer the question?

HalynFlake34: Are you?

Allicat21: I can't answer for Ori.

HalynFlake34: That means no.

Allicat21: It means I can't answer for Ori. But YOU can answer for YOU.

Allicat21: Halyn?

Allicat21: Jane?

HalynFlake34 has signed off.

SIXTEEN

kosmøs was a local band we'd started following a year or so ago, and we were totally pumped for their concert. It was at a bar without the bar — a special concert for teens, so no booze was available — just pop, water, Gatorade, and the usual high-octane energy drinks and a few food selections off their menu. A big sign in front read NO OUTSIDE FOOD OR DRINKS PERMITTED, and people were searched as they came in, but that didn't stop lots of them from showing up drunk off their butts.

"This is so awesome," Nick said, bobbing his head as we entered. We snagged a high-top table off to the side; the whole center of the bar had been cleared for standing-room-only concert viewing. That was where we'd be after we ate.

"There's PurpleGrrl." Alli pointed toward the back, to a girl with bright blue hair, before turning to Nick. "Don't say I never did anything for you."

"But she's not purple," I said. "And last time we saw her, she was green."

"It's awesome," Nick said.

"Go talk to her."

"What would I say?" Nick shook his head.

"Are you kidding, Brewster?" Alli said. "This is what you've been wanting. This is your chance."

He frowned, standing up to sneak peeks at PurpleGrrl and then sitting down.

I looked at Alli. "Please tell me that is not how I look when I'm showing my dork side."

She made a sympathetic face. "Sorry."

"Is she looking this way?" Nick asked.

"She's talking to her friends."

"About me?"

"Sorry, Nicky. I don't have super hearing." Alli snuggled into Troy's side.

Nick looked over his shoulder. "Okay, at the break, I'm going back there. I'm going to talk to her. I can't be like *him*." He thrust a thumb at me.

"Thanks."

"Good boy," Alli said. "Oh, hey."

We turned to see Gwyn, looking very hip in a black lace dress and black just about everything else. She was standing next to some dude who looked like he should be in the movies or something. Looking at him, I felt like a zit-faced sophomore in high school. Oh, wait. I *was* a zit-faced sophomore in high school.

Jane was behind Gwyn with some okay-looking guy who

was pretty buff. I hated the way my stomach dropped when I saw him.

"This is my boyfriend, Adam," Gwyn said, pointing to the movie dude.

"And this is Sean," Jane said, motioning to Buff Guy, "Gwyn's brother."

I relaxed slightly.

"You guys seen a girl with blue hair?" Nick asked.

They all shook their heads. "But we'll be on the lookout," Jane said.

"You should join us." Alli patted the seat next to her. "We can squeeze you in."

"We've already got a table," Adam the movie god said. "But thanks."

Sean touched Jane's arm. "We should probably go back before someone steals it."

My eyes were glued to those fingers on Jane's arm. I wanted those to be *my* fingers.

As they walked away, Alli watched them and said, "Wait for it."

"Wait for what?" we all asked.

"Just act natural, but watch out of the corner of your eye," she said. Our heads swiveled to look at Jane's and Sean's backs.

Alli groaned. "How is that natural? Don't stare at them. You guys are pathetic."

We swiveled our heads back to her.

"Corner of your eyes," Alli instructed. "And she'll turn and look at Ori...now."

Out of the corner of my eye, I saw Jane look over her shoulder—at me.

"Called it," Alli said with a satisfied smile.

"Wow," Nick said. "You're good. Now, can you tell me if PurpleGrrl is going to come looking for me?"

"Strike two, Nick. No super hearing and I'm not psychic," Alli said.

"Then what good are you?" Nick asked, shaking his head. "Can you at least tell Ori what's up with that Sean dude, since he won't ask you himself? I know you know that."

I scowled at him before quickly turning my attention to Alli.

She sighed her could-you-be-any-more-stupid sigh. "She wouldn't introduce him as Gwyn's brother if he was anything else. She wanted Ori to know that."

"Just because Sean isn't her boyfriend doesn't mean she doesn't have one."

"She looked back at you," Alli said. "I called it and you should just go with it. Besides, I think she—" Alli stopped, pressing her lips together. "I'm hungry. Let's get some food."

Troy waved down a waiter, and we put in our order. Half an hour later, our pizza arrived and the warm-up band came on. Once the music started it was nearly impossible to talk, so we ate and drank and shouted, resorting to texting each other when it got extra loud.

I sent Jane a text.

✉ WASSUP?

✉ NOT MUCH. YOU? *HALYN CELL 6:43 PM*

✉ WANT TO ALL MEET NEAR THE CENTER PILLAR WHEN THEY COME ON?

✉ **SOUNDS GOOD.** *HALYN CELL 6:44 PM*

I smiled, wondering if I could find a way to stand next to her, even though she was with Sean.

The opening band finished their set and headed off the stage to a chorus of cheers and clapping. It would be another half hour or so before kosmøs came on.

During the break, Nick scooted off his stool. "Okay, I'm going for it. I need to see PurpleGrrl up close to seal the deal." He craned his neck to look over the crowd.

"What deal?" Troy asked.

"The deal," Nick said as if we should all know what he was talking about. "I'll be back."

He was, about fifteen minutes later, face lit up, cell held high.

"Score!" He shoved the phone in my face. "Look at her."

"You took a picture of her?"

Nick shook his head. "Her friend took my phone and did it. But she didn't seem to care." He grinned. "Got her number, too."

"Are you sure she didn't give you a fake one?" I asked, smirking.

Nick scowled at me and then held up his phone again. "She texted me, baby. She loves me."

"What's her name?" Troy asked.

Nick furrowed his brow.

"You didn't get her name?" Troy and I looked at each other. "Unbelievable."

"This is Nick we're talking about," I said.

"Believable," Alli said.

"Not funny." Nick pressed buttons on his cell. "I'm asking her right now."

"'PurpleGrrl, will you marry me?'" I asked in falsetto.

"'PurpleGrrl, should we name our first kid IndigoBoy?'" Alli asked in matching falsetto.

Troy shook his head at us, but he was smiling.

Nick just scowled, then grinned, triumphant. "Kaitlyn," he said, shoving the phone at us again. "Her name is Kaitlyn."

"She'll always be PurpleGrrl to me," I said, pressing my hands to my heart before standing up with the empty pitcher. "Refills?"

Everyone nodded, so I wound my way to the bar, getting in line behind several people. I was still smiling about Nick when—

"Orion?"

I turned to see Jane standing behind me with her own pitcher. My heart did one of those little blips.

"How did you like the opening band? I think you guys are better."

I laughed. "That's nice, but you haven't heard us much. We're just a high school band. There're a million just like us." I cringed as I realized I was repeating Del's words.

Jane's face turned serious. "I don't think so. Your songs, your music..." She shrugged. "All the big bands started small. Why not you?" She nodded for me to move up as the line crept forward.

"So, Sean is Gwyn's brother?"

Jane nodded. "He is. And like mine. You know the story. Known him since we were kids, blah, blah, blah."

"That's like me and Alli."

"Yeah. That's what I thought." She smiled. "Tonight I'm pinch-hitting. Sean's girlfriend got food poisoning, and Sean didn't want the ticket to go to waste. She knows I'm safe."

We moved up again in line, two people ahead of us. I looked at her hand curled around the handle of the pitcher. I wouldn't mind holding that hand, standing close together, leaning in—

Smack. Someone slapped me on the back.

"Little bro! What's up?"

What was Del doing here?

"I remember you." He glanced at Jane with glassy, unfocused eyes and smiled. "You refused to let me take you home. Broke my heart." He pressed his hands to his chest.

"I didn't refuse," Jane said, smiling back, "I already had a ride, remember? And I seriously doubt anyone could break your heart. My guess is it's the other way around."

Del grinned wide and was about to say something when the bartender barked, "Next!"

"Go ahead," I said to Jane, who thanked me and stepped away from us to go to the bar. I looked at Del. "So how's it going?"

"Peachy," he said, and I got a major noseful of beer breath. "I'm sleeping on Chad's floor, working my ass off, no help from the family. You?"

Why did I bother?

"You should call Vela."

"Yeah, I know." His face softened slightly. Only Vela seemed able to do that to him. Then he straightened up, glancing over at Jane still standing at the bar. "So did you trade in your guitar girlfriend for the real thing?" He didn't wait for me to answer. "She's cute."

Don't even think about it. Her.

"She's great," I said, hoping he'd think we were together and leave her alone.

Jane came up then, holding her pitcher carefully.

"You play?" Del asked, nodding down at her shirt. For the first time I noticed it said ST. ELIZABETH'S ACADEMY LACROSSE on it.

She nodded. "I made JV again, which is great because it means I'll get to play more. A lot of the sophomores on varsity will be sitting on the bench."

They started having this big conversation about lacrosse, with Del actually asking her questions and not just making it about him, which pissed me off because only he could sound so coherent when he'd had a few beers. I went to get my own pitcher filled, watching them over my shoulder. Jane's eyes never left his face. She listened to everything he said, and then said something back. She seemed to be asking the right questions, laughing at all the right places, even squeezing his arm in sympathy at one point.

"Five bucks."

"Huh? Oh, right." I turned back to the bartender, handing her the money before returning to Jane and Del.

"So your sister's in college now?" Del was asking.

Jane nodded. "Sophomore at CU-Boulder." I was glad they were talking about Jane's sister. Let him go after her and leave Jane alone.

"Good for her," Del said. "Me, I'm taking a break from school." He glanced at me. "But maybe Ori already gave you his own version?"

"He told me you were around," she said. "I think it's great you're taking time to figure things out. Not everyone has the guts to go against expectations and do something different."

I stared at her. She was brilliant to say that.

"That's Del exactly," I said. "He's totally his own person." I tried to keep the sarcasm out of my voice because I knew she was trying to be nice.

Del grinned, dropping his arm heavily on my shoulder, which made the Coke slosh onto my shirt. I stepped back, grunting my annoyance, but he didn't seem to notice. "'Course, Orion here is the real trailblazer. Mr. Musical Prodigy. Mr. Big Rock Star. Did you know I gave him his first guitar and his first start? Bet he didn't tell you that."

"That was nice of you," Jane said, her eyes flitting to me. I looked away, angry at Del for calling me those names in front of Jane like *I* was the one who thought I was a prodigy or a rock star. And why did he have to take credit for my guitar playing?

"Del!" Chad was shoving his way toward us. "Hey, Ori."

"Hey, Chad."

"Just been talking to my little brother and his girlfriend," Del said, smacking me on the shoulder so the Coke sloshed again. *Argh.*

"Oh, I'm not his girlfriend," Jane said, and Del immediately raised an eyebrow at me. Before, it would have been "Well, then, let's get you to be his girlfriend." Now I was sure he was trying to figure out how he could get Jane for himself. My heart sank, and not just because of Del. Alli had been so wrong. Jane may have looked back at me earlier, but the speed with which she had corrected Del proved she didn't want to be anything more than friends. I wasn't sure why this bummed me out so much. What did I expect? I was Orion Taylor.

"This is Jane," I said to Chad, pushing to make my voice neutral. "We met through our new bass player."

"Cool," Chad said, nodding at her. "Let's get back, bro." He punched Del lightly in the arm. "The ladies are waiting."

"See you later," Del said, looking right at Jane before following Chad into the crowd.

"So," Jane said, looking in the direction he had taken. "That's Del."

"Yep."

"He's very..."

Charming? Good-looking? Stupid? Drunk?

"...interesting," she finished. "It was fun talking to him about lacrosse." She sighed. "I feel bad for him, though. It must be hard to be back home after the freedom of college."

"Whatever," I said, with more force than I intended, but I was stinging from how much attention she was giving him, for dissing me in front of him. *I'm not his girlfriend.* "Del always manages to come out on top."

She looked at me, her eyes soft. "I'm sorry."

Why? Because she didn't want to be my girlfriend? Because Del always got what he wanted?

"Don't be," I said shortly. "It doesn't matter."

She looked down at her pitcher. "I guess I'd better get back."

"Me too."

I watched her go, my own pitcher heavy in my hands. Maybe I should have been grateful to Del for getting that out in the open so that I wouldn't make a fool out of myself later.

Yeah, I'd feel grateful. Right after I stopped feeling pissed and humiliated.

SEVENTEEN

"What happened?" Nick asked when I set the pitcher on the table. "You're a mess." He poked my damp shirt, which clung to my chest from the spilled Coke.

"Del's here," I said. "Semidrunk."

"We'll just stay out of his way." Alli poured us each a Coke, acting like Del's being here was no big deal, and I appreciated it. I gave her a look that told her so, and she smiled to let me know she got it.

The lights dimmed right then, and kosmøs came on. Everyone's attention turned to the stage. Thank God for a good band. Their music completely transported me, and I forgot all about Del and Jane and everything else.

We jumped up and pushed our way to the middle of the crowd, clapping and singing along, swept away in the crash of the drums and cymbals, the slash of the guitars. I got a text about halfway through.

✉ WE'RE @ THE CENTER PILLAR. YOUR BRO IS WITH US
WHERE R U? *GWYN CELL 9:23 PM*

Why was Del with them? What about the "ladies" Chad
had talked about?

✉ NOT SURE WE CAN GET THERE.

✉ LET'S TRY TO MEET AFTERWARD. *GWYN CELL 9:26 PM*

✉ K.

"I thought we were going to meet Jane and Gwyn," Alli
shouted to me.

I shook my head.

She gave me a look, but I pretended not to notice. Twice I
caught sight of Jane's group, and once Jane gave me a half
wave and I raised my hand in return, but it was pretty lame.
Then Del stepped in front of her, so I couldn't really see her
but had a great view of him getting a little too close to her,
his hands brushing her hips, then her arms, while they talked
and talked and talked in spite of the loud music.

Someone jostled me and I turned. The girl looked a little
younger than me, though it was hard to tell under all the
makeup she wore. Her face lit up and she danced closer, bump-
ing her hip against me. I gave her a half smile and then looked
over her shoulder to see if I could spot Jane and Del again.

"That was fun!" the girl said after the concert was over. She
was giving me those goo-goo eyes that Alli and Troy often
exchanged. I nodded as we got caught up in a surge for the door.

"I lost Troy," Alli said after we were outside the bar. She
glanced briefly at Goo-Goo Eye Girl. "And you are?"

"Stacey Trudeau," the girl said. "I'm with him." She
pointed to me.

Alli raised her eyebrows, and I shrugged. "And do you know 'his' name?"

Stacey shook her head.

"Good," Alli said, steering me down the sidewalk to the front of a shoe store. "Too young," she muttered to me, and then: "Where's Jane?" before snagging Nick and pulling him over. "You guys stay here, away from jailbait, while I go look for Troy. He's not answering my texts."

But before she was even two feet away—

"Orion Taylor?"

A girl with her hair and face all made up was staring at me with wide eyes. She was probably a year younger than me and smelled faintly of popcorn.

Alli turned around and took a step toward me as I tilted my head at the girl.

"Do I know you?"

She giggled, looking over her shoulder. Two girls who I assumed were her friends were watching us. The girl nodded to them and they nodded back, one of them holding up a cell phone. Before I knew what was happening, she was on her tiptoes, pressing her lips against mine. Shock paralyzed me as she wrapped her arms around my neck, trying to push her tongue into my mouth. That woke me up. I shoved her away.

"Hey!"

She looked momentarily hurt, then slipped something into my pocket. "Call me," she whispered before raising her voice to her friends. "Did you get that?"

Her friend with the phone gave her the thumbs-up.

The girl raised her fists in the air. "BoyMagnet kissed Orion Taylor!" Then she trotted toward her friends.

Alli and I whipped our heads around to stare at each other.

BoyMagnet?

Alli took off, grabbing the girl with the camera phone by the arm. I don't know what she said, but suddenly the girl was handing over her phone and Alli was pushing a bunch of buttons.

I saw Jane, Gwyn, and their crew down the block, eyes on me. Jane waved at me, and I waved back.

"What's going on?" Troy stepped around several people to join us.

"Anyone seen Kaitlyn?" Nick said. "She said she'd meet us out here."

"What's Alli doing?" Troy asked, looking down the sidewalk at the girls.

"Making sure some pics aren't blasted all over the Internet," I said. "She's always thinking."

"What did they take pictures of?"

"BoyMagnet planting a fat one on Taylor," Nick said. "It was crazy."

"BoyMagnet from our site?" Troy asked.

Alli was heading our way, looking triumphant. BoyMagnet and her friends had already disappeared.

"I deleted them before she sent them to anyone," Alli told us.

"Thanks," I said, just as Nick said, "There she is!" and started back toward the entrance. PurpleGrrl was waving at him.

"I'll go get the car, folks," Troy said. "Meet here in five."

Stacey was standing in front of me within seconds.

"Wow!" she said. "That was so wild how she just came up and kissed you! I mean, wow!"

"Yeah, well..." I looked past her to Jane, who was now talking animatedly with Del. She pointed back at me, and Del's eyes followed. Our eyes met for a few seconds, and then he was shaking his head at Jane like he didn't believe what she was saying.

Well, believe it, Delphinius Jonathan Taylor. Girls dig me. At least until the RSB wears off.

"So what grade are you in?" I asked Stacey, still watching Jane and Del.

"Tenth." But her voice squeaked a little.

Alli narrowed her eyes and Stacey lowered hers.

"Eighth," she said miserably.

Well, that explained why she hadn't been repelled, hadn't known right away that my hometown was Dorkville. Younger girls like Vela's friends didn't seem to see that. Or maybe it just took them longer.

My phone jingled in my pocket.

"Sorry," I said to Stacey as I pulled it out.

✉ **WHAT R U DOING??? GO 2 JANE!!!!** *ALLI CELL 10:43 PM*

I glanced at Alli, who was giving me her don't-be-stupid look as she clutched her phone.

"We need to go," I said apologetically to Stacey. "It's my mom. Curfew."

"Oh my God!" she said, eyes wide in fear. "I have to find my ride. I have to be home, too!" She took off running toward the bar, her phone to her ear.

Alli stared at me, shaking her head.

"What?"

"They're just talking, Ori," she said. "Get your butt over there."

If things had been different, I might have been able to do that. Walk over and step in front of Del and start talking to Jane, get her to look at me the way she was looking at Del, get her to smile up at me with that smile she was wearing right now. I bet her eyes were bright, those amazing eyelashes high-lighting them, that small dimple in her left cheek showing itself.

But things weren't different. She'd made that clear.

"She doesn't want to talk to me."

"Why would you say that?"

"Just—trust me on this one."

I turned so that I wouldn't have to see her eyes on me, only feel them boring into my back.

Del said something to Jane, and she said something back before putting her arms around him, hugging him. He hugged her back, wrapping his arms around her. Tight.

I blinked.

How long were they going to keep hugging? Would he take her home? Would they make out later? Would I have to answer the door when she came to see Del and point her to the bathroom?

"Friendly hug," Alli said. "It doesn't mean anything."

They were still hugging, Del's mouth close to her ear as he whispered magical Del Spell words to her.

"You have no idea what you're talking about," I said, flip-ping my phone open. "I'll get Nick."

COLORADO ROCKS

We are an up-and-coming band, nameless but open to suggestions. Feel free to post your band name ideas on our blog. (We don't want to use one of those band name generators — we want it to come from you or us.)

Countdown to BATTLE OF THE BANDS:

90

days

Countdown to LES PAUL:

50

days

BAND NAME: to be named later

| PROFILE | MUSIC | PIX & VIDS | ABOUT/FAQ | CONTACT | **BLOG** |

Sunday, March 7

NICK: Anyone else check out kosmøs Friday night? They rocked the house. Great to meet you, PurpleGrrl.

Everything is coming together — we're making progress toward the Battle. Definitely a force to be reckoned with. Hey. Is that too long for a band name? A Force to Be Reckoned With? Yeah, it's too long. And awkward.

We're going to be checking out a new band soon. I'm not saying their name, because I don't want to give them any press but it's a week from this Friday. You can probably figure it out.

🎱 BoyMagnet

So, PG, you met Nick, huh? Big deal. I KISSED ORION TAYLOR! I told you I was a BoyMagnet. I would have pix but some psycho girl came over and wiped them off my friend's phone before she could send them out. He's even cuter up close, even if his ears kind of stick out.

PurpleGrrl

Okay. So you forced yourself on him and kissed him. But did he kiss you back?

Nick — I'm going to try to go to that gig Fri night. Got to find out what all the fuss is about.

BAND NAME: to be named later

| PROFILE | MUSIC | PIX & VIDS | ABOUT/FAQ | CONTACT | BLOG |

We are an up-and-coming band, nameless but open to suggestions. Feel free to post your band name ideas on our blog. (We don't want to use one of those band name generators — we want it to come from you or us.)

🔊 OzoneLayer

The FUSS (what a stupid word) is that Slash and Burn ROCKS, a lot more than kosmøs. What's with that stupid symbol instead of an O anyway?

BoyMagnet

I did NOT force myself on him. And of COURSE he kissed me back. I'm a boy magnet.

PurpleGrrl

But it sounds like you were like a stalker with the camera phone and everything. Not very magnet-like.
Ozone: The symbol is cool!

🔊 OzoneLayer

Not again. I thought we were talking about S & B's gig coming up.

PurpleGrrl

Don't say their name!

BoyMagnet

Doesn't anyone want to know what it was like kissing Orion Taylor?

🔥 DragonBreath

NO!

🔊 OzoneLayer

NO!

Countdown to
BATTLE OF
THE BANDS:

90

days

Countdown to
LES PAUL:

50

days

Gold's Guitars supports this band.   •   303-555-GOLD
This site updated and maintained by A. Wilcox.

COLORADO ROCKS

We are an up-and-coming band, nameless but open to suggestions. Feel free to post your band name ideas on our blog. (We don't want to use one of those band name generators — we want it to come from you or us.)

BAND NAME: to be named later

| PROFILE | MUSIC | PIX & VIDS | ABOUT/FAQ | CONTACT | BLOG |

 ### PeacefulWarrior
NO.

 ### PurpleGrrl
No way.

 ### BoyMagnet
Fine. But Orion was a magnet too, pulling me over to him.

 ### PeacefulWarrior
If I may interrupt, two magnets would repel, not attract, each other.

 ### BoyMagnet
I wonder where DominantSpecies is.

 ### PurpleGrrl
You do? Why?

 ### BoyMagnet
Never mind. Orion's going to call. You're all just jealous. Halyn won't even contribute. She's the most jealous of them all. She's

This page is currently undergoing routine maintenance. You will be unable to post or read new messages at this time. We are sorry for the inconvenience.

Countdown to
BATTLE OF
THE BANDS:
90
days

Countdown to
LES PAUL:
50
days

EIGHTEEN

We sat in OT Studios on Monday, waiting for Gwyn to arrive for rehearsal. Alli was explaining how BoyMagnet or one of her friends must have had web access from her phone, which was why BoyMagnet was able to post about the kiss right away, and how Alli might need to have that same kind of access for damage control and wished she'd thought to pull out her laptop at a hot spot to stop the posts, blah, blah, blah.

"So anyway," Alli said, "it's all off the site now. Hardly anyone saw it."

"You are the best, Al," Troy said, then looked at me. "Maybe just be a tad more careful next time, Ori."

"I didn't do anything!" I protested. "How was I supposed to know some strange girl was going to try to kiss me?"

"I think it'll be good for our image," Nick said. "Girls need to be falling all over us. Especially girls with colored hair. Didn't Kaitlyn look great with blue hair?"

No one answered, but that didn't seem to bother Nick. He kept going on about how great she was, how they were going out next weekend—so more blah, blah, blah. All I could think about was Jane hugging Del.

When Gwyn arrived, Jane was with her. For a moment I was frozen in place. Then I hustled inside to get some snacks.

Unfortunately Del was in the kitchen.

"What are you doing here?"

"Needed a suit for an interview coming up. Vela let me know the parents were out."

You could have waited until I was out, too.

His face lit up. "Hey, Jane."

What was *she* doing in here?

He walked over and gave her a hug. "Thanks for the pep talk the other night," he said. "It helped."

"I'm glad," she said, smiling up at him.

Did she need me to point the way to the bathroom? Maybe I should go there myself and vomit.

"Excuse me," I said, ducking around Del to get to the cupboard where the chips were.

"So, can you help me pick out a suit?" Del asked.

"No," I said at the same time Jane said, "Sure."

I looked at her. Then at Del.

"I was talking to Jane." He smiled at her. "Upstairs, to the left of the bathroom."

Jane said, "I'll be up in a minute."

So now she was helping him pick out suits? And she was going up to his bedroom when she hadn't ever been inside our house before?

"Are you mad at me?" she asked.

"Why would I be mad at you?" I opened the fridge and rummaged around, looking for the salsa.

"I don't know. That's why I'm asking."

Her directness was unnerving. "I've got a lot on my mind. School, work, the Battle."

"Right." She tapped her fingers on the counter. "So it doesn't have anything to do with the other night at the concert? You and Del?"

"There's nothing with me and Del."

She sighed. "I wish you two weren't having these issues. He's so great and you're so great and—"

"I just said there wasn't anything." I pulled out the salsa. "And how would you know he was great? You talked to him for, like, five minutes at the concert." Which wasn't true, because I'd seen them talk for what seemed like forever. But I wanted it to be true.

"It was a lot more than five minutes," she said. "And plus, we've talked some since and he's really—"

"What? Nice? Friendly? *Great?* I can't believe he suckered you, too." *And that you've been talking to him and not me.*

"He didn't sucker me," she said, an edge to her voice. "I've been talking to him about you and—"

"Don't." I leaned against the counter, just inches away from her, looking right at her. "Don't talk to him about me. You think you know him because you've had a few conversations with him, because he's asked you to help him pick out a suit, but you don't. You don't know him and you don't know me. None of this is any of your business."

She stared at me for a few moments, breathing in, then out, never taking her eyes from mine. "I thought you were starting to be my business," she said evenly. "I guess I was wrong." She stalked out of the room, and I heard her footsteps going upstairs. To Del's room. To Del.

I snatched up the bag of chips and the salsa and strode down the hall to the garage.

"Where's Jane?" Alli said, looking over my shoulder. "She said she was going in to help you."

"She's helping Del."

"Del? With what?"

"It doesn't matter," I said. "Have a snack and let's get back to rehearsing."

Jane came into the garage just as we were all getting our instruments. She signed something to Gwyn, who nodded. Then she left.

I felt Alli's eyes on me, but I ignored her, pulling my guitar strap over my head and adjusting the mic. When she came up to me after rehearsal, I just said, "Don't."

"Okay," she said. "For now."

Later, Nick and I were playing video games in the family room.

"So what's up with Jane, dude?"

"Who knows."

"She hanging with Del?"

"Apparently." I pushed some buttons to add another weapon to my arsenal.

"Is it, like, serious?"

"I don't know and I don't care." I moved my guy around the wall, gun at the ready. If I squinted a little, I could imagine Nick's guy was Del behind the helmet and body armor.

"I hear you, bro," Nick said, pushing some buttons so that his guy disappeared from the screen. "I thought you two had the vibe, but I guess not."

"Where'd you go?" I pushed another button, and suddenly the screen was bathed in green; my night-vision goggles were engaged.

"I can fix you up with one of Kaitlyn's friends if you want."

"No thanks," I said, pressing hard. Then I pointed to the screen. "You're dead."

"Dang," he muttered, flicking a few buttons. "I've only got one life left."

We readied for another round.

"If it was anyone but Del…" he murmured as he took a shot at me and missed. "But you're just friends with Jane, so no big, right?"

"Right," I said, getting a direct hit. Nick's guy crumpled to the ground and bled out, and the screen went black.

"Ouch," he said. "That was quick."

I grunted, wishing I could get Del out of my life with the push of a button.

NINETEEN

Two days later, I was at work when my cell vibrated in my pocket and Jeff Beck announced a text.

✉ **CAN YOU MEET AT OUR CHIPOTLE?** *DEL CELL 5:45 PM*

I snapped the phone shut and slid it back inside my pocket. Now what did he want? He'd wanted to take my guitar money, and he'd gotten Jane's friendship. What else was there?

I tried to focus on work, tried to ignore all the memories of going to Chipotle with Del, but they kept popping up. Riding there on bikes before he could drive, and then once a week like clockwork when he could. And I remembered the last time, just before he'd gone to college.

Summer. Del 18, Ori 15. "So this is it," Del said, raising his burrito. "Our last burrito until I come home at Thanksgiving."

Ori tapped his burrito to Del's, and then they both took a big bite.

"'Course, you'll be coming up so we can eat at the one in Greeley," he said.

"You know it." Ori would get his license in November. Del's car was now his, so he'd be able to drive up anytime he wanted, as long as his parents said it was cool. Until then, his mom said they'd go up some weekends and that he could take the bus up on his own.

"So I was talking to my roommate about you," Del said. "He grew up near Greeley and said there are a bunch of places you guys could play. I'll check them out when I get there and let you know."

"Cool," Ori said. "That would be awesome."

"And you guys can stay with us. There's a one-guest-per-room policy in the dorm, but I'm sure there will be other guys on my floor who will take Nick and Troy."

"Thanks, Del. That's really great."

He grinned at Ori. "What are brothers for, dude? And make sure you take care of my car while I'm gone. No accidents."

"It's *our* car." Ori raised an eyebrow. "But let me know if you think you're going to need it up there. I can live without it."

"I should be fine," Del said. "Besides, you need your own wheels to take out all your girlfriends."

"What girlfriends?" Ori shook his head, picking up his drink and taking a big slurp through the straw.

"They'll come," Del said, nodding in his knowing way. "And when they do, you'll have the chickmobile all ready to go."

I blinked quickly as my cell vibrated and twanged again.

It's Del, I told myself. *Don't look at it.*

But what if it was someone else? Like Jane?

✉ I JUST NEED TO TALK TO YOU. PLEASE. *DEL CELL 5:46 PM*

Del rarely said please.

✉ COME ON, DUDE. CHICKEN FAJITA BURRITO? U NO U WANT ONE. *DEL CELL 5:46 PM*

Damn, he was good.

✉ FINE. I GET OFF AT 6.

✉ WANT ME TO PICK U UP? *DEL CELL 5:47 PM*

✉ I'LL MEET YOU THERE.

When I got to Chipotle, Del was already at our table by the window, my burrito neatly wrapped in foil across from him. He'd ordered and paid already.

We ate a few bites in silence and then he spoke.

"So, your girlfriend seems to think we need to help each other out."

"She's not my girlfriend."

He smiled. "Yeah, she was pretty clear on that, wasn't she? But don't give up, bro. She could change her mind."

The burrito lay heavily in my stomach. "So what do you want?"

"Jane seems to think you might actually help me, even though you've said no in the past."

Money. He was back to that again. "Jane doesn't know me very well."

"Look," Del said. "I just want to get these school debts that Mom and Dad didn't cover off my back. They don't give any breaks for people who change their minds halfway through." He rolled his eyes at this. "I want to start saving some money so I can move out of Chad's place. I'm paying them room and board now, so I'm getting a sense of what I'll need on my own."

I didn't point out that he didn't change his mind about going to school; he quit after they put him on academic probation. He could have stayed and gotten his grades up, but he acted like it was the school's fault that he had failed most of his classes.

Del never used to be a quitter.

"Do you have any idea how hard this is for me, Ori? You're my little brother. I shouldn't have to ask you for help."

Guilt crept in, unbidden. I knew it was hard for him to ask me for help. He had always been the one helping me. He'd actually gotten our band an interview with a place in Greeley, just like he'd promised. They had said we were too inexperienced and to try again when we'd been together longer.

"It won't take long," Del had said when we'd met him after the interview. "Pretty soon *they'll* be calling *you.*"

"You've already got a guitar for the Battle," Del was saying now through bites of his burrito. "You don't need a new one. And I can pay you back by the end of the summer. Easy."

Right again. I did have the loaner guitar. I'd been playing it all along, could easily keep playing it through the Battle. I looked at him, sitting across from me at the table we always sat at, eating our burritos like we always did. I could almost pretend the last few months hadn't happened, that he hadn't come home hating everything about me, hadn't taken over our car, hadn't made friends with the girl I really liked and had us angry at each other because of him.

Almost.

And then there was the fact that the Les Paul was my dream guitar. *That* was the guitar I wanted to be playing when we got up onstage in front of all those people at the Battle, in front of Roy Stone and the rest of his band.

But it wasn't just that. It felt wrong to give him my money, like I was giving in to him again. He might be nice to me for a while, but sooner or later he'd go back to being Mr. Hyde, treating me like crap. And he'd have my money, too.

Jane needed to learn to butt out.

"I can't give you my guitar money."

"Why not? Why can't you do this one thing for me after everything I've done for you?"

"I just can't," I said. "I'm sorry."

Del shook his head, eyes dark as he stood up. "If you think a new guitar is somehow going to make you a star, you are truly delusional, little bro."

"The local news is covering us at our next gig," I blurted out, immediately regretting how stupid it sounded, like I was trying to show him our band was something, that *I* was something. "People are talking about us."

"People talked about me," Del said. "And then it passed."

"I'm not you."

"That's for sure." His eyes locked with mine. "Just trying

to help, Ori," he said as he stepped away from the table. "That's what brothers do."

When I got home, I flew downstairs and flipped my iPod to ELO's "Fire on High," skipping ahead past the eerie intro to the guitar riff. Cranking up my amp, I busted out, strumming so fast my fingers blurred.

Wham. Rocking it over Del's face.

Slam. Rolling it over Del's words.

I hit it harder and harder right up until the last chord reverberated through the basement.

"Let's see you do *that*, Delphinius Taylor," I muttered under my breath.

And then I slammed my fist into the beanbag chair Vela liked to sit in, the large indentation staring back at me like a giant, accusing eye.

"Shut up," I said out loud. Then hit the beanbag again.

COLORADO ROCKS

We are an up-and-coming band, nameless but open to suggestions. Feel free to post your band name ideas on our blog. (We don't want to use one of those band name generators — we want it to come from you or us.)

BAND NAME: to be named later

| PROFILE | MUSIC | PIX & VIDS | ABOUT/FAQ | CONTACT | BLOG |

Sunday, March 14

Alli: Matt's Sports is coming up on April 10th. Come out and show your pride for the band!

NICK: And we're checking out that band we don't want to mention this Friday.

 BoyMagnet

Who else is annoyed about the censorship on this site? Every time we write something someone doesn't like, the webmaster gets rid of it.

 PeacefulWarrior

They have a right to have only what they want here. It's their site.

 PurpleGrrl

I agree with PeacefulWarrior.

 BoyMagnet

Of course you do. You agree with everything here because now you know Nick and think you're all that. You're a suck-up, just like Halyn. Where is she btw? Halyn?

Countdown to
BATTLE OF
THE BANDS:
83
days

Countdown to
LES PAUL:
43
days

COLORADO ROCKS

We are an up-and-coming band, name-less but open to suggestions. Feel free to post your band name ideas on our blog. (We don't want to use one of those band name generators — we want it to come from you or us.)

Countdown to
BATTLE OF
THE BANDS:

83

days

Countdown to
LES PAUL:

43

days

BAND NAME: to be named later

PROFILE | MUSIC | PIX & VIDS | ABOUT/FAQ | CONTACT | **BLOG**

🖉 PurpleGrrl

Maybe she ran off with Orion. You're just mad because he hasn't called you and DominantSpecies isn't around anymore.

🌜 BoyMagnet

No way Halyn is with Orion. And how do you know he hasn't called? And I couldn't care less about DS.

♕ DominantSpecies

That hurts.

🌜 BoyMagnet

You're back.

♕ DominantSpecies

And not sure why.

🖉 PurpleGrrl

Anyone going to their gig at Matt's in April? I'm planning to be there. I wish they had one sooner. And I'm not a suck-up, BoyM. I just think it's their site so they can do what they want. Wouldn't you want to have full control over your site or blog?

🌜 BoyMagnet

Fine. I get it. And maybe I will go to Matt's Sports. We can hang out.

🖉 PurpleGrrl

That's the spirit.

TWENTY

That Friday we headed to Rockin' Ryan's to see Slash and Burn. The place was *packed*. I mean wall-to-wall bodies with absolutely nowhere to go. We pushed our way to a wall on the far side. At least we could lean against it and have a decent view of the stage, a *real* stage, with lights and everything.

Man. If Slash and Burn drew this kind of crowd, the Band to Be Named Later was in big trouble.

I scanned the crowd, hoping Del wasn't here somewhere, or Jane, even though part of me wanted to see her.

"Anyone seen Kaitlyn?" Nick was craning his neck above the crowd.

"Not this again." I groaned. "Can't you just text her and find out where she is?"

"She hasn't answered."

"She will," Troy said, patting Nick's arm. "Don't worry."

"How do you know? You don't have Alli's special abilities."

He looked down at his phone. "She just got here." He pushed off through the crowd.

Slash and Burn started to play about fifteen minutes later. Nick was back after their second song, PurpleGrrl in tow. I nodded at them, my attention on Slash and Burn. Roy Stone was pretty killer on the guitar, which made me nervous. Was I that good? I had no idea.

At the break, Troy and I started talking about the band, while PurpleGrrl and Nick went to get drinks.

"He can really play," I said to Troy.

"Yeah, but he's not as good as you," Troy said. "He's more mechanical. You're more—I don't know. Better."

My phone vibrated in my pocket.

✉ THESE GUYS R 2 SAFE, Gwyn texted me. I THINK WE CAN KICK THEM.

I was relieved that Gwyn wasn't mad at me, too. I'd seen that closing-ranks thing a few times with girls and Del. Maybe Jane hadn't said anything to her.

✉ HOPEFULLY, I texted back. BUT IT WON'T BE EASY. WHERE ARE YOU?

✉ NEAR THE BACK. WE GOT HERE LATE *GWYN CELL 7:48 PM*

✉ YOU CAN SQUEEZE IN NEXT TO US.

✉ COOL. SOMEONE JUST BARFED RIGHT NEAR OUR FEET *GWYN CELL 7:49 PM*

Okay, gross.

✉ LEFT WALL, FACING THE STAGE.

They showed up a few minutes later, and we made room.

"Madness," Adam said, signing as he talked. "I can't believe all these people for a band I've never heard of."

"I'm glad I'm not the only one," Nick said.

"None of us had heard of them," I said. "Then suddenly everyone seems to be talking about them."

"Where's Jane?" Alli asked. I glared at her before looking at Gwyn, who was busy texting.

Gwyn closed her phone, then opened it again, reading a reply. She shook her head.

"She okay?" Adam asked, signing it, too.

Gwyn showed him her phone. He sighed.

"Is it Jane?" Alli asked, glancing briefly at me before looking back at Gwyn. "What's wrong?"

"Al," I said. "It's not our business."

"It should be *your* business," she whispered to me.

Not after I'd told Jane *I* wasn't *her* business. But I wasn't going to tell Alli that.

Gwyn raised an eyebrow at us but didn't say anything.

"Today's her dad's birthday," Adam said.

"Oh, man." I pressed my lips together, shaking my head slightly. Poor Jane.

Alli looked at me, confused.

"Her dad died when she was little," I said, wishing I'd known about his birthday. I'm not sure what I would have done, but it would have been nice to know.

"Oh my God." Alli put her hand over her mouth. "I'm so sorry."

"It's cool," Adam said. "It's just that she and her mom

and her sister"—Gwyn poked him, but he didn't seem to notice—"usually get together and look at photos and talk about stuff—"

Gwyn kicked him.

"Ow! What?" He looked at her, and her hands flew quickly in the air, shouting silent things at him none of us understood. "Okay, okay. I'm sorry." He looked at us apologetically. "Apparently I'm telling you too much personal stuff." He put his arm around Gwyn and kissed her cheek. "Gwynnie is a private person and respects other people's privacy. She thinks I talk too much."

"You do," Gwyn said, but she was smiling.

I fingered my cell phone in my pocket. Should I text Jane? Let her know I was thinking about her? But she hadn't been the one to tell me. And I'd told her to mind her own business.

Slash and Burn started their second set, and I tried to focus on them and not think about what Jane was doing right now. When they were finished, we all looked at one another.

"They might be unpleasant," Troy said, "but they can *play*."

"Seriously." They hadn't been nearly as mechanical after the break, and we all agreed that we'd better kick rehearsals into high gear if we wanted to beat them at the Battle.

Once we were outside, we ran into some people from school and talked long enough that the Slash and Burn guys were coming out with their equipment. I was about to tell Roy Stone they'd played really well when he spoke.

"Well, if it isn't O-rion," he said. "You learn anything in

there, boys? Will he choke or will he not?" He said it like the Clash song. Please.

"Got a name yet?" the bass player asked us.

"Maybe," Troy said.

Roy laughed. "That means no." He motioned to his bandmates, and they lugged their equipment to a truck at the curb.

"Hate that guy," Nick said.

"Don't," Troy said. "Put that energy into your playing."

"Still think they see us as a threat?" I asked Alli.

"Absolutely," she said. "And they'll be at Matt's to check you out. But you definitely need to kick it up a notch. They've had a lot more experience than you guys."

Great. They were going to grind us under their drum pedals.

Nick walked PurpleGrrl down the sidewalk to say goodbye. When he got back, he clapped me on the shoulder. "Kaitlyn and her friends will be at Matt's for our gig," he said. "And I think one of her friends might be into you, Taylor. If things don't work out with Jane, I can hook you up."

I groaned and turned toward the car. Everyone needed to butt out of my nonexistent love life.

Nick was chattering away about PurpleGrrl as we pulled away from the curb, so I tuned out, still thinking about Slash and Burn. I looked over my shoulder to where Roy Stone was now standing at the corner, talking to a few guys I didn't recognize.

Wait. Yes, I did.

One of them was Del, who was smacking Roy on the arm like they were old friends. My heart sped up, my jaw clenching. Had he been at the concert the whole time? Why? And how did he know Roy?

I faced front, hoping no one else had noticed. I had no desire to discuss the possible reasons my brother was fraternizing with the enemy.

Allicat21: Someone has to make the first move.

GuitarFreak516: She already did. She went to Del.

Allicat21: What do you mean she went to Del?

GuitarFreak516: She's in me and Del's business. He's asking her stuff and they talk almost every day.

Allicat21: How could you let this happen?

GuitarFreak516: It's Del.

Allicat21: And you're Ori. When is that going to count for something?

GuitarFreak516: I hope you're staying out of it.

Allicat21: Not by choice, because sometimes these things require an intervention. But she's completely incommunicado.

GuitarFreak516: Because she's with Del.

Allicat21: I doubt she's "with" with him. She's just talking to him. He's not her type.

GuitarFreak516: He's everyone's type. Besides, how would u know? Is this one of your girl radar things?

Allicat21: No. It's just obvious. Take action, Ori. I'm serious.

GuitarFreak516: I can't compete with him.

Allicat21: Not if you're not in the game.

GuitarFreak516: It isn't a game.

How could she not get it? She'd known Del almost as long as I had. She'd said herself that it was like he cast some spell over girls, and she'd been sucked into it herself.

Allicat21: You're right. You can't compete. Not until you figure out who your real competition is.
Allicat21 has signed off.

Whatever. I ran downstairs to the basement and pulled out my acoustic, turning up some Rodrigo y Gabriela so that I was forced to concentrate on my fingering and my speed and not the fact that Del had been hanging out with Roy Stone or talking to Jane. The music calmed me down a little, enough so I didn't feel like killing him. I was tired anyway and trudged upstairs to my room. When I passed Del's, I was startled to see Vela sitting on his bed.

"What are you doing?"

She shrugged. "Just...looking around."

I glanced around from my position in the doorway. "Not much to see." He'd cleared out just about everything except the furniture and some pictures and books.

"Notice anything missing?"

I snorted. "How about everything?"

She stood up and walked over to the bulletin board above his desk where all his pictures were, touching each photo like she was taking a mental inventory. She pointed to a spot in the middle.

"He took it with him."

"Took what?"

"The picture of you and him after he won the champion-ship."

"So?"

I stared at the empty spot in the middle of the other photos.

"So, out of all these pictures, it was the only one he took."

COLORADO Rocks

BAND NAME: to be named later

| PROFILE | MUSIC | PIX & VIDS | ABOUT/FAQ | CONTACT | BLOG |

We are an up-and-coming band, name-less but open to suggestions. Feel free to post your band name ideas on our blog. (We don't want to use one of those band name generators — we want it to come from you or us.)

Countdown to
BATTLE OF
THE BANDS:

78

days

Countdown to
LES PAUL:

38

days

Friday, March 19

Troy: My boys are only a wee bit nervous about what we saw at Ryan's tonight. Alli, Gwyn, and I know the truth — that we will take it all at the Battle. Who's excited for spring break? We're hitting the slopes, man. Can't wait.

🌀 BoyMagnet
OMG. Slash and Burn ROCKED.

🔥 DragonBreath
Were you there? I didn't see you.

🌀 BoyMagnet
Maybe because you don't know what I look like. Though I'm surprised you didn't notice all the guys around me.

🎸 PurpleGrrl
I was there, too. Hung out with Nick and the band for a while.

🌀 BoyMagnet
I hate to be a downer, but there is no way the band can compete against S & B. There's just no contest.

⚜ DominantSpecies
Agreed, BM.
So this girlie band and S & B were there? Any fights break out?

COLORADO ROCKS

We are an up-and-coming band, name-less but open to suggestions. Feel free to post your band name ideas on our blog. (We don't want to use one of those band name generators — we want it to come from you or us.)

BAND NAME: to be named later

| PROFILE | MUSIC | PIX & VIDS | ABOUT/FAQ | CONTACT | **BLOG** |

📶 OzoneLayer
BM. Good one.

🎵 BoyMagnet
Don't call me that. And are you back for good?

⚲ DominantSpecies
Aw shucks, BM. You missed me.

🎵 BoyMagnet
I told you not to call me that. And I did NOT miss you!

🖊 PurpleGrrl
She totally did, DS.

⚲ DominantSpecies
Can you blame her?

📶 OzoneLayer
DS, you're dangerously close to joining this chick freak show. Come back to us, man. Let's find out if there was a fight at the S & B gig.

🎵 BoyMagnet
I DID NOT MISS HIM. AND YES, I AM SHOUTING!!!

🖊 PurpleGrrl
Ozone: No fights. And S & B was good, but their originals

Countdown to
BATTLE OF
THE BANDS:

78

days

Countdown to
LES PAUL:

38

days

COLORADO ROCKS

We are an up-and-coming band, nameless but open to suggestions. Feel free to post your band name ideas on our blog. (We don't want to use one of those band name generators — we want it to come from you or us.)

BAND NAME: to be named later

| PROFILE | MUSIC | PIX & VIDS | ABOUT/FAQ | CONTACT | **BLOG** |

were kind of blah.

DS: She totally missed you.

♆ DominantSpecies

I know.

🔊 OzoneLayer

What's the point of a rivalry if there's no rivalry?

🐾 BoyMagnet

I HATE YOU ALL (STILL SHOUTING)!

🔊 OzoneLayer

Something BM and I finally agree on. And I know: Don't call you that.

✏️ PurpleGrrl

We're just kidding, BoyMagnet.

✏️ PurpleGrrl

BoyMagnet?

✏️ PurpleGrrl

Great.

Countdown to
BATTLE OF
THE BANDS:

78

days

Countdown to
LES PAUL:

38

days

TWENTY-ONE

The following week was spring break, which meant people were all over the place. Troy's family had gone to Winter Park for the week, so Nick, Alli, and I went up on the ski train to ski and snowboard with him for a couple of days. Gwyn was in Florida and Jane had gone to Mexico, not that it mattered, since we were barely talking, because why should she talk to me? She had Del for that now.

So for most of the break it was just Nick, Alli, and me hanging out at a different house each day. Nick and I jammed almost every afternoon, either at OT Studios or Gold's, counting down the days until everyone was back in town. When they were, it became a frenzy of activity trying to get ready for our gig at Matt's Sports. We definitely wanted to do "Focus," so we were practicing that one the most, since it was the newest song. At one point during a break, Gwyn and Troy started an impromptu jam session that totally rocked.

"Can you guys do that again?" I asked. "That was amazing."

They both shrugged and grinned. We ran through "Focus" again and then went back to one of our covers.

I looked at Alli. "Do you think Slash and Burn will really show?"

"Definitely," she said. "But you're ready."

I hoped she was right.

When I walked into Matt's Sports with my guitars, I knew right away that playing at a sporting goods store was going to be a tad different from playing in a bar, even one as low-rent as FX.

An area near women's apparel had been cleared for us and our equipment, and there was a smaller area for people to stand—our area was marked off with blue painter's tape. Difference number one. Difference number two: We were used to playing at night and it was the middle of the day, which made me feel more exposed.

But there seemed to be a decent crowd. Gwyn's boyfriend, Adam, was near the back with Sean and a girl I assumed was Sean's girlfriend, who was pretty hot. PurpleGrrl was talking to Nick near the water bottle display. Jane was in the back with Del, her new best friend. I couldn't understand what he was doing here. We hadn't talked since I told him he couldn't have my guitar money. He made it pretty clear he thought this whole band thing was stupid and yet here he was, standing in the back. For someone who acted like he didn't care about our music anymore, he was sure keeping up on what we were doing. And the two of them were talking and laughing like they'd known each other for years. How could Alli say he wasn't my competition? He was so confident, so cool, so...everything I wasn't. And look at how Jane was looking at him, her eyes locked on his face like nothing else mattered.

Stop.

After setting up her camera in front of the "stage," Alli walked up to me, then turned to survey the crowd.

"I don't see BoyMagnet."

"Good."

"I see Jane," she said.

"I see Tarzan."

She sighed, then stepped away to check her camera.

I forced myself to look away from them and over at Vela and her groupies, who were holding up a sign:

**Orion Taylor and
the Band to Be Named Later
You Rock!**

Grinning, I gave them a thumbs-up. Vela and her friends were always good for a few well-placed, ego-boosting squeals, and I definitely needed that right now. Their support, along with the fact that the local television crew was really here, setting up not far from Alli's camera, made me feel better — even though the TV camera was one of those big professional ones and looked like it could swallow you whole.

Alli bounced over. "I totally called it."

"What?"

She nodded toward the front door. "Slash and Burn are here."

"They're heading to the front," Nick said. "Probably to try to intimidate us."

I appreciated that he said "us" and not "you," though I knew he really meant me. He'd be safely tucked behind his drum set, and Troy and Gwyn always stood a few feet behind me except for a few parts of each song, so it was really all me. I was glad we had decided not to do any ballads—anything with just me and my acoustic and Roy Stone in my face could only mean certain humiliation.

"Crap," I muttered.

"You're the Intimidator," Nick said, slapping my back. "Do your intimidation thing right back."

I shot him a look.

"I'm serious, man. Don't let him get to you."

I pressed my lips together. Roy was literally four feet from where I stood, arms crossed over his chest, feet apart— defiant. His bandmates stood in a similar manner, except for one, who was gawking at the television cameraman. He smacked Roy on the arm and pointed. Roy turned around, did one of those don't-tell-me-you're-here-for-these-guys looks, then said something to the cameraman. The dude nodded, so Roy pulled something out of his pocket and handed it over.

Figured Slash and Burn had business cards.

For one insane moment I wished that I was six again and Del was nine and he was pushing Roy's head into that bucket of muddy water so I knew he had my back. Then I shook it off. I was old enough to handle my own damn back. I turned said back on Roy and the audience, sucking in a breath as I fiddled with my amp. We might not have had business cards, but that TV station was here for *us*. And maybe I wasn't the Intimidator, but I could *not* let Roy and his hoodlums mess with me. We had to rock this place.

"It's all about the music," Gwyn said, giving my arm a squeeze.

"I know."

"We love you, Orion!" I looked in the direction of the voices. Vela and her friends were jumping up and down like I was a real rock star. Roy rolled his eyes and shook his head. I took a deep breath and picked up the loaner.

Matt, the owner of the store, walked up to the mic and introduced us.

"I just want to say that I'm happy to help showcase new talent in our area. Thanks to Ed Gold of Gold's Guitars for introducing me to this band. And don't forget, folks, we're having a rockin' sale in the shoe department today." He smiled at his own joke, and I couldn't help smiling, too.

"Thanks, Matt," I said into the mic. "We're happy to be here and really appreciate this chance. And I may have to get a pair of shoes after our set."

"What kind of shoes, Orion?" a girl shouted from the back. I didn't recognize her, but she was a Del girl, beautiful face, long dark hair, and a tight V-neck tee.

"Don't know yet," I said, and people chuckled. "Maybe you can help me." Whoa. Where did *that* come from? I strummed a few chords and raised my eyebrows at the beautiful girl. She smiled and tilted her head. I kept my eyes on her.

Slash and Burn who?

"I'm sure you'll recognize this first one," I said, then looked over my shoulder at Nick. He nodded, then pointed to me. I looked at Troy, and we launched into Guns N' Roses' "Sweet Child O' Mine." Troy and I always had a good time with this one, bouncing toward and away from each other as we got into it.

The crowd melted away as we played, and I hit every screeching note perfectly. When we finished, sweat was pouring down my neck and the sides of my face. Girls were screaming and waving tube socks in the air. Salespeople were snatching them away, returning them to their racks.

I grinned as we went right into a second cover, playing just as hard and good as the first. Roy and his gang tried to stare me down, inching a little closer to the blue tape that separated us.

I ignored them and played to the beautiful girl in the back and to PurpleGrrl, skipping over BoyMagnet and her friends, who had shown up just as we started the first song. I sang to my sister and her groupie friends, then back to the beautiful girl, who was now on the other side of Del.

Jane on one side, beautiful girl on the other.

But I kept playing, like there wasn't anyone else in the room, and pretty soon that was what it felt like. It was just me and the music, and nothing else mattered.

We played three more covers and then hit our originals,

starting with "Suburban Nightmare" and ending with "Focus."
I purposely looked in Del and Jane's direction when I sang
the chorus for "Focus."

But you can't do it anymore
Step back from me
You can't hold me in your grip
I've set myself free
Because I see now that your power
Was power I gave you
Power I can take away
When I walk away, from you

This was followed by a brief guitar riff with Troy and me,
before I repeated the final refrain:

When I walk away, from you
Far far away from where you are
You don't matter anymore, far away
I now have my focus

The crowd went crazy after the last note. It was amazing.
The Slash and Burn guys were looking around like they
couldn't believe it, then Roy was glaring at me like I'd just
smashed his guitar or something.

"You're going down," he said over the applause. "And I
mean *down*." He jabbed his finger toward the ground for
emphasis.

Instinctively, I leaned back. It wasn't like I was afraid of him or anything. I mean, he did outweigh me by about thirty pounds and his muscles were ripped, so he probably could lift me up with one hand and snap me in two with a flick of his wrist, but still. He was in high school, just like me. He had to be, to be eligible for this particular Battle. He was just threatening me on a musical level.

Right?

"Up," Nick said, standing beside me. "We're going nowhere but up."

"Definitely," Troy said, coming around to the other side of me with Gwyn. Together we formed a solid wall of what I hoped was pure intimidation, though it might have been just a bunch of sophomores and one junior trying to look tough.

Roy laughed, but his eyes still held anger. He took another step toward us, leaning close. "You're not nearly as good as you think you are."

I held his gaze, but out of the corner of my eye I could see Del watching us.

Was my brother going to come up here?

Did I want him to?

But then he turned his attention back to Jane and the beautiful girl.

"We're going to crush you," Roy said. Then he smacked his buddies and turned on his heel.

"That guy has serious problems," Nick said.

"I told you," Alli said. "You're a threat."

"But they're good," I said. "We need to keep rehearsing or we won't beat them." *And they might beat us up.*

We started to break down our equipment, but I could tell

everyone was doing what I was doing: watching Roy and his band head for the door. I guess we all just wanted to make sure they were gone so that we could breathe a little easier. But then Roy stopped next to Del, and they high-fived. Del said something that made them both nod and smile before Roy pushed through the door and was gone.

Jane was staring at Del with an odd look on her face. Like she couldn't believe Del was talking to Stone, either.

"What the heck was that with Del and Roy?" Nick asked. "Since when do they know each other?"

"No idea," I said, shrugging.

"Don't worry about it," Troy said. "Alli's right. They are so afraid of us. Why else would they be up in our faces?"

My spirits lifted, especially when I caught two girls looking at me, smiling. I smiled back, then shifted my gaze. The beautiful girl was heading toward us, winding her way to the front.

I looked over my shoulder, but there was no one behind me.

As she got closer I could see that she was older than me. Maybe a senior, possibly even Del's age.

"You were amazing," she said, crossing the blue tape to stand within inches of me. I could smell her shampoo, see her cleavage without dropping my eyes, which I did do once because it's basically a reflex.

"Thanks," I said, my voice rising a bit, "but it takes a whole band."

"Maybe," she said, acknowledging the others with a brief glance, "but you're the one up front making us all crazy." She ran her finger down my arm, then wrapped her hand around my bicep.

"Um, well, hopefully not too crazy."

"RSB! RSB!" Alli shouted.

RSB?

While I was trying to remember why those initials sounded vaguely familiar, the beautiful girl planted a beautiful kiss on my lips. Surprised, I pulled back.

And that was when I saw Del with his arm around Jane's shoulder.

And her arm around his waist.

Grabbing the girl by both arms, I pulled her close and kissed her hard, wrapping my arms around her. It felt great. I'd never kissed a girl so incredibly hot, someone Del always got to kiss and I barely even got to talk to, especially in front of the girl I used to like (still liked?), who was now hanging out with my brother.

The kiss was good. I knew it was. I could tell by the way she relaxed into me, opened her mouth wider, gripped the back of my head with her hand.

RSB.

I heard Alli's voice in my head: *Rock Star Blindness.*

And I should care because...?

"Okay, Romeo," Alli said. "That's enough." Hands were gripping my arms, pulling me back and away from the girl.

"Hey," I protested.

"Wow," the girl said, blinking as if she were waking up. "I mean, you're cute in an average-guy kind of way, but wow. I didn't expect that. Maybe we can do it again sometime."

She slipped a piece of paper into my pocket, tapped a painted fingernail on my lips, and sauntered through the dispersing crowd toward the door. Stopping next to Del, she gave him the once-over, then looked back at me and wiggled her fingers. I wiggled mine back, aware of Jane's eyes drilling a hole in my forehead.

Alli shook her head at me. "What was that?"

I shrugged. "She just—and then I just—but it wasn't—"

"Whatever," Alli said impatiently. "At least she isn't someone who would brag about it on the website." She scanned the crowd, eyes narrowed. "I didn't see anyone taking photos."

"Did she give you her number?" Nick asked, one arm around PurpleGrrl's shoulders.

I pulled the scrap of paper from my pocket.

"Do you think it's legit?"

"It doesn't matter," Alli said, "because he's not calling her. It was an RSB thing, and if he calls her he'll be totally humiliated because she'll be over her RSB and feel stupid that she gave her phone number to a sixteen-year-old, and then she'll totally blow him off."

"Can you just let it go, Al?" I said, sliding the paper back in my pocket. "We need to break down our equipment."

"Do *not* call her," Alli hissed, and then said, "By the way,

Jane's gone. Nicely done," before she headed over to her camera.

"I don't like you anymore," I called after her.

"It'll pass," she called back, waving a dismissive hand.

Nick clapped me on the shoulder. "Don't listen to her, dude. Call that girl." He handed his keys to PurpleGrrl. "Kaitlyn's going to help me get my stuff in the truck. See you later?"

"Yeah. My mom should be here soon."

I unhooked my guitar from the amp and rolled up the cords. Then I packed both guitars in their cases and headed for the door, where I passed a few people still hanging out.

"Orion, how could you?" I glanced toward the voice and saw BoyMagnet's eyes pinned on me. "She's so not your type."

"Give it up, BM," some guy said.

BoyMagnet's face turned bright red, and she whipped her head around to face him. He was only about an inch taller than her, with short, spiked hair and some pretty sharp-looking glasses. Not a bad-looking dude.

"DominantSpecies?" She sounded incredulous.

"The one and only," he said, trying to stand taller.

"I've seen you before," she said. "At FX and the Grog and Rockin' Ryan's. Are you following me?" She sounded rather pleased.

"I don't follow anyone," he said. "I lead."

She laughed, he smiled, and that was when I left, shoving the door open with my butt as I gripped both of my guitar cases.

Several people stood around on the sidewalk outside the store, talking.

"Great set, Orion."

"Great kiss, Taylor." I got a few slaps on the back as I looked around the parking lot. I didn't see my mom, but I did see Del a little ways down the sidewalk, talking animatedly with Vela, who was hugging him around the waist.

I stepped off the sidewalk, barely missing being hit by a car coming down the lane.

It was Del's—*our*—car pulling up to the curb.

Jane was driving.

"Jane?" My voice sounded small and far away. I took a few steps forward, blocking her way.

"There's my ride," Del said, brushing past me. Jane climbed over to the passenger seat and Del got into the driver's seat.

"Hi, Jane!" Vela scooted next to the passenger-side window, waving. Jane smiled and waved back. I could see how bright her eyes were, could see those amazing eyelashes, but could only imagine that dimple in her right cheek because she was looking at Vela, not me.

"Jane?" I didn't know why I was saying her name, why I was standing there looking at her through the windshield when she wouldn't meet my eye.

"Come on, Ori." Vela was next to me, tugging gently at my arm.

I stepped backward up onto the sidewalk, clutching both of my guitars.

We stood in silence as the car pulled away.

Vela reached down. "Let me help you carry something," she said. "Mom's here."

UNNAMED BAND ROCKS
THE STORE AT MATT'S SPORTS

by Gregory Burns

Garage bands seem to be as plentiful as mismatched socks, and we often want to get rid of them just as quickly. But the band that played at Matt's Sports Saturday afternoon made this music lover and reporter sit up and take notice. For as young as these guys (and gal—the bass player is a girl) are, their sound is polished and cohesive. Orion Taylor on lead guitar and vocals apparently has been playing since he was seven years old, astonishing a guitar teacher with his gift for playing by ear. His voice is distinctive, melodic, able to hit the highs and lows and hold them at the right time. Truly remarkable for a sixteen-year-old.

Troy Baines on second guitar manages to hold his own with Taylor, fingers flying as he rips it when it counts.

Gwyn Farcosi is on bass, and people will be asking where she came from for sure. Her play is understated enough to provide the bass support the band needs without getting boring. She has laser concentration and didn't miss a beat the entire set.

Nick Brewster on drums knows how to keep the rhythm, revving it up when he needs to, slowing it down or quieting the percussion as the song calls for it. His pure enjoyment of playing comes through, and the entire crowd felt it.

This band is definitely a band to watch. Now, if only they can come up with a name.

Young Local Groups Get Their Fifteen Minutes
by Courtney Calavera, *DMS* reporter

It's great to see some local establishments giving young bands some exposure. And this band — they still don't have a name, which is a bit frustrating — deserves the coverage. Their command of the covers was near professional level, and their originals were very strong.

Lead vocalist and guitarist Orion Taylor really pushed in their song "Focus." The intensity of his performance transported us all out of a small sporting goods store and into some big concert arena. He sings like he means it, and the audience feels it. Troy Baines on second and backup really kicks it up, following Taylor wherever he goes and sometimes striking out on his own, forcing Taylor to follow him.

Nick Brewster keeps a mean beat, and Gwyn Farcosi really cranks on the bass.

Over at Stella's on Pearl Street, I heard a young girl play melodic guitar, sounding a lot like Sheryl Crow in both her vocals and methodology. She's a freshman at Metro State and

click here for full story

COLORADO ROCKS

We are an up-and-coming band, nameless but open to suggestions. Feel free to post your band name ideas on our blog. (We don't want to use one of those band name generators — we want it to come from you or us.)

BAND NAME: to be named later

| PROFILE | MUSIC | PIX & VIDS | ABOUT/FAQ | CONTACT | BLOG |

Saturday, April 10

NICK: We totally brought the house down at Matt's Sports! I can't believe how well we played. We are really rockin, gang. Nothing can stop us. We did have one or two rival bands in the audience, for intimidation or support, we weren't sure, but it's always good to have a little pressure but still be able to play. Thanks to Gwyn for being such a great addition to our band.
And there was a TV crew filming us for a show on local indie bands. We'll post that link when we have it.

TROY: Keep the names coming. We really want to have a band name before the Battle. We do NOT want to have to resort to one of Brewster's names.

NICK: Hey! What's wrong with those names?

ALLI: And I understand this blog may have brought two people together. We're so proud.

ORION: It always comes back to the music. Nothing else matters. You can only count on the music. Which is why I'm not thinking about anything except the fact that I will order the Les Paul tomorrow! Look at that countdown — only 16 days!!!

Countdown to
BATTLE OF
THE BANDS:
56
days

Countdown to
LES PAUL:
16
days

BAND NAME: to be named later

| PROFILE | MUSIC | PIX & VIDS | ABOUT/FAQ | CONTACT | **BLOG** |

We are an up-and-coming band, name-less but open to suggestions. Feel free to post your band name ideas on our blog. (We don't want to use one of those band name generators — we want it to come from you or us.)

🌀 BoyMagnet

So what if Orion kissed that girl. I've found someone and it's not him.

📶 OzoneLayer

Does that mean you'll shut up about this crap now, BM?

📝 PurpleGrrl

BoyMagnet, you're here! I thought you'd quit for good. Are you the one Alli is talking about? Who's the guy? Dragon-Breath?

🔥 DragonBreath

No way!

🌀 BoyMagnet

I'll never tell. But I will say that people are not always what they seem.
BTW, I liked the orange, PurpleGrrl.

📝 PurpleGrrl

Mysterious.
Thanks on the orange.
Hey, anyone notice that guy in Orion's face at the end?

⚜ DominantSpecies

That was Roy Stone, lead singer for Slash and Burn, space cadet.

Countdown to
BATTLE OF
THE BANDS:

56

days

Countdown to
LES PAUL:

16

days

BAND NAME: to be named later

PROFILE   MUSIC   PIX & VIDS   ABOUT/FAQ   CONTACT   **BLOG**

We are an up-and-coming band, nameless but open to suggestions. Feel free to post your band name ideas on our blog. (We don't want to use one of those band name generators — we want it to come from you or us.)

🎸 PurpleGrrl

Wait a sec, DS. You were there? For someone who hates this band, you sure are around them a lot.

♟ DominantSpecies

Maybe they're growing on me, PG.

🎸 BoyMagnet

Way to be open-minded, DS.

🎸 PurpleGrrl

Did BM just give DS a compliment?
Hmm. I'm thinking I know what's growing on DS. And it's not the band.

🔊 OzoneLayer

Let's get back to the guy in Taylor's face. Did anyone throw a punch?

🎸 PurpleGrrl

No. The Roy guy just pointed his finger a few times and then left with some of his friends.
Alli, is it BM and DS who got together?

🎸 BoyMagnet

Don't call me that!

🔥 DragonBreath

Sounds like a rival band.

Countdown to
BATTLE OF
THE BANDS:
56
days

Countdown to
LES PAUL:
16
days

COLORADO ROCKS

BAND NAME: to be named later

| PROFILE | MUSIC | PIX & VIDS | ABOUT/FAQ | CONTACT | **BLOG** |

We are an up-and-coming band, nameless but open to suggestions. Feel free to post your band name ideas on our blog. (We don't want to use one of those band name generators — we want it to come from you or us.)

OzoneLayer
I smell a fight brewing.

PurpleGrrl
There's not going to be a fight. Orion's a lover not a fighter. And maybe you are too, DominantSpecies?

BoyMagnet
Leave him alone, PurpleGrrl.

DragonBreath
Hurl time.

OzoneLayer
Get in line.

Countdown to
BATTLE OF
THE BANDS:

56

days

Countdown to
LES PAUL:

16

days

TWENTY-TWO

✉ SAW YOU ON TV! COOL. *CHAD CELL 8:00 PM*
✉ IT'S ON THEIR WEBSITE TOO. WE'VE GOT A LINK TO IT.

I wanted to know if Del had seen it, if Jane was with him after driving away together in our car after our gig at Matt's Sports. But I didn't ask, because maybe I really didn't want to know.

I tried to play, to push out the anger and frustration through the music, but it wouldn't go away, just kept gnawing at me.

"Dammit!" I smacked my palm against the wall, ignoring the sting.

"Ori?" Vela's voice was soft, timid.

"WHAT." I didn't turn around. Instead, I bent down and fiddled with my amp.

"Maybe you shouldn't have kissed that girl," she said. "But I guess they were already together so it wouldn't— didn't matter." She stopped, sighed.

Why was she doing this? I didn't need my little sister's pity party. I turned the knob to HI, sending a screech through the speaker.

That didn't faze Vela. She sat on the floor like she planned to stay awhile.

"I thought Jane liked you."

I'm not his girlfriend.

"Well, she didn't." I strummed some more. "She never did."

"It seemed like she did." She tugged at a strand of loose carpet. "I can't believe she's with Del. I mean—"

"Can we not talk about this?" I strummed loudly.

"Sorry." She sat back, leaning on her hands. "What song were you playing?"

"Nothing really. Just a bunch of sounds."

"Play something for me."

"I'm not in the mood."

"You're always in the mood."

I narrowed my eyes at her but couldn't help smiling.

"Remember," she said, "I'm unhateable."

"So you've said."

"So we all know."

I chuckled. "Okay, fine. What do you want to hear?" I adjusted the amp again. "Something fast. No ballads."

" 'Roll with the Changes'?"

Mom's favorite REO Speedwagon song. Ancient classic but it definitely had some fun guitar riffs.

Vela stood up and struck a dance pose. "Just keep on rollin', big brother."

It felt good to hear her call me that. "Will do, little sister."
And we were off.

The next afternoon I pulled up to Gold's in my mom's car.
Even though I could have done it over the phone, I wanted to
order the Les Paul in person.

"OT! Great to see you." Ed clapped me on the shoulder.
"You ready to order that baby?"

"You know it." I pulled out the cashier's check my mom and
I had gotten at the bank as he walked me back to the counter.
He clicked the mouse as he looked at the computer screen.

"Come back here and make sure I'm ordering the right one."

I grinned because we both knew he knew exactly which
Les Paul it was, right down to that ebony fingerboard. I'd
made him look at it often enough.

"That's it."

He pushed the mouse over. "You do the honors."

That was the most satisfying click I'd ever heard.

Ed and I high-fived, and then he slipped the check into
the register. "So I heard the gig yesterday was fantastic. I'm
sorry I couldn't make it."

"Yeah, it was great." I tried to sound enthusiastic as I
fought down images of Roy in my face and Jane driving off
with Del. But hey. I'd just ordered the Les Paul, and thanks
to Vela, I'd had a great little jam session last night. I looked
over at a certain guitar that was currently gleaming near the
window display, the late-afternoon sun hitting it at just the
right angle.

"I know you're closing in a little while, but do you think I could play the Les Paul for just a few minutes?" I nodded toward the Jam Room.

Ed smiled. "Absolutely. Help yourself."

My plan was to play "Suburban Nightmare." That song always got my blood pumping, cranking up my mood.

But what came out instead was something I didn't even think was a song.

We used to be friends.

I frowned. Why did *that* pop into my head? I didn't want to think about Del right now.

We used to be brothers.

I felt my chest constrict and my body tense. I did not need this in my head. I tore into "Eruption," one of my favorites of Eddie Van Halen's screaming instrumentals. No words, just music, loud and screeching. I was swinging back and forth, then taking lunge-steps in time to the beat, then jumping, scissor kicking. . . .

The crowd is crazy with excitement. Nick grins at me, and I know what he's thinking: They're "erupting" just like the title of the song. They are on their feet, clapping, dancing, screaming, and I'm right there with them, moving everywhere as I play.

Sweat flies off my face as I shake my head, edging closer to the bottom of the stage, where security staff hold back a wall of screaming girls.

"Orion! Orion!"

I grin and look straight at Jane in the front row, able to see her amazing brown eyes, those eyelashes, as the light crew shines the spotlight—

Then I point to the girl next to her, motioning her up onstage.

She screams and looks at Jane, then back at me, pointing to herself.

I nod.

As security escorts her to the stairs on the side of the stage, I see Jane, her amazing eyes wide with surprise, then disappointment. I nod to her left. She turns to Del, who is smiling at her, putting his arm around her, but she is looking at me, shaking her head, shouting something. If I could read lips like Gwyn can, I might think she was asking for a second chance.

Too late, *I mouth to her.*

Way too late.

Eruption. Not a bad band name.

I finished the song with some serious stomping, breathing hard, sweat on my forehead—just like in my fantasy. I looked through the Jam Room glass and saw Jane and Del— just like in my fantasy.

Jane and Del?

They were standing near the sheet music, talking.

What the hell were they doing here?

I set the Les Paul on the guitar stand and backed into the far corner, but not before Del glanced over. Our eyes locked for a few seconds, and I was determined not to look away, but then he did. Reaching for Jane, he pulled her to him. She looked over at me, then up at him, and then he was kissing her, his arms around her, and before I knew it I was shoving the glass door open, heading for the back.

"Ori!" The door slamming behind me shut out Jane's voice. I dashed out the delivery door into the alley, running toward the street.

Del leaning in to Jane.
I just needed to get to the car.
Del's lips on Jane's lips.
That was all I needed to do.
Del's arms around Jane.
Just get to the car.

Except Jane was there, on the sidewalk, standing next to Del's car—*our* car—which was just two cars away from Mom's. Jane's back was to me as she talked to Del, her hands moving quickly, emphasizing whatever point she was making. Del wore his charming smile as he responded.

I flipped around and ran back down the block, passing the alley and turning onto the next street, which was residential. Crouching behind a row of juniper bushes, I pulled out my phone.

✉ CAN U PICK ME UP? I'M NEAR GOLD'S.

✉ KAITLYN'S HERE. BESIDES, U NO I CAN'T DRIVE ANYONE ELSE UNTIL MARCH. *NICK CELL 4:32 PM*

Stupid Colorado driving laws.

✉ I'M BEGGING U DUDE.

I waited, shifting to a more comfortable position on my heels.

✉ WHERE R U? *NICK CELL 4:33 PM*

"Can you just tell me what's going on?"

We were squished in the cab of the Brewsters' truck, PurpleGrrl—she just wasn't Kaitlyn to me—between us, heading toward a coffee shop about a mile from Gold's.

"Thanks for coming," I said, then looked at PurpleGrrl. "I guess we're two for the price of none."

She laughed.

"Yeah," Nick said. "I figured if I was going to get in trouble for driving one person, I might as well have two. And I didn't want to leave Kaitlyn by herself." He patted her leg and she smiled at him. "So, what gives?"

"We just need to hang out for a while until I can go back for the car."

"He's a man of mystery," Nick told PurpleGrrl.

I called Ed on the way, apologizing for leaving the Les Paul in the Jam Room, saying I'd had to deal with something and would be back later. I hung up before he could ask any questions.

We ordered coffee and Nick got a scone, complaining that we should have gone to Crown Burger so that he could have fries.

"Okay," I said after we finished our coffee. "I think we can probably go back."

"But I'm not done with my scone!"

"Can't you eat it in the truck?"

"Do you see this?" Nick asked PurpleGrrl. "I'm doing him a favor, and he's ordering me around."

PurpleGrrl smiled. "Let's get his car, and then we can go back to your house."

Nick stood up. "I can eat my scone in the truck."

"Just drive by once and tell me if anyone is near the car," I said when we got within a block of Gold's. I leaned down and pretended to tie my shoe.

"Who are we looking for?" Nick asked.

"No one. Just tell me if anyone's there."

"Okay, we're looking for no one, but someone might be there." Nick pressed the gas as the light turned green.

"I don't see anyone," PurpleGrrl said, and I started to raise my head. "Wait," she said, and I ducked back down. "There's some guy at the front of a guitar store."

"That's Ed," Nick said. "He owns the place. I think he's closing up."

"Anyone else?"

"No."

"Any cars you recognize?"

"Besides your mom's?" Nick asked. "No."

"Okay," I said. "Turn down the side street, and let me out." When Nick pulled up to the curb, I opened the door.

"Thanks, guys. I owe you."

"That you do, Taylor," Nick said. He saluted and drove off. I walked down to the corner and hurried to my mom's car.

"Where'd you run off to?"

Del stepped out from the shoe repair shop next to Gold's. My eyes flicked behind him.

"I had to take Jane home," Del said. "But I'll see her again. We have plans."

So why did he come back? Did he just want to hang around and gloat?

I didn't look at him as I stepped up to Mom's car, fumbling for the keys in my pocket.

"These things happen, bro," he said. "I'm sorry." But he didn't sound sorry. He sounded smug, pleased, and I wanted to leap around the car and smash his face in.

But of course I didn't.

"I have no idea what you're talking about or why you're here, and I don't care."

I climbed in and closed the door. I didn't slam it like I wanted to — he would have been expecting that, wanting it.

And the last thing I wanted to do was give Del what he wanted when he was so good at taking it anyway.

TWENTY-THREE

"I've decided not to talk to Del until he's nice to you." Vela sat down across from me while I worked on my math at the kitchen table Monday afternoon.

"That's nice of you, Vee, but not one of your better ideas," I said. "First of all, you're the only one he likes in this family, so you need to maintain that connection, if for nothing else than to make sure Mom doesn't go too crazy worrying about him." I took a bite out of one of the Oreos I had stacked next to me. "And second, I don't need Del being nice to me, coerced or not."

"Ooh, good word, Ori. That was on my vocab test last week."

"I know. I helped you study for it, remember?"

"Right." She grabbed one of the Oreos. "So when's your next rehearsal?"

"Friday. You and your friends can hang out if you want."

"Thanks. Maybe we will." She took a bite of the cookie.

"Hey, Vee, you know I'm getting my new guitar on the twenty-sixth. Want to come?"

Her face lit up. "Seriously?"

"Sure. The whole band is coming. We're going to jam a little there before I bring it home."

"I am so there."

The next two weeks before I could get the Les Paul were filled with homework, rehearsals, and work at Gold's. It was good to be busy, to do things that kept me from seeing Del and Jane kissing, an image that would pop up in my mind if I didn't keep going, going, going.

The only good thing about the Del/Jane situation—if there could be a good thing—was that any leftover guilt I had about spending my money on the Les Paul instead of on Del was completely gone. I felt absolutely nothing except the now-familiar anger that continued to grow inside me, getting bigger and heavier each day.

I did dread checking my e-mail, though. Not because of what might be there, but what wasn't. Not that I expected to hear from her, or even wanted to, but we'd had so many conversations through e-mail, I just automatically looked for "HalynFlake34" in the From column even though it had been weeks since we'd written each other. When I didn't see it, my heart dropped, which was stupid because *she was kissing Del.* I should have hated her. I did hate her. True, I'd never told her my real feelings, but didn't girls just know that kind of thing? Alli did. Alli would have known in a second if I liked her. But Jane...

"Forget it." I spoke the words out loud, hoping I could actually listen to them this time. But it was hard. So I went down to the basement, cranked my amp, and lost myself in the music.

On April 26, I was standing in Gold's, looking at a very big box on the floor. I'd seen boxes like this before, had unpacked more guitars than I could count, but this one looked different somehow.

Inside that box was the Les Paul. *My* Les Paul.

"This is so cool!" Vela said, and Mom smiled back at her, nodding.

"Come on, Ori, open it!" Nick was bouncing from foot to foot next to me.

I grinned and took the X-Acto knife from Ed, slicing through the tape and plastic strips keeping my Les Paul captive. Tossing the lid aside, I pawed through the foam blocks until I could see the guitar case, wrapped in a thin plastic film.

"It's like a mummy," Troy said.

I unwrapped it quickly, then snapped open the case to reveal the guitar, gleaming black and beautiful in front of me. Everyone let out a collective "Whoa," including me.

"Wicked," Nick said.

"*Awesome*," Gwyn signed.

Vela knelt down next to me. "It's so shiny."

I stared at it for a few seconds before reaching in slowly to lift it out. It felt strong and solid in my hands, and as I stood up, I pulled it against my body. Then I strummed. Even out of tune and not connected to an amp it sounded fantastic. Grinning, I ran my hand over every inch of it, feeling the curves, the edges, getting familiar with it. It was so smooth under my touch, so beautiful, that I was suddenly overwhelmed with emotion. I had to blink quickly to fight back a few tears threatening to make a fool of me.

"Here's the strap," Ed said, tugging it out of the box. I attached it to the Les Paul and pulled it over my head, adjusting its position.

"Looks good," Nick said.

"Like it was made to be in your hands." Troy nodded as he looked me over. "It's unbelievably perfect."

"Let's go," I said, leading the band to the Jam Room.

I tuned the Les Paul while Troy and Gwyn tuned their guitars.

Nick sat down behind the drum set that Ed kept in the Jam Room.

Then we were ready.

The Les Paul was ready.

"Let's rock," I said, starting the opening chords to "Suburban Nightmare."

The Les Paul screamed, launching us to new heights. When the song was over, everyone was shouting and clapping and smacking one another on the back.

"Did you hear that?" I said. "Isn't it amazing?"

"We are going to totally dominate Slash and Burn," Nick

said. We played one more song, barely noticing the small crowd that had gathered outside the Jam Room to watch and try to listen through the thick glass. When we finished, they all clapped and cheered, and I raised one fist in the air, the other hand resting on the Les Paul.

After we filed out of the Jam Room, everyone wanted some time to hold the Les Paul. I handed it over reluctantly, hating the feeling of emptiness it left against my body.

Mom was smiling at me.

"What?"

"That's how I felt when you boys were born and other people wanted to hold you. I didn't want to let you go, even though I was exhausted." She looked over at the guitar, now in Gwyn's capable and careful hands. "It's not quite the miracle of a newborn, but it's close." She squeezed my arm. "I'm so proud of you, Orion. You worked hard for that guitar, and it will be such an important and memorable part of your music."

Her words got those emotions going again, but it was cool. She understood my passion. She supported it.

I smiled, surprising both of us by giving her a hug in front of everyone.

COLORADO ROCKS

We are an up-and-coming band, nameless but open to suggestions. Feel free to post your band name ideas on our blog. (We don't want to use one of those band name generators — we want it to come from you or us.)

Countdown to
BATTLE OF
THE BANDS:
40
days

Countdown to
LES PAUL:
0
days

BAND NAME: to be named later

| PROFILE | MUSIC | PIX & VIDS | ABOUT/FAQ | CONTACT | BLOG |

Monday, April 26

ORION: Five words: I GOT THE LES PAUL!!! It screams! It's the most awesome thing I've ever played in my life. We will completely dominate at the Battle.

PurpleGrrl
Awesome! I can't wait to hear you play it.

PeacefulWarrior
One does not win the Battle by a new guitar alone. The proof is in the playing.

DominantSpecies
Well said, PW. I'm looking forward to watching this band bite it while Slash and Burn takes it all.

PurpleGrrl
DS: I thought you'd be nicer now that you're with BoyM.

DominantSpecies
I don't do nice. And why would you think I'm with BoyMagnet?

PurpleGrrl
It's a small cyberworld after all.
And you've stopped calling her BM.

BAND NAME: to be named later

| PROFILE | MUSIC | PIX & VIDS | ABOUT/FAQ | CONTACT | **BLOG** |

We are an up-and-coming band, nameless but open to suggestions. Feel free to post your band name ideas on our blog. (We don't want to use one of those band name generators — we want it to come from you or us.)

📶 OzoneLayer

Here we go again. Take it over to a site that cares, why don't you?

❄ Halyn

I'm so happy you got your Les Paul, Ori.

🌀 BoyMagnet

She's calling him Ori like she knows him or something.

🖊 PurpleGrrl

Maybe she does.
Good to see you back, Halyn. Hope things are ok.

Countdown to
BATTLE OF
THE BANDS:

40

days

Countdown to
LES PAUL:

0

days

TWENTY-FOUR

I could hardly concentrate on anything else, knowing the Les Paul was downstairs, waiting for me to take it for another spin. I finally took my homework down to the basement so that when I got stuck or needed a break, I could just pick it up and play.

Needless to say, I took about ten breaks, trying every song we were planning to play in the Battle, plus some favorites. It felt so right in my hands, like it was made for me, and I found myself smiling like crazy thinking about strumming this baby in front of a crowd. I even brought it into the bathroom so that I could see how it looked in the mirror. I had rigged up my gooseneck desk lamp on top of the cabinet above the toilet and aimed it down where I was going to stand, and then I turned off the overhead light.

I wear faded jeans, a ripped and faded yellow T-shirt, knowing the black Les Paul will stand out against it. I wait in the center

of the stage, which is completely black, counting in my head—one,
two, three—before strumming the first chord.

The crowd cheers immediately, and I play a few more chords
before the spotlight catches me, holds me in place. The Les Paul is
so shiny the light bounces off, no doubt blinding anyone out there
lucky enough to be in its sight line.

"Ori, are you in there?" Vela's voice in the crowd. No,
outside the bathroom. I scramble to turn on the overhead
light, banging the Les Paul against the sink.

"Damn." I rubbed my fingers across the body, checking
for nicks. Whew. Still smooth, still gleaming.

"Are you okay?" she asked. "What are you doing?"

"I'll be out in a minute."

"I wanted to see your guitar again, but it's not down in
the basement anymore."

"I'll show it to you later, Vee, okay? Geez. Can I get a
little privacy?"

"Sorry. I'll be in my room." I heard her footsteps retreat.

I waited until I heard her door close before glancing at
myself in the mirror. My hair was disheveled, two zits making their home on my right cheek. I was clutching the arm of
the Les Paul, my other hand on the body. I looked young,
goofy, not at all like the guy I saw in my rock star fantasies.

Still, I had the Les Paul and I could make it scream.

RSB. Bring it on.

Allicat21: Did you see Halyn's comment on the blog?
GuitarFreak516: No.
Allicat21: You should look.

GuitarFreak516: No thanks.

Allicat21: She was happy about the Les Paul.

GuitarFreak516: So now I don't have to look.

Allicat21: I think you should talk to her.

GuitarFreak516 has signed off.

When I got home from work on Friday, I immediately grabbed the Les Paul and took it out to the garage. I wanted to hear it big and loud in our rehearsal space.

I ran through a bunch of different riffs, switching around from slow to fast, just warming up. Then it was time to get back to the fantasy Vela had interrupted on Monday.

I stand front and center on the Red Rocks stage, my head down, the Les Paul quiet. I raise my head and position my hands on the guitar, which sends a ripple of shouts and applause through the crowd. They are waiting, their anticipation palpable. I strum once, and the crowd screams its recognition. I strum again, and they are on their feet, stomping and clapping as the spot lights me up. Nick gives me some drums just before Troy and Gwyn kick in.

The girls are shrieking, hands outstretched toward me. I smile and point to them, and the shrieks get louder. Any one of them could be mine, any of them.

But the one I want —

The Les Paul squealed before going tinny.

"What the —"

Del was behind me, holding the cord from the Les Paul above the amp.

"I just wanted to see it for myself." He sauntered toward

251

me, his eyes on the guitar in my hands. I backed up, hugging it tightly, anger smoldering inside me.

"Vela was freaking out about it yesterday," he said. "Couldn't stop talking about how great it was." He stopped in front of me, reaching out to brush his fingers across the body of the Les Paul. "It's a beauty, that's for sure."

Our faces were only inches apart now, which was why I could smell it—the beer on his breath.

When was this going to end?

I pulled the guitar strap over my head and leaned the Les Paul against the wall a safe distance away, keeping one eye on Del.

"Why don't you go inside and say hi to Vela."

"Don't tell me what to do." His fists clenched and unclenched at his sides.

I realized mine were doing the same.

"Why are you doing this? Why can't you just leave me alone?"

"I'm trying to help you!" His voice rose. "All this is going to go away, and you can't even see it! You're so stupid!"

"You're not trying to help me!" I shouted back. All that anger I'd been carrying around with me, that had been growing and spreading through me, was looking for a way out. It was just beneath the surface, burning my skin. "You're just trying to make yourself feel better. You're pathetic!"

"Is that why Jane is with me and not you?"

Before I knew it, my fist was up.

I swung—

And missed.

Del was more accurate. My head snapped back, warm blood immediately running out my nose and down over my mouth.

"Don't even try," he said, fists in front of his face, ready for more. But he swayed a bit, and that was all I needed.

Ignoring the pain in my nose, I swung again, this time connecting with his jaw. Adrenaline raced through me as I watched his head jerk to one side.

"You can't stand it!" I yelled. "You can't stand to see me doing better than you. It's killing you, isn't it?"

"Shut up."

"I only have this one thing and you can have anything, but it doesn't matter. You still want to take it away from me!"

I threw another punch, this one hitting his temple.

He staggered back but got his footing and came at me, punching me again.

"I said shut up."

"You're just a worthless screwup!" I screamed at him. "I can't believe I ever wanted to be like you!" Pain was shooting through my hand, traveling up and down my fingers and across my knuckles, which were already starting to swell. My face was throbbing so much I could hardly stand, hardly breathe. I stumbled back, just out of reach of Del's lethal fist.

"Shut up, goddammit!" He snatched the Les Paul and held it like a bat. I lunged for him, my "NOOOO" cut short in a cry of pain as my body protested the quick movement.

But he was already swinging, swinging toward the concrete wall. My heart stopped, my breath froze, and in that brief moment while I waited for the sound of crunching wood, for my beautiful Les Paul to be reduced to splinters, I had a small, stupid thought: four days. I got to play the Les Paul for four measly days before Del came along and took it away, just like he took away the car. Jane. Everything.

And then I heard it. Not the sound of smashing wood, but Del's labored breathing from the sheer effort of stopping the Les Paul from connecting with concrete. His muscles quivered, his bloody hands shook as he held it just an inch away from the wall.

"Shut up," he murmured, but there wasn't anger there anymore, only...something else. I wasn't sure what. He shoved the guitar at me, and I clutched it to my chest with my good hand, my breath escaping shakily. I watched as he slid to the floor, dropping his head in his hands.

"Ori! Del!" I had no idea how long Vela had been standing there, tears streaming down her cheeks. "Oh my God!"

Then Mom was there, glaring at both of us.

"Get in the car." Her voice was like steel. "I'm taking you both to the hospital."

TWENTY-FIVE

"No broken bones for either one," the doctor said, slipping the X-rays in the catch above the lighted wall. "Just badly bruised. Some ice and ibuprofen and they should be back in the ring in a couple of weeks."

Mom scowled.

"Sorry," the doctor said, glancing at both of us. "Guess that's not too funny right now."

"When can I play my guitar again?" I asked.

"If you take care of it, probably in a couple of weeks." He turned to give more instructions to my mom, but I tuned out, staring at the poster on the wall of the human skeletal structure. All those bones connecting fingers to knuckles, knuckles to hand, hand to wrist, and on and on. All those little pieces making a hand that could move across strings or pluck them or strum them with a pick.

No playing for two weeks? He might as well have told me I couldn't breathe for fourteen days.

We rode home in silence, Del in the front seat, me in the back. My parents had decided he needed to be home again, and he hadn't protested.

No one had asked me what I wanted.

When we got home, he trudged up to his room and shut the door, and I went immediately to the garage. The Les Paul was lying on top of its case, not on the tarp where I'd left it. I'd expected to see bloodstains, but it shone like it had when I'd first taken it out of the box that day, black and gleaming.

"I cleaned it up for you," Vela said softly. "I didn't think you'd want to come home to..." She gestured to the Les Paul before letting her hand drop to her side.

"Thanks," I whispered, not trusting myself to speak any louder. I bent down to look at the guitar, shivering involuntarily as I thought about how close it had come to being smashed to pieces.

But it hadn't.

Del had swung with full force and stopped just before impact.

Why?

He had to know that one of the worst things he could do to me besides take Jane was ruin my guitar, the guitar I'd bought instead of giving him a loan. Why hadn't he done it?

I sighed, putting the Les Paul back in its case before standing up.

"I'm going to take this downstairs," I said, and Vela nodded. I looked away quickly, knowing I was partly to blame for the pain I saw in her eyes. "Thanks again."

After I'd tucked the Les Paul safely in a corner of the basement, I looked over at the loaner still leaning against the wall where I'd left it a few days ago. In all the excitement of the Les Paul, I'd forgotten about it and hadn't returned it to the guitar mentor who had loaned it to me.

I pulled it out and looked at it. It was a basic Stratocaster, nothing flashy, really. Just a battered and worn electric guitar that had gotten me through weeks of rehearsals, one of Vela's birthday parties, and two almost-real gigs. Stroking the body with my good hand, I felt every nick, every cut, each one no doubt with a story behind it. I thought I'd put a few on it myself.

Tears stung my eyes, and I shook my head angrily. Why did I feel like crying? What was wrong with me? Del would love that. Little Ori crying. Little Ori was such a baby.

Rubbing my eyes, I sniffled hard, sucking in a deep breath and releasing it. Then I held the loaner against my chest for a few moments before placing it gently in its case, snapping the clasps shut.

When I went upstairs later, I noticed Del's door was slightly ajar. I held my breath, listening for sounds of life inside. But it was quiet. I tiptoed by, peeking in as I passed.

He was lying on his bed, his hands over his head like he was protecting it. He looked small and vulnerable curled up like that, battered and scratched, someone who'd been through some crap, some he'd caused, some that just had come at him.

Golden boy full of promise now reduced to this lump on

his bed, working at a job he didn't particularly like, not sure what the future held, most of his friends gone. He'd lost everything familiar, everything he knew.

And I'd told him he was a worthless screwup, pushing the knife in deeper.

I turned away, feeling something I'd never, ever felt before. It was so foreign, so uncomfortable, that I let out an "Ahhhh" before slumping into my own room, settling heavily onto my bed.

The foreign feeling was still there, waiting for me to do something. But I'd never felt sorry for Del before, the brother I'd idolized since I was a kid, so the pity just twisted up my insides and made me feel a little sick.

Then I thought about it. If the object of my pity got a whiff of what I was feeling, he'd pummel me to a bloody pulp—more than he already had. And if the object of my pity could actually pummel me to a bloody pulp, he probably wasn't someone I should be feeling sorry for in the first place.

I smiled a little at that, but I still locked my door before I went to sleep.

No one ever tells you how sore you are after a fight. The next morning, I felt like my head had been cranked through a meat grinder. My nose was swollen, my right eye was slightly blue and yellow, and my hand throbbed. Del looked just as bad, which gave me an odd feeling in the pit of my stomach. I had done that? Del was always the tough one, not afraid of anyone. I'd never been in a fight, but I'd always thought I'd feel cool hitting someone.

But I felt like crap. And it wasn't just because the hospital painkillers had worn off.

After the lecture from Mom and Dad, Del and I steered clear of each other, and I knew he was doing what I was: listening and watching to see when one of us was going to the bathroom, downstairs, or out for the day. The first two days he stayed in his room, opening the door only to use the bathroom or accept food from Mom, or when Chad came over with some of his stuff. After that, he got up early, before me, took a shower, and headed out to work or who knows where. He didn't come home until after I was in bed.

I should have been glad he was avoiding me, but for some reason it bothered me. I found myself looking at his closed door every time I passed, my stomach sinking with each glance.

Later that night, Jeff Beck rocked my cell.

✉ YOU OKAY? *HALYN CELL 10:10 PM*

Why was she texting me? Why wasn't she texting Del?

I pressed Reply.

✉ WRONG BROTHER.

She didn't reply back.

On Wednesday afternoon, the band gathered for rehearsal. I was as ready as I could be with my hand wrapped and pain meds pumping through my veins.

"Okay, we have about four weeks until the Battle," I said. "I should be ready to play in about two weeks. For now, I can finger the chords and watch for mistakes."

It didn't really work. It was impossible to form a chord and then not be able to strum it out, to actually make music.

I ended up putting my guitar down and just listening, correcting everything that didn't sound right.

"You're going to nitpick us to death," Gwyn said after I'd stopped them for the tenth time. "That hand better heal soon."

"Sorry," I muttered.

We ended early, with everyone sneaking me looks every few seconds.

"Would you all just stop that?" I said finally. "Yes, Del and I got into a fight. But the Les Paul is fine, and I'll be fine."

"Where is it?" Nick asked.

"What?"

"The Les Paul."

"In the basement. Safe." I didn't say I hadn't been able to look at it since I'd put it down there.

"And Del?" Alli whispered over my shoulder as I put the loaner away.

"What about him?"

"Where is he?"

I looked at her, then straightened up, purposely putting the guitar case between us as I spoke to the band. "See you guys next time."

I didn't even wait for a reply, just headed inside. After I'd put the loaner away in the basement, I headed upstairs to do homework. As I reached the landing, the bathroom door opened and Del stepped out, practically running into me.

"Sorry," we said in unison. I ducked left to get around him, but he ducked the same way. We both snorted.

"You first."

"Thanks." I stepped past him to my room.

"Your face is worse than mine," he said.

I felt my temperature rise and turned, ready to lash back with something. But I was surprised to see him smiling.

"But not by much."

My anger subsided. "Yeah, well, you're a better fighter."

"You're not bad yourself," he said. "Though I'm not sure it's something to be proud of."

He was gone before I could say anything, even if I'd had something to say, which I didn't.

I stepped into my room, not sure what to make of his comment or my feelings. Opening my closet, I pulled a sweatshirt off my shelf. Something in the corner caught my eye.

The T-shirt had slipped off Del's trophy, exposing the tip of a lacrosse stick. I hesitated, then pulled it out into the light. It wasn't too dusty, since it had been covered up. I brushed my fingers across the nameplate—DEL TAYLOR, CAPTAIN—then set the trophy in its usual spot on my dresser.

HalynFlake34: Alli? You online?

Allicat21: Yep.

HalynFlake34: Sorry I didn't answer any of your e-mails. Just trying to figure things out.

Allicat21: And have you?

HalynFlake34: Not really. I heard about the fight.

Allicat21: They'll be okay.

HalynFlake34: Neither one is answering my texts.

Allicat21: I don't mean to be mean, but why are u telling me this?

HalynFlake34: I don't know.

HalynFlake34: You still there?

Allicat21: Yeah.

HalynFlake34: I guess I just wanted to talk to you.

Allicat21: Because you can't talk to Del.

HalynFlake34: Yeah.

Allicat21: Or Ori.

HalynFlake34: Yeah.

Allicat21: Is it helping?

HalynFlake34: Not really.

Allicat21: Maybe because I'm not the one you should be talking to?

HalynFlake34 has signed off.

TWENTY-SIX

On Saturday afternoon, Del was out in the driveway work-ing on the car.

"Need any help?" I asked, pulling my jacket tighter against the cool May breeze. It always seemed like it should feel like summer once May hit, but it was often chilly and sometimes even snowed. I breathed in deeply, though, enjoy-ing the coolness filling my lungs.

Del laughed. "Since when do you work on cars?"

"I can follow directions," I said. "I've got one good hand."

Del raised an eyebrow before rummaging around in his toolbox. "I need some other tools," he said. "Do me a favor and pull out the owner's manual while I go raid Dad's tool-box." He headed into the garage, and I opened the passenger-side door, flipping open the glove compartment.

A large manila envelope dropped to the floor. I picked it

up to set it aside when a photo slipped out, making my heart flip oddly.

It was a picture of us playing at Matt's Sports.

I slid my hand inside the envelope and pulled out the contents. Everything inside was about me and the band: newspaper and online announcements about our gigs, the reviews we'd gotten, more pictures of us playing at FX and Matt's Sports. It was all in chronological order, the photos attached to the appropriate announcements and reviews.

"That's not the manual," Del said, snatching the envelope away from me and stuffing it under the driver's seat. My eyes darted from his face to the corner of the envelope peeking out.

"What?" he said.

I rubbed my lips together. "Why do you have all that stuff?"

He shrugged, then reached into his back pocket. "Here."

I took a piece of paper from him. It was a photocopy of "Related Strangers."

"Where did you get this?"

"Doesn't matter. You looked at my private stuff, I looked at yours. We're even."

I stared at the words, embarrassment fighting for relief inside me. So now he really knew how I felt. Fine. But I knew how he felt, too. If the stuff in that envelope was "private," it meant something to him. I folded up the paper, tucked it into my pocket, and pulled out the manual, opening it to the table of contents.

"What do you need me to look up?"

*   *   *

The next day, I was online when Alli popped up:

Allicat21: Talk to Jane.

GuitarFreak516: Hi to you too. Why?

Allicat21: Because I said so.

GuitarFreak516: Gee, that really makes me want to.

Allicat21: Fine. Because I think she wants to talk to you.

GuitarFreak516: I'm not stopping her.

Allicat21: You're being really annoying.

GuitarFreak516: So are you.

Allicat21: I give up. If you want to lose out on a good thing because of your pride, go for it.

GuitarFreak516: I will.

GuitarFreak516: Wait. I didn't mean to say that.

Allicat21: Unbelievable. I have no idea what she sees in you.

*Allicat21 status: **Away***

GuitarFreak516: Wait! What do you mean? Did she say something to you about seeing something in me?

Two weeks and one day after the fight, I was back to playing. My hand felt stiff, but I kept working it, doing ridiculous hand and finger exercises to get it back in shape. The first few times I tried to strum, my hand didn't feel like my own, but then I got into it. I couldn't believe how good it felt to play again, especially on the Les Paul, which I'd finally taken out of hibernation because I didn't immediately think of the fight when I looked at it anymore. I texted everyone, and when we got together for our next rehearsal, they all cheered when I got through our covers and "Suburban Nightmare" with just a few mistakes.

"Thank God," Gwyn said. "You weren't fit to play with before."

I grinned. "I know. I'm sorry. It's just that when I can't play—"

"You can't breathe," Gwyn finished my sentence and nodded. "That's what Jane says when she can't write her poetry."

There was an awkward silence as I tried to look anywhere but at Gwyn.

Alli shook her head but avoided my gaze. She wasn't talking to me about Jane anymore. After our IM exchange I'd sent her a bunch of texts, asking what she meant about Jane. She didn't answer and didn't answer until finally she texted back: ✉ I AM PONTIUS PILATE. She would answer all my other texts and e-mails and IMs, just not any that had to do with Jane.

I couldn't blame her. She was trying to help, and I hadn't been too nice about it. Still, even though I wanted to know things, I wasn't ready to talk to Jane, wasn't sure what to say, so I let time go by thinking maybe she would talk to me. I went to school and work, and we rehearsed as much as possible, fine-tuning every song, every word, every beat. Del and I talked, but not about anything important, like two people who had just met, weren't sure if they liked or trusted the other, and were being polite until they found out if they did.

And then, suddenly it was the middle of May, less than a month before the Battle of the Bands.

"We're sounding good," I said after one particularly long

rehearsal. "But I really wish we had one more chance to play in front of a friendly crowd before the Battle."

"Leave it to me," Nick said. And just like that he sweet-talked the administration into letting us play a set at school.

"Our song 'Finals Week' will inspire everyone to kick— you know—on their exams," he apparently told the principal. "And we can charge a small fee and give it to the school."

Maybe the administration had the end-of-school-year giddiness like we did, or maybe it was because the seniors had already graduated and they were feeling generous with fewer students around, or because Nick had asked on one of those amazing Colorado spring days when the sun warms your back and the sky is such a brilliant blue it hurts your eyes.

Or maybe it was the cash.

Whatever it was, they said yes, so on the Friday before finals, we got out of our last class early to set up our equipment on a special platform on the football field. Some of the parents had opened the ticket and concession stands. It almost seemed like it would be a real outdoor concert. Gwyn arrived as soon as she could from her own school, ready to help. I looked past her out of habit.

"She's not coming."

"I wasn't—I'm not...do you need any help?"

Gwyn shook her head, placing her guitar case on the ground and snapping it open. "You know it's not what you think."

"What?"

She gave me a look.

"Oh. Okay," I said, slowly registering. Jane and Del. I

hoped. My heart did one of those little flip things. "You're just now telling me this?"

Gwyn shrugged. "First, I don't do mediator as a general rule. Second, after I decided I would make a very brief exception in this case, it took me a while to be sure."

"Right." I didn't really care *why* she was telling me this. I just wanted to hear more.

"Anyway," Gwyn said, "I told Jane the same thing about you and that girl at Matt's Sports. I assume I'm right that it was nothing?"

I nodded. I never called Brandy and she never called me, even though I was easy to find. Alli had been right about the RSB. Of course.

"Good," Gwyn said, plugging in her bass. "So now you'll talk to her."

I frowned. "Why doesn't *she* talk to *me*?"

"Okay, this is why I don't do mediator." She waved me away to set up her amp before pulling her phone out of her pocket.

I had no idea what to do with this information. I just knew I needed to get away for a few minutes to process it. I jogged across the grass, stopping several yards from our makeshift stage. Then I flipped open my cell, determined to send Jane a text before I chickened out. Just as I started to type, a text came through my phone.

✉ SECOND VERSE: YOU HAVE SEEN THE PERSON I
REALLY AM (I SEE YOU) THE MISTAKES AND REGRETS
I'M SORRY FOR (ARE YOU?) THAT ISN'T THE BEST OF
ME (WAS THAT THE BEST OF YOU?) COULD YOU
HALYN CELL 3:32 PM

Could I what? What was she going to ask me?

I looked up at the stage, where Gwyn was watching me. I held up my phone.

"I thought you didn't do mediator," I called to her.

She cupped her hand around one ear. "What? I can't hear you. I'm deaf, you know."

I waved her away with a laugh as another text came through.

✉ FORGIVE? (COULD I?) IS THERE AN EMPTY SPACE
WHERE I USED TO BE? OR IS THERE ROOM FOR YOU
AND ME (GOOD AND BAD) *HALYN CELL 3:32 PM*

Man, she was awesome. My fingers flew over the keys, responding to each question she'd raised in her poem.

✉ YES, MORE THAN I CAN SAY – NO WAY – YES! – HOPE SO,
WILL BEGGING HELP? VERY EMPTY, PLENTY OF ROOM
WILL YOU BE AT THE BATTLE?

✉ YES!!! *HALYN CELL 3:33 PM*

✉ AND YOU STILL OWE ME A GUITAR HERO CHALLENGE.

✉ DANG. I WAS HOPING YOU'D FORGOTTEN. *HALYN CELL
3:33 PM*

✉ NEVER.

I raised my phone over my head in triumph, ignoring Gwyn laughing at me as I hustled inside to use the bathroom. When I was finished, I headed down the hall. Just as I was turning the corner toward the doors that led out to the field, voices caught my attention.

"Del Taylor was back here again? Really?"

"Kind of pathetic, isn't it?" one of them said. "Hanging around your old high school."

"Yeah," the other one said. "And I heard Tara totally

dumped him last fall. He thought he could do better and was messing around with some college senior."

"What an idiot. Doesn't get much better than Tara Middleton. Think she's still single?"

"Doubtful, dude. And she wouldn't dip below the food chain for you anyway."

A smack, then: "Ouch!" Then a locker closing.

"I used to think Del Taylor was so cool when he was here, but now..."

"Pathetic."

"Yeah, pathetic."

Something welled up inside me, and I spun around the corner in the direction of the voices.

"Del Taylor is worth ten of you assholes."

"Well, if it isn't Orion Taylor," one said. It took me a second to register that he knew my name. Most of the upperclassmen knew I was Del Taylor's brother, but very few knew my name.

"Standing up for your brother," the other said. "Admirable."

"He can stand up for himself," I said. "But you probably know that, which is why you're giving him crap behind his back." I smiled. "I have an idea. Why don't we give him a call so you can say those things to his face?" I pulled out my cell phone and held it up.

They looked at each other before the first one shoved his hands into his pockets. "Aren't you supposed to be playing with your band right now?"

"We have time." I flipped my phone open. "Let's see.

270

Why don't you tell me your names? Then I can tell him exactly who has such nice things to say about him."

"I've got to go," the second guy said, shifting his eyes nervously. "I want to get a good seat."

"Yeah."

They took off down the hall. I slid my phone back into my pocket, feeling better than I had in days.

It took us over an hour to set everything up, and we were going to be playing for only a little over thirty minutes.

But it was worth it.

We rocked the high school. People were dancing, and some were even singing along. Who knew they'd been listening to our band long enough to know the words to some of our originals? Too cool. Looking out over all those people looking at *us*, listening to *us* and singing along, was one of the greatest moments of my life.

"Living the dream," Nick shouted over the applause after we'd finished a song. "Living the dream, baby!"

We ended with "Finals Week," and everyone went wild. Shouting, screaming, fists pumping in the air—it was such a high we could hardly contain ourselves.

Troy and I amped up the finish, jumping up and down while we played because we couldn't *not* jump up and down. When we'd smashed the last chord from our guitars—me on the Les Paul—the crowd was clapping and screaming. Caught up in the moment, I leaned into the mic and shouted, "Now go kick some finals ass!"

They screamed, whooped, and clapped even louder.

PurpleGrrl, Alli, and Adam were in the front row, cheering louder than everyone else. And because Jane and I were almost back on track, it was like she was there, too.

I looked over my shoulder, grinning at Nick, who was off his stool, juggling his sticks. We were giddy, we were ecstatic, so when I saw someone shouting and clapping off to the side and in the back, it didn't register at first.

But then I recognized Del's whoop, the way he was clapping over his head, the wide grin across his face.

Most people were heading for the parking lot as they shouted "You guys rock!" "Take the Battle!" "Orion Taylor, we love you!" over their shoulders.

And there was Del, grinning like a crazy man. My eyes stayed on him for a few more seconds before I turned away, the sun warm at my back, the sky so blue it hurt my eyes—

Till they watered.

TWENTY-SEVEN

✉ R U ON UR WAY HOME?

✉ NO. JUST GETTING 2 PARKING LOT. *DEL CELL 5:05 PM*

✉ WAIT 4 ME.

I wasn't sure if he would. The new Del would have taken off, just for the satisfaction of knowing he'd left me behind. He might even have waited at the exit so that he could actually witness my humiliation in person. But I felt like we were with in-between Del now, and I wasn't sure what to expect.

He was standing by the car when we showed up with our equipment.

"You're not going to piss him off again, are you, Del?" Nick asked. "'Cause he really needs that hand."

Del smiled slightly. "Don't plan to."

"Don't hit him," Nick said to me as he passed by, holding one of his drums. He was followed by PurpleGrrl, Alli, Troy,

Adam, and Gwyn, all carrying part of his drum set along with their own stuff.

"Don't worry," I said after him. "I won't." I set my guitars down near the car and flexed my fingers. "So, thanks for coming."

"No problem."

We stood awkwardly for a few more seconds.

"You didn't leave right away," I said. "I figured you'd have to get to work or something."

"Nah," he said. "I'm off tonight. A few people stopped me, wanted to say hi. You know how it is."

I nodded.

"Funny, though," he said. "I started to say hi to a couple of guys I remembered from last year, and they practically ran away like they were afraid of me. Like I might hurt them." He shook his head, perplexed. "Did they know about the fight?"

"I didn't say anything, but maybe word got around," I said, remembering the jerks in the hall. No need to tell him about that and actually give him a reason to hurt them. "So how did that interview go? The one you had to wear a suit for?"

"I called and cancelled," he said. "It occurred to me that I hated wearing a suit and really didn't want a job where I'd have to wear one every day."

"Smart move."

He shrugged. "It means I'll still be piecing together these stupid minimum-wage gigs, but oh well."

I glanced back at Nick and company. They were standing

around Nick's truck, talking. Alli looked over and gave me a wave. I waved back.

"Are you coming?" Troy called.

I looked down at the guitars resting between Del and me.

"I can give you a ride home if you want," Del said.

I hesitated. It had been a long time since we'd driven together, been alone together for any length of time. Not that the school was very far from our house, but still. A lot had happened.

Like his hating me.

And making me look stupid.

And taking Jane.

And almost smashing the Les Paul.

But not smashing the Les Paul.

And having that envelope full of stuff about me.

And coming to watch us play.

"I'm covered," I called back to Troy. He waved in response.

I hoisted my guitars into the trunk after Del released the latch. Then I climbed into the car, sitting awkwardly as he got in and snapped on his seat belt. When he turned the ignition on, the stereo blared rock music through the speakers. He turned it down before pulling out of the parking lot.

We drove in silence for a few blocks, getting used to the feel of each other in the car.

"So," Del said as he pulled through an intersection, "great set."

"Thanks."

Silence for another mile. Then: "That song you sang today and at Matt's Sports—'Focus,' was it?—interesting."

I had a feeling he knew it was about him, at least in part. "Yeah."

And that was it. He turned up the radio, and we didn't talk anymore, even though the car felt heavy with the weight of everything left unsaid.

Jane answered on the first ring when I called and we agreed to meet at a Starbucks neither of us had ever been to—no connections, no memories—neutral territory. I was waiting on the sidewalk when she arrived. She stepped up in front of me, and we just looked at each other for a few seconds.

"So, can we just rewind this whole thing and start over?" I asked.

"Sure," Jane said. She stepped back a few paces, then stepped forward, holding out a hand. "Hi, I'm Jane Garfield, aka Halyn. I've been waiting for you." I liked the reference to my song.

"I've been waiting for you, too."

Then we went inside and talked for a long time, getting everything out.

"She meant nothing, that girl," I said. "I just saw you with Del and flipped out. You have to know the history. It's just such a stereotype, but he's the better-looking one, the one who always gets the girls, and I'm the dorky younger brother and—"

"You're not dorky."

I smiled at that. "I am, but that's okay. But anyway, before, he would never even look at any girl he knew I liked or thought I liked. And then he did it with you. So I'm sorry for being a jerk."

"So you like me."

"Did I say that?"

"I think you did."

"Huh. Do they have instant replay here?" I looked around, hoping she didn't notice my cheeks, which I knew had to be turning a very stupid shade of pink.

"Well, I'm sorry for *my* jerkiness," she said. "I was just so mad when you pushed me away, even though you were right that I was butting in. I just hated to see two really great guys not getting along and I thought I might be able to help because—" She stopped. "I'm making excuses for butting in, aren't I?" Sighing, she took a sip of her latte. "Darn. Gwyn says I do that."

I smiled.

"Anyway," she continued, "Del seemed to need someone to talk to, so I listened. And I know this sounds crazy, but being with him and talking to him kind of made me feel closer to you." She looked down at her cup. "But he also really made me feel like I was—well—" She stopped, blushing.

"It's the Del Spell," I explained. "It happens."

She admitted to liking the attention, especially right after seeing me with Brandy. "It just seemed like every time I turned around there were girls all over you—at the auditions, at the gigs, and then BoyMagnet kissed you....But when I saw you with that totally gorgeous girl at Matt's Sports, I just lost it. I mean, why would you want to be with *me* when you could be with someone like *that*?"

"RSB," I said.

"What?"

"That's what Alli calls it. Rock Star Blindness. Girls go wild for average-looking or ugly musician-type dudes, then it wears off."

"Well, I don't have RSB," she said. "And I think you're way above average-looking." Then we both looked away, embarrassed. "He wasn't you," she said softly. "He was never you."

I stood up and so did she. Then I wrapped my arms around her and kissed her in front of the world. Long. Hard. Like we might never break apart. But then we did because we needed to breathe.

"Can we rewind that part and play it back exactly the same way?" Jane asked.

"Absolutely."

And we did.

TWENTY-EIGHT

"Ori. Ori!" Alli was striding toward me on Battle day, her eyes bright with excitement. We were at the Sports Complex, where three stages were set up around the soccer fields. While one band played on one stage, other bands were setting up at another. They would continue rotating around until all the bands had played. "There's some bigwig guy here to see your band!"

"What? Where?"

"In a limo on the street. You should totally go."

"Now? Don't they want to hear us play first?"

"I don't think so," Alli said, handing me a business card. "Some guy gave me this and said they wanted to talk to you now. His exact words were 'We want them before everyone else gets to them.' He said it wouldn't take long."

I felt my heart thud with excitement. Could this really be happening? We were just another high school band, weren't we?

"It's got to be a joke," I said.

"Only one way to find out." Nick grabbed my arm. Troy, Gwyn, and Alli followed behind.

"I see it," Troy said, pointing to what was indeed a limo double-parked on the street.

When we got closer, a guy stepped out wearing jeans and a T-shirt.

"You guys the Band to Be Named Later?"

"Who wants to know?" Nick asked, trying to look around him into the limo.

The guy looked us up and down, then said, "Do it."

Suddenly three more guys emerged from the limo, spraying us with shaken-up pop cans and pelting us with water balloons.

"Suckers," the attackers shouted after us. "Stone said you'd fall for it!"

"Run!" Nick shouted, turning on his heel. We all joined him, ducking to avoid being hit with any more water balloons.

"I can't believe we fell for it," Troy said, trying to catch his breath beside me. "And why wasn't Roy around to see the joke?"

Troy was right. If Roy wanted to make us look like fools, he'd want to be around to see it. Unless…

"Oh, no." I kicked it into hyperdrive.

"Ori! Wait! What is it?"

"No one's watching our equipment!" I shouted over my shoulder.

We got back to the stage where our equipment was stashed and couldn't believe what we saw. Everything was dripping in orange paint, including a person who was splayed over a guitar case.

"I'm sorry," the person said. "I tried to stop them."

"Del?"

He pushed himself to his knees, shoving the guitar case away. "I hope it's not ruined."

I stared down at the Les Paul case. It was upside down, and I could see where the paint had seeped inside.

I couldn't bring myself to unclasp the case and look. I knew the Les Paul had to be destroyed.

The whole park seemed to fold in on itself. I dropped to my knees, weak and dizzy, before collapsing facedown in the grass with my arms over my head.

"Dude, what are we going to do?" I could feel Nick next to me and someone on the other side, Troy probably.

I didn't respond. I could barely breathe. I was wet and sticky from the limo sneak attack, and I couldn't stop thinking about all that effort, all those rehearsals, working and saving for the Les Paul—and now we couldn't play.

We couldn't play.

We were out of the Battle of the Bands.

The enormity of it overwhelmed me, leaving me paralyzed, unable to think or move or feel.

"Leave him for a minute," Del said. "Why don't you guys see if you can get something to clean your equipment."

I heard murmuring, then footsteps moving away from me. I kept my head down for another minute, then looked up.

"They're gone," Del said.

"Why don't *you* go get cleaned up." This was the first

time I'd gotten a good look at him. He was completely covered in orange paint. It was even inside his ears.

"I will," he said. "I just want to make sure they aren't coming back." He stayed where he was, sitting a few feet from me. "Why are you all wet?"

I told him about the fake record executives in the limo.

"Classic Roy Stone," he said.

"Speaking of which," I said. "I saw you talking to him a few times. What gives?"

"We played against them in lacrosse," Del said. "He thought he was a badass on the field, too."

"So why were you acting all buddy-buddy with him?"

Del shrugged. "Keeping close to your competition," he said. "Figured if I found something out and I wasn't pissed at you, I'd tell you about it."

"And?"

"They didn't say much, but I could tell they saw you as real competition." He nodded to the equipment. "Obviously."

I sat up, sighing heavily. "Maybe this was payback for thinking I was actually going somewhere."

"It isn't," Del said. "We'll figure something out."

"There's nothing to figure out. It's over." I fell back on the grass, staring up at the sky.

Del chuckled. "Okay, now you're sounding like me, and that's not good." He ran his orange-stained fingers through his sticky hair and looked over his shoulder, like he was making sure no one was coming. Then he breathed in and let it out. And did it again. Breath in, breath out. "So here's the thing."

I looked at him.

"You were right. What you said during the fight."

"Del—"

"No. Let me get this out because I won't say it again and I'll deny it if you ever try to pin it on me."

I smiled slightly.

"No one knew me in college, Ori," he said. "I went from being the Man at Falcon High School to Taylor, Del, student ID number 43579." He looked away. "It sucked and I guess I didn't know how to handle it. I stopped going to class, doing the work, and the next thing I know I'm on academic probation with some debts and shit to pay off." He shook his head. "Then I come home and here you are with this great band that's getting written up in the papers and online and there are girls after you—*you*, not me. Well, some of them were after me." I raised an eyebrow at him, and he smiled. "But I'm just saying, you know. You had this great thing going, and you were right. I was pissed because it felt like we'd changed places, and I hated it. Hated you. I wasn't used to looking up to you. You're supposed to look up to me. You always had until recently." He sighed again. "But who wants to look up to a screwup?" He held up his hand. "And don't say I didn't screw up, because I did."

"Yeah, you did," I said. "But who doesn't? I should never have said that crap to you."

Del shrugged. "I kind of had it coming." He scratched at the paint on his elbow. "But I can't believe how much it bothered me when you said you didn't want to be like me." He looked over his shoulder. "And if you tell anyone I said that, I'll kill you."

I suppressed another smile. Del cared what I thought. *Del* cared what *I* thought.

"You know you're still that guy, right?" I said. "The one who can do anything?"

Del smirked. "Maybe not anything, but I guess I can do something."

I was about to respond when someone spoke behind us.

"Orion?"

We turned around to see —

"Tara?" I said, trying to register the fact that Del's old girlfriend was standing in front of me. "What are you doing here?"

"A friend's brother is in one of the bands, so we came out to watch. And I knew you were playing, so of course I wanted to check it out. Chad's been sending me links and stuff about your band." She looked at the equipment. "What happened?"

"Someone sabotaged it. Del tried to save it."

She looked at Del, noticing him for the first time.

"Huh." She turned back to me. "This is terrible. What are you going to do?"

Before I could answer, Nick was there. "This is all they had," he said, pulling a flat dolly with water buckets and cloths on it.

"They are moving us to second-to-last," Troy said. "But I don't know how we're going to play wet instruments. The guitars might be okay, but Nick's drums..."

"It's hopeless," I said.

"Boxes and string," Del said. "That's all any of you need

to make music. Boxes and string." He nodded toward Nick, Troy, and Gwyn. "This is your band, Orion. Take charge of it."

I looked at him. He never called me Orion. Then I looked at my friends. My band. *My* band.

"Nick," I called. "Where's the loaner?"

He bent down to peek under the stage. "Right where you stashed it. Safe and sound and unpainted."

"Excellent." I turned to Tara. "When does your friend's brother's band go on?"

"Second, on Stage B." She pointed to the stage at the top of the field.

"Think we could talk to them?" I said. "See if they might consider loaning their equipment?"

"Good idea," Tara said. "Let me call them." She stepped away and started punching buttons on her cell.

"Man, she is *so* fine," Nick said, watching Tara.

Del sighed. "I really blew it with her. Which reminds me," he said, turning to me and lowering his voice. "Don't blow it with Jane. She was smart enough to see me for who I was. Or more to the point, who I wasn't." He crossed his painted arms. "She's really great, so just don't screw it up."

"I won't."

"They're up for it," Tara said as she walked over. "Let's go over there so you can decide what you need."

"Thanks," Del said to her.

"I didn't do it for you," she said. "I did it for Ori."

"Understood," he said. "But I still appreciate it."

She frowned, like she wasn't sure how to react. "You should wash up before you're permanently stained. You look like a giant carrot."

Del grinned.

"Orion or the Band to Be Named Later or whatever the hell you are," one of the Battle assistants barked. "You've got about ninety minutes before you go on."

"I can't believe we don't have a band name for the Battle," Nick said. "It's humiliating."

"Oh, man," I said, looking across the field. "It's Slash and Burn." Everyone turned toward Stage C. My breath caught in my throat as Roy Stone and his band ripped through their opening chords. They were on their game, hitting their notes perfectly, whipping up the crowd. My heart sank. How could we possibly compete with that? We didn't even have a name.

Then my brain did a rewind.

Maybe we did.

"I like it," Nick said when I told them my idea for our band name a few minutes later, and the others nodded in agreement. Just before we were supposed to go on, I walked over to the MC who was going to introduce us and whispered in her ear.

"Nope, it's not too late," she said, scribbling on her notes. "I can do that."

I smiled as I pulled the strap of the Stratocaster over my head and pressed it against my hip. It felt right at home there, like it belonged.

And it was worth every freaked-out moment we had with

the sabotage to see Roy's face when we walked onstage, me carrying the paint-free Stratocaster, everyone else set up with borrowed equipment.

And then Roy Stone and everything else was out of my mind because the MC was introducing us with our new band name and we were waving from the stage to shouts and cheers. The huge soccer fields between the stages were full of people. Some were just chilling, some were in line at the concession stands, but a lot of them were filling in the area in front of our stage. Dozens and dozens of people.

And I didn't feel like hiding in a bathroom stall.

I grabbed the mic like I owned it. "We want to send a shout-out to Flash Drive for lending us their equipment after an unfortunate situation." I leveled a look at Roy, then returned my gaze to my family, who had squished into the middle of the pack. "Also thanks to our families, who put up with all our crazy rehearsals." I waved to my parents and Vela, whose friends screamed and jumped up and down. "And to some of the fans we have from our Colorado Rocks site. Thanks for coming out." I pointed to a group hanging out with BoyMagnet and DominantSpecies. "We're dedicating this first one to my brother, Del Taylor," I announced without a tremor or crack in my voice. "He took a hit for us tonight. Literally."

We tore the house down with our first two covers. The crowd could not get enough of us. Some of the security guards were walking around trying to calm people down so that we could play our original and let the next band come on.

More cheers, which grew louder when we started the

opening chords to "Suburban Nightmare." The Battle didn't allow multimedia, so Alli's video extravaganza would have to wait for our next gig. But it didn't matter. It was all about the music.

The applause, the whoops, the whistling rolled over me and through me. I looked out over the sea of faces and realized I wasn't in one of my little rock music fantasies. This was real. These people screaming and calling our name were real. The music on the Stratocaster was real. And what I felt inside— the rightness, the knowing, the truth of it—was real.

"Thank you so much," I shouted into the mic. "You all rock!" They were still calling our name when we left the stage.

"B.A.S.! B.A.S.!"

We slapped high fives, whooping it up until the assistant barked again, telling us to get our "crap" off the stage so that the last band could set up.

"You're not the friggin' Rolling Stones, you know," he snarled. Then he stopped. "But you're pretty damn good."

I pulled out my cell.

☒ WHERE R U?

☒ TALKING TO TARA *DEL CELL 9:30 PM*

☒ COOL.

☒ BTW, B.A.S.? *DEL CELL 9:30 PM*

☒ BOXES AND STRING, BRO. B.A.S. IT'S OUR BAND NAME.

☒ WHAT'S MY CUT? *DEL CELL 9:30 PM*

☒ HA! C U @ HOME?

Several seconds went by before I got his reply.

☒ C U @ HOME *DEL CELL 9:31 PM*

B.A.S. got first place, and everyone went crazy. We stepped out onto the stage to accept a very cool guitar-shaped trophy, a check, and a promise of more prizes to come. Of course Nick had to grab the mic and mention that we were available for bookings.

"You can find us on Colorado-rocks.net," he said. "Thank you, Denver!"

We clapped and whooped as we climbed down from the stage to talk to a few reporters and get our picture taken. Behind them, Roy Stone and his band glowered, holding their second-place trophy, a smaller check, and no extra prizes.

In your face, boys.

"Nicely done," Courtney Calavera said, shaking our hands after the photographers were finished. "Check out my piece tomorrow."

Once the hoopla died down, we were back to normal, returning the borrowed equipment.

"We still need to talk to those record execs," Nick said as he hefted an extension cord over his shoulder.

I sighed. "That was fake, Nick, remember? Slash and Burn getting a few laughs."

"Not *those* record execs," Nick said. "*Those* record execs." He pointed to a man and woman striding toward us. When they caught our eye, they waved.

Rock *on.*

B.A.S. Takes It All at the Battle of the High School Bands

by Courtney Calavera, *DMS* reporter

It's a relief to finally have something to call this young local band after covering them at two other gigs (see Archives, keyword: Calavera). Of course, none of them would tell me what the initials stood for — at least O.A.R. spells it out on the site. But maybe B.A.S. will when they get big.

And I do mean when. B.A.S. whipped the crowd into a frenzy that didn't let up even when they'd left the stage and the next band was setting up. My sources tell me that they've already garnered interest from record companies. Let's hope they have some good people advising them so early in their career.

In a surprising twist, second place went to Slash and Burn, long favored to take it all at the Battle of the High School Bands this year. The crowd was abuzz afterward at the upset, noting that this was their last shot, since all the members graduated in May. "Who cares?" lead singer Roy Stone said when a nearby reporter asked how they felt about second place. "This is Little League. We'll be household names by this time next year."

Red in the Face took third with a respectable, though not spectacular, heavy metal original.

Another band to watch: Flash Drive, led by female vocalist Sela Rochester. They had a clean sound with great female backup vocalists and dancers. B.A.S. gave a special shout-out to this band for lending equipment. It was unclear what had happened to B.A.S.'s equipment; rumors were flying about sabotage and orange paint. If I get the real story, I'll report it here.

In the meantime, I recommend catching any of these bands when you can. I know B.A.S. is already booked at Rockin' Ryan's, and I'm sure the others will have good gigs as well. I've

click here for full story

BAND NAME: B.A.S.

| PROFILE | MUSIC | PIX & VIDS | ABOUT/FAQ | CONTACT | BLOG |

Monday, June 7

ORION: Thanks to everyone who came out to see us at the Battle. It was great to meet some of you in person after the show.

PeacefulWarrior, we'll have to jam sometime, even though I know you are down in Pueblo.

PurpleGrrl, love the red. So does Nick.

DragonBreath, thanks for the lids—we'll wear them with pride.

OzoneLayer, you missed a helluva scene before our set.

And Halyn, what can I say? Looking forward to writing more songs together.

ALLI: BoyMagnet, I'm sure everyone is happy to know you officially have a boyfriend and it's DominantSpecies.

BAND NAME: B.A.S.

| PROFILE | MUSIC | PIX & VIDS | ABOUT/FAQ | CONTACT | BLOG |

But you didn't have to push him into Ori.

OFFICIAL BAND NAME: B.A.S.
(And no, we aren't going to tell you what it stands for. Enjoy the mystery of it.)

BoyMagnet
Wow. Halyn and Orion! And PurpleGrrl is going with Nick? Like full on? Now things are making sense. But I do want to know: Who kissed Orion first? Me or Halyn?

PurpleGrrl
Why do you care? You're with DS now which, btw, I would think was BIZARRE if I hadn't met him myself. DS, you DO do nice.

GreekSalad
What's with the girl crap? I thought this was for the band.

DominantSpecies
Welcome to hell, GreekSalad.

PurpleGrrl
Some things never change.

PeacefulWarrior
Some do.

BAND NAME: B.A.S.

| PROFILE | MUSIC | PIX & VIDS | ABOUT/FAQ | CONTACT | BLOG |

🔲 OzoneLayer
I want to hear about the scuffle. Did the cops come?

PurpleGrrl
And some things don't.

BoyMagnet
Thank God.

PurpleGrrl
Yeah.

TWENTY-NINE

"You ready?"

It was the beginning of August, and I was carrying yet another box to the trunk of the car. Del had decided to give UNC another try. He'd lost his lacrosse scholarship, but if he got his grades back up, he might get back on the team at some point.

"I'm always ready," he said, taking the box from me.

I cocked my head. In the right light, his skin still had a faint orange tinge to it.

"What's the latest on Tara?" I knew they'd been texting and talking again, but Del hadn't given any details.

"We're getting together in Fort Collins next weekend."

"That's great."

Del shook his head. "I think it's the whole last good-bye, closure thing. Last I heard, she was seeing someone."

"That sucks." I shifted the boxes so that he could fit the last one in.

"Yeah, well, I guess it's part of that I-screwed-up-and-deserve-the-fallout crap." He waved his hand impatiently. "It is what it is, but at least she's talking to me. Maybe we'll be friends." He shrugged. "Tell me about the big meeting."

B.A.S. had met with another indie record company a few weeks ago. This was the one that was part of our prize for winning the Battle; the other was the man and woman who had come up to us after the Battle. The indie record company had been scouting the talent, and we'd met with them last month.

"Good," I said. "They like our originals. They want to hear more. See if we can come up with enough for a whole album."

He shook his head. "You did it. You really did it."

"It's still not for sure," I said. "But it's looking good." I gazed down the street. He followed my gaze as the now-familiar white Taurus turned the corner at the end of the block, coming toward us.

"Lucky dog," Del muttered. "If you ever get tired of her..."

"You got my back, bro?"

Del nodded, his familiar lopsided smile twitching at the corner of his mouth. "Always."

I laughed.

"How's the Les Paul?"

"Good." It hadn't been touched by the paint; just part of the inside of the case had gotten "oranged," as Nick called it. It was funny, though. I found myself picking up the Strato-caster as often as I picked up the Les Paul. The owner of the loaner had offered to sell it to me cheap, and I had been thinking of taking him up on it. A lot of rockers played a different guitar for each song; why not me? Besides, it had gotten me this far. I had a feeling it could take me all the way.

"Hey, there." Jane was coming around the front of the Taurus — tall and tan, with those amazing eyes looking right at me.

Me.

She and Del exchanged hugs. Friendly, you're-cool-but-that's-it hugs. Then she slipped her arm around my waist. "I'll miss you," she said.

"I'll be back tomorrow."

"I'll still miss you."

"I'll miss you, too."

"God, can we all vomit now?" Del shook his head as he put the last box in the car, but I could see that he was smiling.

Our parents and Vela came out then, followed by Alli and Troy from her house, just as Nick pulled up with PurpleGrrl.

"Quite the send-off," Dad said as they all gathered around to say good-bye.

"We just want to make sure he's really leaving," Nick said, then: "Ow!" after Del punched him in the arm.

"Are you sure you don't want us to come with you?" Mom asked.

"Ori's got me covered," Del said. He looked at his watch. "We should hit the road." He held the keys out to me. "How about you drive?"

"It's about time," I said, snatching the keys before climbing into the driver's side.

"Call me or text me when you're on your way home tomorrow," Jane said, leaning on the window.

"I will." I desperately wanted to kiss her, but no way could I do that in front of Del and my parents.

"So," Del said as I backed down the driveway and into the street. "Feel like a burrito?"

"You know it." I cranked the tunes, then glanced at him. He was leaning back, relaxed, his sunglasses dropped slightly down the bridge of his nose. It was weird to think about everything that had happened over the last several months, how much things had changed, how much *I* had changed. It almost felt like I'd dreamed it all.

But when I took one last look in the rearview mirror, I could see Jane and the others standing in my front yard, solid and real, waving at us.

A girl, a gig, a guitar, and a brother, not necessarily in that order.

Rock and roll, baby.

ACKNOWLEDGMENTS

Thanks to the insightful feedback from my ever-amazing (and brutally honest) Wild Folk critique group, who made me realize I had two books in one and helped me remember that I wanted to write a story about brothers.

Big thank-yous to my wonderful editor, Julie Scheina, at Little, Brown, and the fresh eyes of Pam Garfinkel, editorial assistant, for helping me take Orion's story to another level. Eternal gratitude to copy editor Christine Ma for keeping me honest with her careful readings (yes, that's multiple!) of the manuscript, and high fives and fist bumps to designer Erin McMahon and cover photographer Chris Borgman for the truly rockin' cover and interior pages. You had your work cut out for you, and the result is fabulous!

Thanks to Josh Calisti at Guitar Center in Denver for explaining the ins and outs of the arrival of a new guitar, to Red Rocks for hosting so many awesome bands over the years, to all the bands who play there, and to my favorite radio stations for playing the music I love (in order of their appearance on the dial): KTCL Area 93.3, KBCO 97.3

World Class Rock, KQMT 99.5 The Mountain, KIMN Mix 100, KRFX 103.5 The Fox, KALC Alice 105.9, and KBPI 106.7 The New Music Revolution. You all ROCK, and I'm so grateful that you do.

Although I can't play an instrument or sing, I do love music, especially rock and roll. I will always be grateful to my dad, John Vega, for letting me sit at his feet while he played the guitar and sang, and for introducing us to the Beatles when we were kids. Thanks also to my brother, John Vega Jr., whose ability to play by ear and to write and sing his own music continues to inspire and amaze me. Bring back No Exit, bro! I'm grateful for the hilarious made-up songs and guitar playing by brother John and brother-in-law Wayne Applehans on our family camping trips over the years. Thanks to niece Jordan Applehans and nephew Aaron Applehans for sharing your talents on the piano. Finally, kudos to brother-in-law Josh Massaro for bringing some percussion to the family beat.

But most of all, thank you to the love of my life, my husband, Matt Perkins, who is not only the best concert partner a rock-loving girl could ask for but also the one who introduced me to the awesomeness that is southern rock. Honey, I appreciate your tolerating the not-always-peaceful coexistence of Neil Young and Lynyrd Skynyrd in the same record collection. Let the good times keep rolling, baby.

Waiting for You

I'm always alone,
even in a crowd,
the voices soft, but mostly
   loud
I always felt there was
   someone for me
I was waiting and so was
   she.

CHORUS:
When you came through the
   door,
I knew it was you I'd been
   waiting for
It was all I could do
Did you know it too?
I'd been waiting for you.

I'd see someone
just walking along
And then she'd turn and I'd
   be wrong
So I'll keep waiting, just
   moving on
Until you finally come to
   hear my song.

[CHORUS]

There you were, smiling at me
Your eyes a light only I
   could see
Sometimes you know when it's
   right
I just want to be with you
   tonight.

[CHORUS]

And we will laugh and even
   cry
Together we can fly
I always felt there was
   someone for me
And now you're here, hope
   you'll always be.

CHORUS REDUX:
Then you came through the
   door,
I knew it was you I'd been
   waiting for
It was all we could do
We both knew it was true.
I'd been waiting for you.

But no more waiting...for
   you
No more waiting, no more
   waiting
   ...it's you.

Lyrics by Denise Vega • Music by Zachary James Carabelos and Melissa Rankin • Performed by Zachary James Carabelos and Melissa Rankin • You can download a free version of the song with information about the book at www.denisevega.com, or support the musicians and buy a clean version (without Denise talking about the book!) on iTunes, Amazon, Spotify, and more. Search for "waiting for you carabelos."

Check www.denisevega.com for information on additional songs from *Rock On!*